W

AM

Looking

After

Lily

Also by Cindy Bonner

Lily

Looking After Lily

A Novel

Cindy Bonner

Algonquin Books of Chapel Hill
1994

Many thanks to Mary Caldcleugh, Mark Gretchen, and Margaret Rose of the Corpus Christi Library Systems for their help in finding research material. I'm also indebted to Evlyn Broumley at the Weatherford Public Library for working with me through phone calls and the mail. To Chuck Thomasson I'm grateful for his prompt answer to my legal question and for saving me hours of time. And finally, to Peggy Cleaves for simply listening.

Published by
Algonquin Books of Chapel Hill
Post Office Box 2225
Chapel Hill, North Carolina 27515-2225
a division of
Workman Publishing Company, Inc.
708 Broadway
New York, New York 10003

Library of Congress Cataloging-in-Publication Data
Bonner, Cindy, 1953–
    Looking after Lily / Cindy Bonner.—1st ed.
       p.   cm.
    ISBN 1–56512–045–0
    1. Man-woman relationships—Texas—Fiction.
  2. Outlaws—Texas—Fiction.   I. Title.
  PS3552.06362L66   1994
  813′.54—dc20   93-33730
                                            CIP

10 9 8 7 6 5 4 3 2 1
First Edition

To Susan Rogers Cooper for the years of encouragement and friendship. And for loyalty.

Looking

After

Lily

1

The day I walked out of court, I didn't have anything more in mind than getting the hell away from Bastrop County, and quick. One minute the jury was acquitting me of Willie Griffin's murder, the next I was hot-footing out of there.

Well, there was a little more to it than that. For one thing, I was still limping from the thigh wound Tom Bishop gave me with his pearl-handled Colt's. I had other, healed-up bullet holes in me, from Mr. Milton's over-and-under, that pained me in wet weather. But the wrench in my gait kept me mad. I was too damned young to be walking like an old man already—twenty on the last day of May just past. One other problem—I

1

was about to leave my little brother in that shit-hole of
a jail.

Our lawyer didn't hold out much hope for getting
Shot off his charges of robbery and assault. But at least
it wasn't murder he was facing like I had been. He'd got
caught, though, and landed in jail coming to bust me
out, and that was what hurt me about having to leave
him there. I knew, though, that he could take care of
hisself. He was plucky, buck-strong, *and* he didn't have
any murder charges pending against him. That was the
main thing.

Now the story might have come different if Shot *had*
been out there on the streets of McDade with us the day
Mr. Milton and Tom Bishop killed our older brothers, Az
and Jack. Shot might have been facing murder for killing
Willie Griffin just like I had been, like Bob and Charlie,
our pals, had been. They couldn't prove against us was
all. There had been too much shooting to say rightly
whose bullet was the one to take Griffin out of the fight.
Willie was our friend, though, and if I shot him, I sure
didn't mean to.

Course, if my little brother *had* been out there on the
street that day, it's for pure certain the outcome would've
been different because he's a crack shot. Always has
been. I remember him shooting a hawk out of the sky
with one round from Pa's old cap and ball when we
weren't but six and seven, if that. Pa whaled both our
butts bloody for taking his pistol without asking, but

Shot got his go-by name after that. His real one's Marion Simon, after our ma's side of the family, but Shot just seemed a more natural, rightful thing to call him. And I believe if he'd been there at McDade last Christmas Day, Tom Bishop and Mr. Milton would not have come away alive.

So that's what all troubled me as I left the courthouse. I felt bad for deserting Shot since he'd been coming to my rescue when he got hisself arrested. But I was also still just a mite ticked off at him not going into town with us last Christmas Day. Anyhow, I sure wasn't planning to stick around long enough to attend his trial. There was plenty of folks who still thought me guilty as a skunk with hydrophoby to maybe get up a lynching party if their mood struck ugly. It was the feeling bad part festering in me, though, that made me duck back in that jailhouse long enough to say goodbye to my brother. He was, after all, the only brother I had left.

But Shot, he didn't have it in his mind to let me make it a quick adios. I was standing there beside the bars, bare-headed, in the same ragged clothes I'd worn since they'd caught me last December—just washed up enough so's I could stand trial in them. And I raised up my hand at him, told him about the acquittal, and said I'd read about him in the newspapers.

I had already turned around to walk back into the outside sunshine, when he said, "So? Tell me where you're going. I'll meet up with you when I get out."

I answered, "West," and kept inching towards the doors. I didn't really have nothing planned good yet. Just getting out of town.

He said—and now this was with the jailer and the other prisoners and everybody else standing there listening—he said, "Take Lily with you. Take care of her for me, Woody." And well, dammit, I almost reached back and knocked him to the ground for asking that of me like that. For one thing, Woody was Jack's name for me, and it sort of shook me hearing it come all the sudden out of Shot. And for another, he should of known I didn't have time to put up with toting around no little girl, especially not a pregnant little girl.

"I'll fetch her if Wash Jones don't bring you clear," I said to him, pretending he had a chance in hell in court.

He shook his head at me. "She ain't got no place to go till then. And anyway, Wash says it don't look too promising for me." He gave me one of those sad-dog looks he could put on so good. "She ain't got nobody, Woody. Take her with you. You owe me that much."

"Goddammit," I said, stepping right up close to the bars, and his face. "What the hell're you asking me for?"

"Who else is there? I already wrote to Aunt Violet, and she says they're too crowded. Her brother's sick and she's got his whole family there. I can't think of no place else." His features turned ornery. "Anyway. You owe me. You wouldn't be carrying that leg if I hadn't picked that lead outta you. And you'd more likely be dead." He stuck his arm out through the bars and pointed his finger at me. "You know it's the truth. You owe me, Woody. You take her with you."

He was right, of course. I owed him my life and I knew it. So I said I'd take her, and we gripped our hands together, but I never gave him my word on it. Still, when I stepped out of that jailhouse into the sunshine again, I turned towards the boardinghouse down Elm Street where I knew Lily was working, and I trod that way, cussing her, cussing Shot, and cussing myself the worst.

She'd forsook her family and upbringing for Shot. She'd even made a half-hearted attempt, back last January, to sneak us a pistol so he could pull it on the guards and break us out of that stink-hole. Sharp as Shot was about most things, he was plumb ignorant when it came to that little, big-eyed girl, though. He wouldn't take her gun, said it would just get us deeper in trouble, and he wanted to live to someday watch their baby-child grow up. Appeared to me like he'd lost a few screws and I told him so, seeing as how at the time it looked like I'd be the one to swing for Willie Griffin's murder. Bob Stevens and Charlie Goodman had already skinned out on acquittals by then, and that pocket pistol of Lily's looked like my only hope.

"You'd understand," Shot told me, after he'd sent her away that day, "if you ever once fell in love."

And so that was all the stuff I was reflecting on and puzzling over as I walked out of that cold place. And all

I had wanted to do was get the hell out of Bastrop. But I reckoned if I owed Shot my life, why, I owed his girl just as much.

See, she *had* been there on the street in McDade that day, and it was her that plucked me bleeding from that ditch and rode me out to Jack's house, where Shot was waiting with his penknife and a bowl of cobweb poultice to doctor me with. Not only that, but Wash Jones had called her as a witness for my defense, and it was her testimony that cast the first doubt that I'd been the one to shoot Willie down. So I limped on over the six blocks to Elm Street, turned left, and found the boardinghouse setting neat off the road underneath a spread of broad pine trees.

Lily was in the kitchen cooking supper for the people staying at the place, using her apron to lift a hot oven of beef bits and taters off the stove. When I came in the back door, she saw me, jumped, and I thought was about to dump that stewpot all over the floor. Her belly pooched out underneath her apron, and it was my niece or nephew, after all, curled up inside there, so I slid over a bench real quick for her to set the pot on. It seemed like the least thing I could do.

She said, "You scared me half to death. You're out?"

I nodded and looked down into that pot of hash. The smell was steaming up at me, making spit come in my mouth.

"You hungry?" she said, noticing what direction

my eyes were aimed. "I could skim you off some if you want."

I stuck my hands in the pockets of my britches and shifted from foot to foot. My leg was giving me misery after walking the mile to get there. And too, I'd been in jail about half a year by then and wasn't yet used to my freedom. I said to her, "Shot says for you to come along with me."

She was getting down a plate from a crate cupboard, a saucer really, and she piled a spoonful of the hash onto it. "Where you going?" She handed me the plate and a spoon.

I shrugged. "I dunno. Some place."

I gobbled up the food, and I don't expect I was much mannerly about it. Shot had told me she was a fine cook and he hadn't lied about that. I started thinking she might not be so bad to have along, at least till I'd purged myself of the poor jail chow I'd been forced to eat for the last six months.

"San Antone maybe," I said, around a mouthful of food.

"San Antone? That's pretty far away. I can't go that far away. Marion's trial's coming up pretty soon."

She wrung her hands in her apron and looked unsettled for a second. Then, like her mind kicked back in gear, she flung open the firebox on the stove and reached in with her apron for a pan of toasty biscuits. I helped her with that too, and she gave me one to sop my gravy.

"You don't have to go," I said, stuffing the biscuit whole into my mouth. "It don't make no difference to me."

She gave me a look like she didn't quite catch that last part, which she probably didn't with me blowing biscuit crumbs through my teeth. Then the door from the kitchen to the house opened, and a tall lady with a bunch of keys pinned to her waist peered in at us.

"That food almost ready?" the woman said, and then she spied me eating. Her shoulders straightened stiff. I tried to hide the saucer behind my back, to stop my mouth from chewing. I stood there sucking at the wad of biscuit.

"Yes ma'am, I'm nearly done," Lily said, acting nervous about the woman.

"Lily? Who is this vagrant?" the woman said, harshlike, staring mean at me.

"Don't mind him, Miz Dillard." Lily waved a floury hand towards me. "He's just my brother-in-law."

The woman frowned harder at me, and to Lily said, "We charge for board. He'll have to pay. And if I catch you feeding people for free, kin or not, I'll have to let you go. You understand?"

"Yes'um," Lily said, and she seemed to have shrunk up about six inches, which she could ill afford. She wasn't really even full-grown yet—only a month or two past her sixteenth birthday—and so stubby she'd have made a good armrest.

The landlady went back into the house, and I recommenced with my all-out chewing. Lily was picking up biscuits and putting them in a big, cloth-wrapped bowl.

"Good food," I said, feeling I owed her something since I'd got her in trouble. I was still hearing what she had just called me—her brother-in-law. It made me feel funny thinking about it like that. It was true, of course. Shot had sure enough married her over in Austin just after Christmas. So that made her kin, all right. Made me her brother-in-law. And thinking that, I realized she was just about the only kinfolk I had that wasn't locked up or pushing up daisies. At least any place close around.

"You have money?" she said, concentrating on the biscuits.

"Nope." I licked my fingers and set the saucer in the dishpan. "The pay ain't too good where I've been."

"How're you gonna get to San Antone?" She raised her eyes at me.

"I was hoping you had some I could borrow," I said. I sluiced off my hands in the dishwater, then had to wipe them dry on my shirt, since there wasn't any dishtowels around, save the one underneath all the biscuits.

Lily just kept watching me. Seemed to me her face was all eyeball, like she was part possum or hoot owl. Made me feel itchy having them glued on me so straight.

"You gonna get a job when you get there?" she said.

"I reckon."

"You ain't made plans?"

"Nothing past getting there."

I dabbed the back of my hand against my mouth. During all those months in jail, I'd grown a sort of mustache, and I found a few crumbs clinging to it. I brushed them onto the floor, then thought maybe I shouldn't have done that. I tried to grind them in with my foot, but Lily didn't seem to notice. She flopped the cloth ends up over the pile of biscuits in the bowl.

She said, "What about your papa's farm?"

"It's foreclosed."

"No, it ain't. I went and paid the taxes."

"Did Shot tell you to do that?"

"I didn't ask him. I figured he had worries enough."

I shook my head. "I ain't going nowhere near McDade. You go on ahead."

"I ain't going back there, either." She stopped fiddling with the bowl of biscuits and leaned on the table like she was either tired or thinking hard. "Marion mentioned once about leasing it out."

"To who?" I almost laughed. "Ain't nobody around there gonna deal with me in business."

"You've got a lawyer, don't you? It's a way to get some money. Maybe he'd lease it out to somebody, give you whatever he gets. Marion thought there was a way to do it. Then after his trial, we could meet you over at San Antone."

"We?" I stared at her and the smile slid out of my mouth. "Ain't gonna be no we. They got him cold on this. Got folks to testify they seen Shot shoot them men in Austin. Got witnesses say they seen him come outta Billingsley's store with that strongbox from the safe. They got him guilty. The only question is how long they're gonna give him for it."

Maybe I shouldn't have been so blunt about it. Thinking back, I see now it was a mistake. But for one thing, I wasn't much used to speaking to a female, and for another, it just didn't seem healthy for her to keep fooling herself. She'd been hanging around Bastrop since February, and it was June already. She'd been going over to see Shot every day they'd let her, telling him this and that about how things were going to be once he got passed the trial, like they were about to be back together full-time again. And Shot just let her go on thinking like that, because I guess he felt too soft about her to just say flat-out, "I'm gonna be at Huntsville for a while, hon, and then we can do all this you got planned."

Anyhow, I just blurted it out for him, right there in the kitchen and she like to have collapsed before I caught her. Tears were brimming out of her like rain, and I was sorry I'd opened my mouth. I wasn't much for comforting a person, and I didn't do too good then, either. Oh, I held her all right—by both shoulders and at arm's length, just kind of amazed and puzzled by how she was churning up all that water.

Mrs. Dillard came in again and she saw Lily bawling and me holding her out like the Thursday newspaper.

The woman shook her head and got real mean-looking. She said, "Goodness sakes. Are you still here?" to me and I didn't know what else to do. I said, "Your supper's all cooked. And now me and Lily's got to go. Could you give her her wages now so's we can get along?"

Lily's head started shaking and she clutched at my sleeves. She babbled something, some kind of protest that I couldn't understand for all her sputtering. But I wasn't giving her any choices now. I steered her towards the back door, and she went on outside. Then I turned and looked at Mrs. Dillard's narrowing eyes. I pushed my hands down in my pockets and waited for her to come across with Lily's pay.

"I know now," she said to me, pointing. "You're Haywood Beatty, aren't you?"

"Yes ma'am. That sure as hell is my name."

"I heard they were about to let you out but I didn't believe it."

"Acquitted me. I was acquitted fair and square. You got Lily's pay now?"

She gave me one more mean look and I gave her one right back. And then she went to the crate cupboard, reached up in there for a fancy tin can, and prized the lid off.

There was a lot of cash money inside there, and I had to keep my mind turned away from the sight. Not too many months ago, I might have been tempted to snatch that money can right out of her stingy hands and light out on the run. Or else I might have made a note of the exact spot on the cupboard where she put it and come back some dark-moon night. But six months' worth of smelling the stench of sun-starved bodies, and of sweating the gallows rope, had sort of tamed me down.

She said, "If I'd had any idea there was a murdering scoundrel in my house, why I would've called for the sheriff to come put you back where you belong."

I pasted on a smile that hurt my cheeks, chomped down on my tongue to keep from spouting off, and held my palm out for the six dollars that ugly woman counted into my hand. It would've served her right if I had bashed her down and stole her tin can.

"Thank you kindly," I said and reached to tip my hat before I remembered I didn't own one no more. It had got left somewhere on the street in McDade, along with the blood and souls of my brothers Jack and Azberry.

Lily was outside, sitting on a pine stump in the yard, eyes dried up and waiting for me. She had a little gripsack laying at her feet. "How much did she give you?" she said, rising as I came up.

I looked and saw the door standing open to a little lean-to room off the carriage shed where I reckoned she must have been sleeping all these past months.

I opened up my hand. "Six bucks."

"She owed me eight."

I started to turn around and go back for the extra two dollars. We'd be needing all we could rake up. But

Lily grabbed ahold of my elbow, and it struck me I hadn't had so many girl touches in all my life. It felt kind of funny having a sister.

"It doesn't matter," she said. "Just let it be. Miz Dillard's been a trial to me. And anyway, I've got one-sixty in here." She patted her clothes bundle and I nodded.

We started walking around towards the back road, and I got to say, I was glad she picked that route. I wasn't too anxious to be showing my face. Even if this wasn't McDade, trials were big news in those parts, and all five days of testimony, the courthouse had been jam-packed. I figured if the biddy Dillard had recognized me, she wouldn't be the only one to. I felt more comfortable sort of easing into it, going around down through the outhouse alleys and by the horse lots.

"Still," I said, having to slow down my pace for Lily. Even with me crippled she wasn't keeping up. "Two dollars is two dollars. With your one-sixty, we're still coming out forty cents in the hole on this deal."

She glanced sidewise at me, kind of dipping her head. Then she laughed, and it was plumb mirthful sounding. I had never in my life seen anybody go from one mood to the other so fast. She had to stop walking, she got such a kick out of whatever had set her off.

I wiped at my lip, thinking maybe I still had some hash gravy stuck in my mustache. She kept on laughing. "What?" I said, getting kind of touchy about it.

"I said one-sixty, and you thought—" She busted up

again, and it took a second for her to get ahold of herself enough to speak. "I meant one hundred and sixty, Haywood. Not one dollar sixty."

"Oh," I said, still not liking that I was the butt of some joke.

Then it dawned on me what she was saying. I looked at her, and a smile started on my face. It got even bigger when I noticed where she was leading me and what we found when we got there. Mollie, Shot's pretty paint mare, standing in a box stall just inside the boarding-house stables.

hile Lily was inside the jailhouse saying her goodbyes to Shot, I rode over to see Wash Jones, my lawyer, and Shot's lawyer now, too. In fact, Wash Jones had been doing lawyer work for our family clear back to when Pa was still alive and got sued in court for shooting a neighbor's cow who kept breaking through our fence to get to our corn patch. Jones had defended for Jack once, Az three times, and now me and Shot. There wasn't hardly anybody that knew me any better.

So before I left town for good, I wanted to thank old Wash for all he'd done. He'd got me out of jail as quick as he could and I knew it. He'd even argued to the judge that the seventy-five-hundred-dollar bond posted on me violated the Eighth Amendment to the Constitution, some words about an excess in bail. Anyhow, the judge must've agreed with Wash because the sum got lowered to fifteen hundred dollars, but there still wasn't anybody I knew with that kind of money. Estelle, Jack's widow, had wrote to say she would try to raise it, but nothing ever came of it. Last I heard, Estelle had moved off to Henderson County to live with some maiden aunt of hers. I reckon her home in Rockdale was just too close to McDade and things she'd have rather forgot.

So I went to Mr. Jones's office, and after I'd thanked him again and we'd talked a while about Shot's trial coming up in a couple of weeks, I went ahead and told him about Lily paying off the tax debt on the old farm-place underneath the Knobs.

"So it's my land again, and Shot's—I mean Marion's. And I figured you could maybe sell it for us and keep whatever you get as pay for what we owe you."

I hadn't talked with Shot about any of this but I was pretty sure he'd see things the same as me. Wasn't any other way I could think of to pay back Mr. Jones what was due him. The money I had in my pocket, the little bit doled out to me by Lily, we would need to get us to San Antonio.

Wash Jones wasn't no fancy-Dan lawyer. He wore a town suit, but it was just of homespun and a little tattered around the edges. He had a tin tobacco ring hanging from his vest pocket instead of the Turkish cigars the lawyer for the State had sported. The paper collar at Jones's neck was unbuttoned and flapped out about his ears.

"Know where you're bound?" he said, pushing himself back from his desk. The wheels on his chair needed a squirt of oil. The squeak they made raised the hair on my neck.

"Thought about San Antone," I answered and Jones nodded.

"Got relatives there?"

I shook my head. "Just an interest. I thought I might try my hand at the cattle business."

"Buying or selling?"

"Punching."

"Oh." His eyebrows bent in the center. "Just so you behave yourself."

"I will."

I stood up to leave and he studied on me a few more seconds. "I've a brother in Parker County," he said, "with some farmland he can't tend to. Got the backstrain and can't go full-speed anymore. Needs a good man working for him, if ever you're interested."

I thanked him and we shook hands. He pulled the tin ring from his breast pocket and gave me his cigarette makings, which I greatly appreciated. I was all the way out the door and headed down to the livery stable before the notion struck me that Wash Jones had been calling me a good man.

Now, I'd been called a great many things in my life. Murderer, thief, coward, outlaw, even bandit, which I never thought was a word ought to go to describe a white man anyhow. But nobody had ever said I was a *good* man. Not to my face or behind my back either, so far as I knew. And although I didn't give one hoot nor holler about ever hopping clods behind a bull-tongue plow so long as I lived, Wash Jones saying I was a good man made it some easier for me to dodge the hateful glances I got out on the street, and fend off one or two abusive remarks made under somebody or other's breath as I passed by.

I bought a light wagon with a spare wheel and a broke-down pulling mule named Sassy. I also bought what all provisions I thought we'd need for the eighty-some-mile trip to San Antonio. By the time I got a cigarette rolled and lit, the first pull of smoke giving me a dizzy head I hadn't enjoyed for nearly six months, Lily was coming out of the jailhouse wiping at her cheeks.

She didn't make a comment about the wagon and mule, or about Mollie tied on behind. She didn't glance to notice the box of stores in the back, or say one thing to me at all. Her face was puffed and splotchedy, and she looked to me near to being wrought up into a fit of desperation. She held out her hand, like she was the queen of Sheba, for me to help her up onto the high-seat. Like I said before, I wasn't much for comforting a person, especially not a female person, and so I ignored her hand and took her by the waist, swinging her off her feet and up into the wagon.

She was heavier than I'd thought, and I had to give

her backside a shove once her feet cleared the railing. She stumbled but caught herself before anything tragical happened, like her falling out and dashing the baby in her belly on the street. Shot would of never forgive me for an accident like that.

I gave the jailhouse one final look, feeling glad to be going, but irritable at Shot for heaping all this responsibility on me. Then I got up beside Lily and took the lines. I popped them down on the mule's rump and we started off.

"You ain't gonna tell him goodbye?" she said, turning to stare back at the red brick jailhouse.

"Already did." I cracked the lines again, and whistling through my teeth said, "Giddup, mule."

Didn't seem to matter how much I throttled her, that old Sassy had her mind set to take it at a walk. If it's one thing in this world I hate, it's a godamighty mule.

We struck the old San Antonio Road about a half-mile from town and Lily had taken to bawling again. At least she wasn't loud about it. That's all the good I can find to say about the first hours of that trip. I tried hard not to look at her, and she kept to herself as much as is possible for two people sitting shoulder to shoulder.

It was a small wagon, but we didn't need much else. Once we got to San Antonio, I planned to get me a job somewhere and maybe find a good family willing to take Lily in till the baby was born. Passed that, I didn't calculate. I'd send Shot word where she was staying. I couldn't see me turning into no family man.

We spent the night in the Cedar Creek bottoms. I lit a fire, and Lily made us coffee and corn mush from the meal I'd bought. I'd got some cans of hogshead cheese too, but they were rancid. The cornmeal had weevils. She made do and didn't complain, but she seemed sickly to me as she climbed in the back of the wagon to sleep. I bedded down on the ground by the fire. Sweat and skeeters kept me awake all night.

In the morning, I took the single-barrel shotgun I'd bought for ten dollars and the box of birdshot, and got us some fresh meat. Killed the first thing I came upon— a rabbit skip-hopping through a little graveyard above the creek. I had to cross a fence to make the kill, but didn't anybody see me do it.

Lily fried rabbit meat in our one skillet. She didn't eat much. I'd forgot to buy salt. We stopped at a little grocery in St. Mary's for a box. Right after that we rolled out of Bastrop County, and I felt my spirits lighten considerable.

During all those miles, we didn't speak much, past me asking now and again if she needed for me to stop for something. She always blushed and shook her head, then when it was me who needed to stop, she'd disappear near about running behind the farthest clump of trees. We were on a mesquite prairie, without much thick vegetation. Sometimes she covered a quarter mile before she found a place she liked to squat and do her business. I never knew a person who could hold their water so damned good.

The second night out, we ran into rain. I put Lily underneath the wagon to sleep, though even that didn't keep her dry. The next day the going got rougher with the road turned to slush and the wagon bogging up to the wheel hubs every few yards. I had to untie Mollie from the back of the wagon and bring her up around front to help that balky old mule with the pulling.

"We ain't ever gonna get there!" Lily said, while I was scraping mire off the wheel spokes with a stick. Her saying that, and screeching it out like she did, made me feel she was blaming me for the rain and the mud.

I looked at her, back where she was pushing and heaving behind the wagon. I said, "If it wasn't for you, I'd have done been there already." And I chunked the stick down into the soft mud my boots were sinking into.

If she hadn't made me mad I probably wouldn't have said it, though it was, in fact, the truth. By myself, I would've just saddled up Mollie and gone. Wouldn't have needed a wagon nor all these provisions. I'd have lived off the land and got there in about two days.

"Leave me here, then!" she screamed. "Just go on and leave me! I ain't wanting to follow you anyhow!"

She gave the wagon another shove and I felt my face get hot. With a folded length of rope I whipped down on Sassy's already raw back, and she took off sudden.

Mollie went too, and Lily fell splat and face first in the mud behind the wagon. I thought she'd probably take to crying again, but instead she jumped up and doubled her fists into knots.

She said with a glare, mud on her nose and chin and all up the front of her dress, "I ain't going another step with you! You just go on! I'll get by just fine on my own!"

She picked up her sodden skirts and started high-stepping through the mud, heading east like she intended on trodding back how we'd come. It was a funny sight, made funnier by her paunch poking out like she'd swallowed a ripe muskmelon seed. But I didn't laugh. I watched her go about twenty steps and got even madder.

"You get your ass back here," I hollered, gritting my teeth together. I thought I sounded pretty mean, but it didn't scare her back. She kept on stomping off. So I looped the lead lines through the left wheel, even though Sassy was mired up to her hocks again, and I slopped through the mud after Lily. When I reached her, I jerked her up by one arm. "I said to get your butt—"

"Don't you cuss at me like that!" She slung me off. "I won't take your cussing."

She lurched away from me so fast, she stumbled to her knees. When I reached to help her up, she slapped my hands. They were sore and wet anyway, and her slapping at them stung.

"Get up from there! Get up!" I said, but she kept fighting me, and then sat down flat in the ooze, glaring, her hair flying wild around her face. She reminded me some of a mama coon I'd come across hunting once, a coon that had her young'uns in a tree nest right above me. That coon baring her fangs had backed me off, and Lily's glaring did the same to me now. I straightened up and took a step away.

"I wasn't cussing," I muttered. "I said butt. I kept it clean."

She took a deep breath, but her chest was still heaving. "You said ass first." She practically whispered the word *ass*.

"But then I remembered and said butt."

"And *butt* is clean to you?" She was getting her lungs back, and her glare wasn't so sharp, but she was still pretty well covered in mud.

"Well. Yours sure as hell ain't," I said, and ventured my hand out again.

She took it this time, and let me pull her up to her feet. Her eyes flicked around us—at the mud, the bogged wagon, at Mollie and the mule. Both animals stood still, tails twitching flies, ears flickering.

"I promised Marion I'd go with you," she said in a hopeless voice. "He made me swear to it."

"And I said I'd look after you."

"I can't abide a filthy mouth."

"But the filthy mud don't bother you none at all."

I thought for a second she was about to start with her weeping. But then she made a little noise that sounded almost like a laugh, except she wasn't exactly smiling. She dabbed her muddy hair out of her face with the back of her wrist, and looked up at me. It was downright pitiful—or almost.

I sort of stooped over. "Climb up on my back."

"I'm just so tired," she said. "And I don't think I can. My feet are stuck."

"Give her a try."

Balancing herself on my shoulder, she uncorked her foot from the mud, and poked it through the loop I'd made with my arm. I shrugged her on up. She wasn't as heavy that way, piggy-back, and I could maneuver in the mud with my boots better than she could in her shoes. I carried her to the wagon and dropped her at the seat.

"You drive," I said, "and I'll heave. But whip the mule hard. She's a damned ornery bitch." I gave Lily a sideways glance. "*Derned* ornery bitch, I mean," I mumbled on my way back down around to the end of the wagon.

3

At San Antonio, we used some of the money to rent beds and a bath at an old town inn. We were both tired of washing in branch water. Leastwise, I knew I was ready for a douse bath. Between the sweat and road dust, I'd begun to grow turkey beads on my neck. Lily wasn't a whole hell of a lot cleaner.

The place where we stopped was owned by a man name of Markin. He was stooped-shouldered, gray-headed, and hard of hearing, and he wore a pair of broad, leather galluses like came from the army. He was as skinny as a walking stick, so I reckon he needed his braces that broad and heavy to hold up his britches. He leaned way out over the plain wood registration table and cupped his ear at me when I asked him if he had any rooms empty. Then he nodded, turned the swivel book towards me.

"Sign in," he said, shouting like it was me who was deaf.

I wrote out my whole name—Nathaniel Haywood Beatty—then glanced at Lily. She had wandered on through the front room, and was looking around, feeling her hand along the stone walls. I bent and scribbled her name right out behind mine, which was probably how come him to figure we were married to each other.

He showed us to a tiny room tucked up underneath the long staircase. The room had one window, one table, one lamp, and one bed. A small bed at that.

"I usually get six bits a week for a room like this," Markin hollered. "But since the door lock don't work, and since I got that wet spot seeping up—" He pointed at the floor, which had a rag rug thrown down. In the middle of the rug was a dark place that Lily went over to squish the toe of her shoe in.

"Got a spring creeping under the foundation," Markin said. "Keeps it cool in here, though. Oh yeah, that windowlight don't open neither." He squinted at me. "Would you pay four bits for this'un?"

"We ain't married," I said. Lily was still squishing in the rug. Awful quiet, I thought. "She's my sister-in-law."

"What's that? Oh." Markin rubbed his gray stubbled chin. "Your sister, you say?"

"In law."

Lily looked over at us both and Markin seemed to study on her a while. Then he turned back to me. "It's all I got. Unless you'd be willing to go into the bachelor quarters. Four bits for that'un, too."

The bachelor quarters, as Mr. Markin called it, was two doors down, a long room with three beds, one of which I got to share with a fellow from Arkansas. He smelled like the sour bear oil he put on his hair, but we each had our own pillow. I turned my nose to the wall and finally got some sleep.

In the morning, I went down to the telegraphing office and sent a wire to Wash Jones, so's he could pass the word on to Shot where we had gone. By the time I got back, Lily had hired herself on with Mr. Markin. I found her out back by the spring well washing bed linens in a big kettle.

"Said he'd pay me two dollars a week and board," she told me, sounding proud of herself. "That's nearly double what Miz Dillard was giving me, and we won't have to scrape up the money for my rent."

"Ain't this gonna be too hard on you?" I said, eyeing the crumbling fieldstone building behind us. It was a little shoddier place than I'd figured on leaving her.

"Not for a while. I got till September." She blushed, stirred in the boiling water with a two-tined fork. Her hair was sticking to her forehead like flypaper. "What're you gonna do?"

It irked me that she thought she could just ask me that outright, and sounding like she didn't think I could hold down a regular job. The way I figured it, wasn't none of her business, anyhow. But after the spat we'd had in the mud on the trip over, I managed to keep my tongue civil.

I scratched my head and looked around the yard. There was a bald-faced, brindle-colored cow in a pen, her sack bulging with milk. "I'd like to buy me a hat for one thing."

She squinted at me, then hung the fork on the kettle hook, and reached into her apron pocket. She drew out a black snap pouch, dug in it, pulled out a few dollars. She held them towards me.

"Get you one then."

It felt peculiar to me taking money from her—like she was the bank and me a pauper. I said, "Maybe you oughta let me hang onto that money for safekeeping. There's liable to be dishonest characters about."

She looked at me again, then at the pouch she was holding. She handed it over. "Don't lose it," she said. "That's all we got."

I nodded, stuck my fingers down inside the pouch. There was still more than a hundred dollars inside. "Where'd you get all this money, anyhow?" I raised my face.

"Marion gave it to me. Before he got thrown in jail."

I nodded. "Where'd he get it?"

She shrugged, but I thought she looked uneasy. "He never did say."

I nodded again, figuring that uneasy look of hers

had answered me. The money had belonged to somebody else and Shot had just made it his. I could imagine how. I'd been in the same situation myself, poking a pistol in somebody's face with one hand and holding the other hand out.

"It's safe with me," I said, drawing out all but three dollars and giving her back the pouch.

I found a brown felt hat with a snake band, and at the same dry goods store, picked out a black-handled .45. I'd always liked a .45, the way it felt inside my palm and on my hip. And this one was pretty near to the one I'd had and turned over to Sheriff Jenkins when he arrested me, as near as I was going to get for twelve dollars. The store clerk threw in the cartridge belt and two rounds of bullets for that price.

I couldn't wear the six-shooter in town, but I thought I'd need it when I hired on with a cattle outfit. Every cowpuncher needed a pistol at his side, and a pair of spurs on his heels—something else Sheriff Jenkins had got away with of mine. My boots were in poor shape after the mud-trekking I'd done, but I figured I'd think on what to do about them while I quenched a burning thirst I'd been growing in my throat for the past six months.

Red's Saloon was the first one down from the dry goods store, and I walked inside like I owned the place. The bartender was a friendly Pollack fellow, told me if I'd stick around long enough, some of the cattlemen would be coming in before dark.

"They do their hiring right here," he said and mixed me up a drink that like to have burned my eyeballs right out of their sockets. I drank down two more while we were jawing.

Pretty soon a couple of cowboys did walk in, and I got to chatting with them. The place was mostly empty at that time of day, but these two boys, who worked at the Diamond M, were in town after supplies.

"Come fall we'll be taking on plenty of new hands," one of them told me. I bought them both a round of drinks.

Hilbert Sullivan was the most talkative of the two, and he started telling me about how his boss was making new headquarters up in the Panhandle. They would be moving the first herds come October. He said if I thought I could wait till the first of September, I could probably hire on with the outfit.

We had another batch of the bartender's strong concoctions, and the Diamond M boys began to take their leave.

"How will I find you again?" I said, and Sullivan slapped me on the back.

"Hell, we ain't leaving yet. We're just leaving here." And he invited me to tail along.

These boys were real honest-to-God cowpunchers, wearing fringed-leather leggins, bright neckerchiefs, and big-roweled spurs on their boots. I felt like a barefoot plowboy tagging along to the other bars in town. And I kept getting stuck paying for the drinks, as these two had a knack for wandering out the doors when I wasn't looking. Also, the liquor went to my head pretty quick, since it had been so long since I'd got lit up. I guess I wasn't paying close enough attention. There was a lot to see.

In one place, a table of fancy-Dans were dealing out high stakes poker, and I wasn't the only one interested in all the money swapping hands. It brought to mind memories of Jack, who'd been the best goddamned card player I'd ever seen. Wasn't nothing for Jack to lay down two dollars and walk out a few hours later with two hundred jangling in his pocket. And he wasn't a cheat neither, nor a sharp, he just had a good mind for remembering what all had gone down on the table, and who was likely to bluff, and who was likely not to. And he practiced a lot, regularly cleaning all of us out of everything we had in our pockets. Jack just plain beat all I ever saw when it came to draw poker. And the worst of it was, we didn't any of us ever learn our lesson. Not right down to the end, after Jack married Estelle and swore off gambling forever.

At another saloon, there was a man with a monkey sitting on his shoulder eating peanuts while the man drank. And that was something else to watch. The monkey'd crack the shell with his sharp teeth, then sit there picking out the nut with his fingers, just like a human being. After he'd eat a bite, he'd grin wide, so you'd think he was friendly. But if you tried to pat him, he'd hiss and growl till you bet you dodged away. After about ten minutes of that monkey, I looked up and saw Sullivan and the other one had disappeared again.

I found my boys at a dancehall with loud music from a stomp and holler band. By then, it was dark and I had so much stinger juice in me my leg wasn't even bothering me. I paid three bits to a long-haired gal for two dances. The band played "Cotton-Eyed Joe" and "Billy in the Lowground," and girls were swinging and spurs jingling, boots and shoes pounding up dust that rose all the way to the ceiling. I'd have kept on dancing, too, except the fiddle player got mad over something, or had just got too tight on the wine that was flowing, and hit the song caller over the head with his fiddle box. Just used it like a war club, and then the whole band got into the fracas. I invited my longhaired gal to leave the dancehall with me but she wouldn't go. I guess it was her job to stay there all night, brawl or not.

Thinking about it, I reckon I've said things to give a person the idea I wasn't hot on women, but a whore was a different matter. A whore ain't rightly a girl, least not in the ways that made me nervous. A whore ain't really too much different from a good taste of whiskey, or a black-handled pistol you've bought and paid for. So as soon as me and the boys left the dancehall, we made a bee-line for a place Sullivan knew about. A place called Annabel's, or at least that's what Sullivan said it was called. There weren't any signs anywhere.

The wine-sipping girl at the dancehall, and all the drinking I'd done, had me feeling frisky. Hell, we were all frisky. We took the first three girls we came to and went out back to the cribs. Mine wasn't no real beauty but she was soft in the right places and had a bed without seam lice. I rolled her till I was spent, which didn't take long. It had been six months after all. Maybe longer. I couldn't even remember my last time with a woman.

"Did you find work?" Lily asked me the next morning before breakfast, while I was sipping coffee and trying to keep my brains from popping out through my ears.

"Maybe," I said, remembering the Diamond M boys, but forgetting I hadn't found out how to reach them.

Later, I counted my money. Our money. *The* money. We were down to forty-three dollars and thirty-three cents. Plus the three dollars I'd left in Lily's pouch.

4

The Pollack fellow at Red's Saloon told me how to get out to the Diamond M, which was most of a day's ride from town. Mollie was up to it, though, since all she'd been doing for the past few months was putting on flesh and growing a long, glistening tail. Usually I would have been against riding a mare for my saddle mount, but Mollie was a butch mare, barren for sure cause we'd tried several times to breed her to Ben, the gray stallion I'd lost in the street fight at McDade. Being butch, *and* barren, Mollie was prone to fits of temper, and Shot had been the only one who could control her good. She got to poking along and tried to throw me when I stuck her with my shining new, jingle-bob spurs.

I sure got to longing for old Ben on that trip out Uvalde way to the Diamond M.

I found Sullivan at the ranch bunkhouse and he showed me to the strawboss, a man name of Castaneda. I wasn't sure how I was going to like working for a Mexican, but I told him I was in the need for a job.

"Any job. I'd even fix that chimney for you," I said, noticing, as I had when I came up, that the dauble was crumbling and chinked on the bunkhouse chimney. My pa, back before he took to drowning himself in liquor, had used to be a chimney man during the winter months, and I'd sort of soaked in some of what he knew. It was all in the batting was what he would say, and this bunkhouse chimney was proof positive of that. Come cold weather, smoke would be leaking out of it like a sieve, from every crack and hole in the column.

We were standing out by the horse pen where there was a whole herd winding circles around the fence. Castaneda looked up when I nodded back at the crumbling chimney. But he just snorted.

"How good are you with a rope?" he said, and he didn't sound one bit Mexican so I figured him for a half-breed, which settled some better with me.

"Damn good," I answered and he motioned for one of his hands to fetch me a rope. He didn't say out loud what he wanted, but a skinny, freckle-faced fellow came over with a twenty-foot hoop so I guessed mind-reading would be part of the job, too.

Castaneda pointed out a pretty buckskin pony for me to catch and I eased up on the pen rail, trying not to favor my bad leg. I didn't want no past injury cheating me out of a job.

I built me a loop, swung her over my head, and cast forward. Every horse in the pen shied away from my throw, and the rope landed splat in the dust.

"Just warming up," I said, pulling in my line like I was dragging a creek for fish. Some of the boys around snickered, and Castaneda spit on the ground.

I whirled her around another time, threw, but the horses had got wise to me now, and I came up empty again. I did that five times in a row, my ears getting redder and burning like coals underneath my new hat. Finally Castaneda called a halt to the game.

"I hadn't got time for a greenhorn in my outfit, Bailey," he said, but there wasn't any devilment in his tone.

"Beatty," I corrected.

He didn't seem to hear me. He nodded at my leg as I limped back towards Mollie. "A horse dump you or what?" he said, squirting another wad of spit. He wasn't chewing, just seemed to have a lot of water in him.

I turned back to face him. "Huh?"

"That gimp leg of yours."

"Oh." I shook my knee. "That." Then an idea started to come to me. I perked right up, grinned at him, sort of. "Had an old bang-tail try to rub me off on a fence last spring. Busting broncs for Mister Holman over at Giddings in Lee County."

"Curly Holman?" Castaneda said. He seemed like he was warming up to me.

"Know him?" I hoped not. I almost crossed my fingers. Old Holman would remember me all right, but not for busting his broncs. Az and me and Shot and a couple of others had relieved the rancher, one summer a while back, of a few head of his short-horned cattle.

"Heard of him." Castaneda took a long time sizing me up then, and I wondered what he thought he was seeing. "You on the dodge from something?"

"No," I said, then sort of added the "sir" under my breath. He wasn't all that much older than me—maybe twenty-five. And he was a Mexican after all. Part Mexican. He had the lightest colored eyes I'd ever seen on somebody so dark. I tried to look them square on without batting mine.

He glanced around at Sullivan who had sidled after me, to say tough luck, I guess. Castaneda blinked at a dusty wind that blew up, spit. He said, "You want work, Bailey, stick around till tomorrow. I got a string of twenty unbroke ponies coming in. Two dollars apiece. I can get somebody else to toss the rope." And he strode away.

Sullivan came up to me and clapped my shoulder. I turned to him. "That mean I got a job?"

"Shit work. For a while, anyhow. If your ass-end holds out." He laughed, and popped me with a length of bridle rope right on the spot he was speaking of.

"It'll hold out," I said, confident, watching Castaneda direct his men over towards a cow pen.

Well, it nearly didn't hold out. By the end of the first week, I could barely walk. My neck, arms, back, and shoulders ached from being flung about. I went to the bunkhouse every night after supper and fell into bed, asleep before I hit Shot's saddle, which I used as a pillow during my stay there. I had scraped knuckles, scraped knees, a broke nose, and, I was sure, three or four cracked ribs to boot. One time I'd been pitched flat on my head and got an apple-sized knot I had to stretch my hat brim out around. The damned thing never did fit me right again, once that knot went down. And I'd been awful partial to that snake band, too.

It was the hardest forty dollars I ever came by and it took me almost a full month to get all the way through the string. But by the time I left the Diamond M, I had ever blessed one of those horses broke good enough so's the regular hands could finish them off. Old Mollie felt mighty nice between my legs going back to San Antonio, and Castaneda had said he'd be in touch. He turned out to be a pretty good Mexican after all.

I put Mollie up at the inn stable, pumped her some water, and forked her hayrack full. Suddenly, watching Mollie munch, it struck me that Lily might not even still be around. I hadn't thought much about her during those weeks, hadn't remembered, even, to send her word where I was at. I walked around the side of the outbuildings and the privy, through the well yard, and she came rushing out the kitchen door. She had a wooden spoon in her hand, her hair pinned up, and it looked to me like her belly had grown six inches. I knew I ought not to be staring at it, but I couldn't seem to help myself. She sort of waddled, flatfooted. I guessed Mr. Markin had put her to cooking now, for she smelled like onions and garlic and woodsmoke.

"I thought you were dead," she said straight out. "I don't know whether to whop you with this spoon or celebrate. What happened? Where've you been?"

I frowned at her. It seemed a strange way for her to be acting, demanding to know my every move. I said, "I found work," and pushed past her, headed towards the door.

She came along with me, backing hair sprigs out of her face. "Is it good work? I've been worried sick."

"What for? You knew I was looking."

"But not that you'd stay gone for twenty-nine days."

I hitched up the three stairs into the kitchen, wincing at the pain it caused me to climb. I had my mind on a cool tub of bath water. The kitchen was all a-clutter and Mr. Markin himself was at the long work table. He nodded and smiled at me, and kept chopping up some kind of yellow pepper.

Behind me, Lily said, "I was just about to start back for Bastrop by myself, but then I had a letter from Marion."

"You got a tub of water drawn?" I said to Markin and

laid down the five cents he charged for it by his elbow.

He moved to get up, and Lily said, "I'll do it." She headed down the short hall to the bath shed.

Mr. Markin slid the nickel back at me. "For you, no charge," he said, talking loud enough folks probably heard him out on the street. He grinned and his teeth showed from under his gray mustache. "You can thank your fetching *sister* for it."

"In law," I said. "Sister *in law*." I looked down the hall where she'd gone. "She's my brother's wife."

He nodded, keeping that sick grin on his mouth. He winked at me. "Whatever."

The wink confused me at first. Then it made me mad. I stood there blinking at him, witless, wishing I was Jack or somebody else with more spunk. Jack would've scared old man Markin with just one look. And Az had had fists like iron. Nobody ever dared to make him cross. Even Shot, who was good at words, could've found something to say right then to put Markin in his place. But me, I just stood there like a lump of dough, burning red, struck dumb, while Markin went back to chopping his yellow peppers, grinning ear to ear like he knew a good secret. Finally, I gathered myself up and turned down the hallway towards the bathhouse.

It was a dim room, or really a lean-to added onto the side of the main building. You could see daylight through the tin cover and slat walls, and were supposed to, so's the steam wouldn't get too wilting. The floor was dirt, and the spigot was across a short span of three feet

or so from the tub. Lily was pumping the water into a
pail and hefting it to the tub by hand.

"You want it hot?" she said, sweat shining around
her mouth and at her temples.

"No. Gimme that." I took the pail from her and
dumped the water into the steel tub. There wasn't but
about an inch yet on the bottom. I picked up the end
of the tub and swung it across the three-foot span and
started pumping the water straight in from the spigot.
"Did you tell that old leech I was your married husband
or something?"

Her face went pasty and her mouth rounded up.
"No, I surely did not."

"Well, just don't go using that trick." I pumped
harder, feeling suddenly dirty. I could smell myself.
"Truth is best where that's concerned."

"I never said a thing like that. I wouldn't." Then her
tone turned snippy. "What makes you think I'd want to,
anyway? You ain't so much, for all your kin to him. He'd
of never gone off like you did for twenty-nine days without a word. And he'd of never not cared what you had
to say in a letter neither."

She turned around and was prissing out. It steamed
me even more watching her high-toned manner, and
hearing her unflattering remarks. I quit with the pump
and reached into my pocket. I flung down a handful of
money on the ground. It didn't roll in the hard-pan dirt,
just made a jingle then sat there, some of it shining back
glints of sun. It made her stop her flouncing and turn

back around. She peered down at the money, winding some stray hair behind her ear.

"That's *some* of the forty dollars I earned. I used part of it on a good pair of leggins for when I trail up some cattle to the Panhandle come fall. It oughta be enough to get you into a nicer place."

She seemed like she held her breath a minute, then lifted her face at me. "You got work trailing cattle?"

"That's right," I lied, but it was a hopeful lie. Castaneda *had* said he'd be in touch. "I'll be gone longer than any twenty-nine days too, so if you can't stand being alone you'd better speak up in a hurry. You can use that money to get yourself back to Bastrop if you want, or wherever. It don't matter to me. One day shines like the next far as I'm concerned."

She gave me a good long look before her eyes puddled up. "It ain't no point to going to Bastrop," she said. "He ain't there anymore." She reached under her cloth apron. "I was gonna show you the letter." She brought a folded slip of paper from her skirts and held it out, then she came the three steps it took to reach my hands.

I went over to one of the wall cracks so I could see the page better. Shot's handwriting never had been too easy to decipher. He wrote:

Deer Lily,

I hope you or safe in Sanantoon by now. I dont no how to brake this to you any smoother then just to say I am done fore. They gave me 2 years but it could be worst.

*Could of been 5 like John Olive had said when he first
arrested me. So dont fret. I will let you no how to rite me
as soon as I no myself. You stick with Woody. He will
keep you safe and see my son gets a proper start in this
hard life. I wish I had beter news but I dont. I love you
and think of you with each breath. Dont foregit me.*
                              Marion

I was stunned. There wasn't any call to be stunned,
but I was just the same. It was less than I'd expected, or
had told myself I did. The truth of it fell leaden on me:
I couldn't believe they'd given Shot two years of hard
time. Not while I'd gone scot-free, though free wasn't
exactly what I was feeling just then. Now I had his
woman to worry over, to pander to, and I didn't have a
mind for that sort of thing. Hell, I hadn't even thought
to send her word from the Diamond M where I was at.

I folded the letter back up and held it out to her. She
tucked it into her skirt again, and I guess she noticed the
starch had gone out of me. She said, "I'll get you some
fresh soap. This cake here's about finished."

I watched after her, and before she made the door,
said, "I'll get you fixed someplace before I head off up
the trail."

She turned back. "I'm fixed right here. I ain't looking
to be a burden to you."

"You ain't no burden," I said, but seeing in her eyes
that she could recognize a lie, I bent my head, picked at
the hard calluses and scales on the inside of my palm. "I

just ain't used to having to account to nobody as to my whereabouts."

"Marion hadn't been fair strapping you with me. We'll just both of us make our own way from here out."

I looked up at her, and she was looking back at me. She sort of smiled—at least I thought it was a smile—then she lifted her hem and stepped up the stairs leading back to the kitchen.

So we agreed to it—that she'd go her way and I'd go mine. Trouble was, there wasn't nowhere for me to go right then. Supposing I *could* hire on with the Diamond M come September, which I was pretty sure I could do, that still left the rest of July and all of August to fill up. But I had the hard-earned forty dollars, so I wasn't in a big hurry to wander out looking for anything else just yet.

I slept off my soreness for a couple of days, didn't see much of Lily except at mealtimes, which she cooked and served. I avoided Markin and his slack-eyed grin as much as possible. And I didn't worry over the promise I'd given to Shot. It hadn't been an actual promise, anyhow, as I recalled it. I hadn't given him my word on anything. If she didn't like my company any better than I liked hers, why force it? That was the way I looked at things. I would make sure before I left town that she had money enough to pay some granny to birth her baby. That much, I told myself, I would surely do. I wasn't about to shuck *all* my obligations.

Now, I reckon there's those that would consider me a sorry fellow for thinking about abandoning Lily as soon as I got the chance to. But those folks might not have understood much about the life I'd led till then, or the upbringing I'd had. See, my ma had died on the same day as Shot was born, and so besides an aunt or two that we hardly ever visited, I hadn't been raised with nothing but men and boys around. What did I know about female needs? And once Pa decided he'd rather drink whiskey than push a plow, the four of us boys were, more or less, left to fend for ourselves. What with now and then stealing a bale of cotton off some farmer, or a few untended cattle from a rancher's grazing land, and later on, holding up stages and dry goods stores and groceries, didn't any of us four boys have much grounding in the whys and ways of family life. And even though watching Jack and Az get cut down last Christmas, and rotting in that Bastrop jail, had turned my mind down a different path now, the truth was, I still figured Lily could do better without me. I decided to let her.

In about three days, as soon as I got over feeling so stoved up, I started visiting Annabel's fairly regular.

And playing cards at Red Meany's saloon. I won a gold fob watch off a San Augustine boy on his way to the silver mines out at Terlingua. But mostly I lost.

I bought me a new set of clothes and a pair of bull-hide boots, and in about two weeks I blew all but nine dollars of the forty, and then I *had* to go looking for work. Money just never had stuck to me for very long. I used three of the nine I had left for a good piece of rope, put on my new clothes, boots, and side-fringed leggins, and I set out to find me somebody looking for a good cowboy.

On my trip to the Diamond M, I'd passed a couple of spreads I remembered, and I decided to try one of those before I struck out cold, going into places I didn't know at all. But when I saddled up Mollie that morning, she balked at leaving her stall. No matter how I spurred her or swatted her rump, she wasn't going nowhere. And then it occurred to me to check her feet.

There was the problem. She had one shoe wore down to nubbin, and another with a loose hobnail. I found a shoe-puller hanging in Markin's shed, and I yanked the two bad ones off her hoofs. I thought she was going to pucker up and kiss me for it.

So with six dollars in my pocket, I headed over to the nearest blacksmith, Poe Terry, his sign said. He charged two bits a shoe. That was scrawled on his sign, too, along with FENCING, WAGON PARTS, KITCHEN WARES, AND ANYTHING METAL.

Poe Terry had the heavy shoulders and neck of a blacksmith, and also a pair of crazy eyes that looked off in two separate directions when he spoke to you, like he was watching your face and somebody else's standing behind you at the same time.

While he worked on Mollie, I practiced with the new jute I'd bought, roping a gate post outside his horse lot. After a minute I said, just by way of conversation, "Don't reckon you'd know of an outfit around here that's looking to hire on a cowhand, would you?"

Poe Terry looked me up and down, or else he was studying the post I was trying to loop. It was hard to tell with him ten feet away, and with those cockeyes of his. He let down Mollie's foot and said, "Do you know anything at all about smithing? I could use a helper around here."

Now, I'd shod a few horses in my time. I wasn't what you'd call an ace at it, but I figured given a little more experience, I could get fast like Terry was. A job was a job after all, and I needed one to set me square, at least till Castaneda gave me another shout.

I said, "As a matter of fact, I know quite a bit about blacksmithing."

Terry took me into the back of his shop. He had a regular tin store back there, with kitchen goods and gardening supplies. He'd been busy making wrought-iron fence curlicues and weathercocks, even furniture of a sort, for sitting on out of doors.

"A feller's got to keep abreast of changing times," he said. "I'm needing me a man to take care of the regular trade, so I can get freed up for this work here." Then he led me back out front to where Mollie was tied. He pointed down at her left hind foot. "I saved you one. Let me see what you can do."

So, I picked out the mud from Mollie's sole, trimmed up her frog, and filed down her hoof. I took down one of the shoes hanging on a wall peg. The forge was glowing, but I pumped up the bellows to make it hotter and heated the iron till it was soft enough to shave. I hammered the shoe to match Mollie's curve, drove in the nails and clenched them down, and when I was done, sweat pouring from my face, old Terry gave me a nod.

"You'll do," he said, and he pitched me an apron and a pair of leather sleeves. "Six dollars a week and we don't work on Sundays. I'll throw in the shoeing of your mare."

So I became a blacksmith's apprentice, and though it wasn't what I had in mind, it was honest work. Hot, but honest. I figured I'd just use the job till September anyway, when I could start up the trail with the Diamond M.

At first my neck, shoulders, and arms stayed tired all the time, but by sometime in August, I noticed the soreness had gone away. I got to where I could shoe two horses in an hour complete, and Mr. Terry stayed, more and more, in the back with his tin and wrought iron.

I wasn't getting rich, but I had enough so's every Saturday on payday, I could visit down to Annabel's. Once I even paid the five dollars to buy an upstairs girl for an hour, though it turned out she wasn't a bit softer than Darcy Jean or Leona out back, who I could get for two-fifty. Either way, I got a free bath first, so from then on, I saved the extra money.

It was at Annabel's I ran into Hillie Sullivan again. That was sometime around the middle of August. When we parted, he said, "See you in two weeks," so I felt sure Castaneda had plans to hire me again. It also reminded me that I hadn't done a thing about finding a granny-lady for Lily.

She'd gotten as big as a hay barn, and every evening when I came in from work, she looked pale and tired from all the cooking and washing and ironing she did for Mr. Markin. Usually for a minute or two after supper, we'd speak. She'd tell me about a letter she'd just got from Shot, or one she'd wrote to him. He was getting along all right, it seemed; getting used to—though I couldn't imagine it—prison life.

"Haven't you got some news I can write to him?" she asked me one night near the end of the month. "Something so's he knows what you're up to? I already told him you're blacksmithing. He asks after you in every letter."

I thought about that for a second. I could hardly tell her I was spending my free time whoring over at

Annabel's, though it was probably just the thing Shot would've liked to hear about. And I didn't want to tell him I'd be going up the trail with a herd of cattle pretty soon, leaving his woman behind to fend for herself, though maybe she'd wrote to him about that already, anyhow.

"I ain't got any news," I said to her and she gave me a disappointed look. She started to go, and then I remembered the folded-up scrap of paper I'd been carrying in my pocket since last Saturday. "Oh," I said, fumbling for it. "I got the name of a midwife here." I drew out the crumpled paper.

Her face went flame-red. She snatched the paper from me and read it. "Where'd you find this out?"

"Mister Terry," I lied. I couldn't very well admit it had been Darcy Jean who'd told me of the woman. "He says she has a lot of experience. She lives out on Olmos Creek, so she ain't far away."

Lily refolded the paper, neater than I'd had it, and raised her face at me. She'd gone back to her natural color.

I said, "I thought you might need to know of somebody. Since I'm gonna be leaving, I just thought I should—"

"Thank you," she said. She shoved the paper into her apron pocket. "Will you be taking Mollie?"

The question caught me by surprise. I'd been taking Mollie everywhere. Hell, I hardly even thought of her as Shot's horse anymore. "I figured I would."

"I figured you would, too," she said, and started towards the door to her room under the stairs.

"Well, ain't that all right?" I said, following her. "I mean, you don't need her, do you?"

"No. Go ahead. I reckon Marion would want you to." She pulled the latch handle on her door and ducked inside.

I took six steps towards the room I shared for four bits with every passing stranger, then glanced back at the door to the one Lily got for free. Why in the hell had she brought that up about Mollie in the first place, if it was all right for me to take the horse? To make me feel guilty was the only answer I could come up with.

I worried on it for the next two days. I laid in bed at night, sweating in the suffering heat, listening to my roommate snore, and I came to the conclusion that Lily didn't want me going with the cattle herd. The Diamond M's or any other. She wanted me here keeping my promise to Shot, even if it wasn't a real, true promise I'd made him; even if we didn't, her and me, see each other but two minutes every day; even though she'd said before I could go my own way. If there was one thing I was learning fast, it was that you couldn't trust a thing a woman said.

So she kept me awake with that festering question of hers about Mollie. And when I wasn't stewing over that, the fellow snoring in the next bed worked on me. I'd had a round of roommates come and go during the past weeks—a barbwire salesman from Ohio, a roustabout for a circus that came through town, and for a few days, a down-on-his-luck farmer running from his furnishing merchant over in East Texas. I didn't make friends with any of them, but hadn't a one of them growled all night long like this newest one did, this drifter from Tennessee.

He sounded like some wild animal, and he smelled like one too, but it didn't do any good to complain. Pa had been a snorer, and Az had done it sometimes when he'd had too much drink. Either one of them you could just roll over, or clamp your hand over their mouth till they stopped. But the one time I'd mentioned the racket to the Tennessean, he'd laughed in my face, rested his hand on the butt of his bone-handled belt-knife, and told me to fold my head up in my pillow if it bothered me so much. That I'd been doing anyhow, for the smell as much as the noise. I guess I should have been grateful that Markin's business wasn't brisk and we weren't having to share a bed.

But it was that racket, or the lack of it, that caused me to come awake so sudden, the night before I was due to head west for Uvalde and the Diamond M. I rolled over in my sleep and found the room, for once, quiet. It jumped me alert. The sounds from down the hall came to me second.

At first I thought it was a summer storm blowing in, and that the sounds were just the upstairs half of the inn creaking in the wind, but the cloth tacked over the open window was hanging straight. And then a current of other noises came along right after the first ones. It wasn't voices speaking exactly, but it was human sounds of some sort. I got up.

I was sweating rivers in the heat clogging the room, so I peeled off my wet handles, and pulled my britches on over naked skin. I took a candle and went barefoot out the door. Listened.

The next room over was empty, had been ever since the spring below Lily's floor had started seeping under the wall. I walked past that door, and then I stopped.

All at once, I knew where the sounds were coming from, and I knew what they were, too. I realized where my bedfellow had disappeared to, and where I had to go. I also knew what I'd find when I got there. And all this knowing sprang on me so quick, I didn't even think about my six-gun. I bolted down the hall, flung open the door to Lily's room, and even being damned sure certain what was going on, I wasn't ready for what I saw.

In the paltry light from my candle, I recognized the fellow from Tennessee. He was face-down and on top of Lily's bed. I couldn't really see her except for one white leg sticking out from under him, but I knew it was her and the man's bare ass was humping down on her.

A sick feeling swallowed me, and I started to back out of the room, thinking this wasn't my business, and maybe Shot knew already what she was up to with other men. But then the Tennessean rose up enough to look back at where I stood. When I saw that he intended to

come after me, it was too late to shut the door. I dropped
the candle and it went out.

"He's got a knife," Lily's voice came, high and
quavery, nearly unrecognizable. As soon as the words
hung in my head, I saw the flash of silver swipe in
my direction, and remembered that long-bladed, bone-
handled knife he wore on his belt.

Lucky for me, I had my night-eyes still from having
just been asleep. I moved faster than I ever had before or
since, and bowed away from the blade. It was a hunting
knife, about eight inches long and sharp on both sides,
and when he slashed at me again, only him yanking
up his britches saved me. I rolled along the wall out of
reach, and bumped into the writing table. It made a thud
scooting across the floor.

The third time he cut out at me, he took a piece of
my elbow. It stung like the blazes of hell, and sent me
a clear message—this fellow meant to kill me, and if I
didn't do something quick, he'd have an easy go of it.

Lily wasn't screaming but she was making scram-
bling noises. I tripped on something dark in the corner
and stumbled. Tennessee came after me. His breath was
loud and foul-stinking. I buried my head in his gut and
butted him backwards. The knife raked across my back,
but his balance was upset enough the blade didn't sink
in deep. I hit him square in the groin, both hands locked
together and coming up solid between his legs, a trick
I'd learned from Az, since he'd pulled it on me enough

times. I knew first-hand how bad it hurt. Tennessee grunted, then all his weight bore down on me. He was as heavy as iron.

We were both on the floor then, grappling in the wet spot at the center and tangling in the sodden rug. I got him turned off me and I was searching for his knife hand. A strength came to me, or else fear made my strength more powerful. I kicked him away from me. He hit the bed and Lily let out a cry. When he came at me again, I got a clear view of the knife flickering in the dim light from outside the single window.

I grabbed his wrist. He was sweaty, slippery. So was I. But I held on, digging my fingernails in, trying to squeeze off the feeling in his hand. Finally, the knife clattered to the floor and hit the rug. My heart was pounding so hard, it was almost all I could hear.

Still the fellow wouldn't quit. He was bent on seeing me dead, and when he dove for the blade, I beat him there. I got a lock on his shoulders, and had the knife under his chin, when the room lit up. Lily had struck a candle, and she sat there on the bed trembling, both her hands wrapped around that little pepperpot she'd tried to sneak to Shot in the Bastrop jail. I hadn't even known she still had the damned thing.

I saw the truth on her then—on her face streaked with tears and sweat, the red welt rising on her cheek, and on her nightdress torn to pieces. He'd been raping her, with her swole-up pregnant and helpless to fend him off. The muzzle of her pistol was pointed at the big fellow's gut, which I had exposed to her when I wrenched his arm backwards. She was cocking the hammer, her eyes wild and wide.

"Don't!" I grunted at her, and in the next instant, I stuck the knife deep into the man's neck and drug it across his throat. His back arched up. I felt him quiver once. Hot blood poured over my hand. I dropped the knife, stood, and let him crumple forward on the floor.

When I looked up, Lily had gone white and terrified. Her eyes were like black holes in her head. She swallowed, raised her face at me. "Did you kill him?" she whispered.

I glanced down at him. A shiver rustled over me. Then came a stillness, a calm almost. I had his blood on my britches. I wiped on more from my hand. He had a dark pool of it under him, and more was spreading out over the floor. I stepped backwards and my bare foot left a print of it on the rug.

I went to the door and closed it softly. When I turned around, Lily was staring down at the dead man in the middle of her room. "We gotta get him outta here," I said.

Her hand rose trembling to her throat. She nodded.

"I ain't going back to jail," I said in case she had any notion of calling the law in on this. She just sat there, ghostly quiet. The little pistol was still in her hands, but forgotten now and resting on her lap.

I squatted down, ran my hands up under his arms,

yanked him onto the rug, and wrapped the ends around him. It didn't cover him completely but he could do the rest of his bleeding inside there. I looked at her. She was still staring, trancelike.

"Go get a bucket and a mop and some rags," I said. "And do it quiet."

She nodded again and kept her eyes at the floor. She didn't move.

"We gotta hurry," I said.

She looked up at me. She was shaking so hard I could see it. Her eyes had gone to all pupil and I thought I might have to slap her sense back. She stood up, and the pistol dropped soundless on the bed. Holding her belly like it was a baby born already to the world that she needed to comfort, she stood up. Her clothes were torn at the top and at the side seam. She stepped around the dead man on the rug. I caught her arm.

"Put something on, Lily. In case somebody sees you." I nodded at the housedress hanging on a nail hook. "Just throw it on over you. Get a mop and a bucket and rags—"

"I heard you," she said. Her voice wasn't yet normal. Her eyes weren't.

"Make sure nobody's up. I'm gonna have to carry him outta here."

I helped her pull the dress over her head. She still looked pretty ragged with her hair frazzling out about her face, and with that welt on her cheek, but I couldn't go with her and risk tracking the man's blood all over the place.

She went without shoes through the door. I watched her pass the stairs, then I closed up the room again. She had taken the candle and I seemed pulled into blinding darkness after its light. I stood by the door, studying the black lump in the middle of the floor.

I'd killed him, sure enough. With my own two hands. And it hadn't been much different than slitting the throat of a boar hog. I thought something must be wrong with me not to feel any more remorse than I did. Maybe I had the killer instinct in me after all. Maybe I *had* shot Willie Griffin back at McDade last December. I'd been wild that day, too, wanting a life—any life—in exchange for my brothers' lives.

I knelt beside the Tennessean, remembering how little sleep he'd given me during the nights before. I lifted back the ends of the rug and felt inside his pockets.

He had money, hard money and cash. He had a watch and a little plug of tobacco. I unwrapped the waxy paper from around the plug and stuck it into my cheek. The money went into my pocket. The watch I shoved back into his.

It took all my strength to drag the Tennessean down the hall and through the kitchen, wrapped in the scatter rug from Lily's room. His head hung out and bumped on each one of the back porch steps. I drug him through the well yard, past the kitchen garden, and Lily went behind me, sweeping the ground with a broom.

Inside the barn, I brought Sassy out of her stall. Lily held the mule still while I bear-hugged the body up over her back. I used my new rope to tie him on, and the damned dumb mule didn't seem to know or care that she was packing a dead man. Mollie, on the other hand, knew the smell of death. She shied from the saddle and whinnied, like she was the one carrying the body. It took Lily with a nosebag full of oats to keep the mare quiet.

When I was done, I stopped for a second to catch my breath.

"Let me go with you," Lily said in a whisper.

"You can't. You've gotta get back inside and make sure there's no trace. Pack your things together. We'll be leaving as soon as I come back."

"We could just go on now. I don't need none of my things." Shadows cast from the barn lantern hollowed out her face.

I put my hand on her shoulder. "No. You gotta stay here and get everything ready. It'll look suspicious if we run out in the middle of the night. We gotta do this so's nobody thinks nothing's wrong. I'll be back before you know it."

She stood there looking doubtful and watched me mount up. She handed me Sassy's lead rope. I dallied it round Mollie's saddlehorn.

This wasn't the first time I'd hauled off a dead body. I'd done it for Jeff Fitzpatrick when he killed that Lee County deputy last December. I hauled the deputy, one Bose Heffington by name, out to the cedar brakes east of McDade, just cause it didn't seem right to me to leave a man lying dead out in the open, but I paid for it later with the lives of my brothers. The next morning we put Jeff on an outbound train, and that night, Christmas Eve, the mob had come calling for me, hunting me down like a coon since I'd been the one seen taking the body off. Seen and also accused of the deed, though this man behind me, this one from Tennessee who snored and stank and abused pregnant girls, he was the first man I was sure I'd killed. Killed him with my own hands and his own knife. It still wasn't settling on me.

I guided Mollie down past the barn. Down the dark back road. Down to the river and a place I'd seen once—a deep bend tucked up in a thicket with a pool of deeper water.

At the river thicket, I found a rock big enough to sink the Tennessean—sink him for a time at least. Time enough for me to get away, head down south to Mexico where I should've gone as soon as I left Bastrop.

I sat down to pull off my boots, and used my good, brand-new rope to tie the rock onto him, curling his legs and arms around it like a lover. I had to wade in knee-deep before the current took him under. For several minutes, I watched, waiting for him to bob up. In my mind I could see him dragging along the pebble and mud bottom, his hair riffling in the waves, eyeballs open, and head half hanging on.

I took off my bloody britches, wadded them up inside the scatter rug, and rolled that out in the river, too. The water burned the cut on my elbow, and my bare foot hit something solid but spongy, something like an arm or a leg. I strangled back the yelp that tried to come from my throat. It was only my imagination going wild, I told myself. The man was gone, downstream. He couldn't have hung up already, but I waded fast back to the bank.

The animals needed a drink, so I let them have it while I pulled on the change of britches I'd brought, the old holey pair I'd worn during my time in jail. Then we set off back to the inn, the unburdened mule behind me, and Mollie's heart thumping against the inside of my thigh.

It was nearing sunup, but deep into the final darkness of night, when I got back to the inn. I almost stumbled over Lily, where she huddled in a corner of the back porch.

"What're you doing out here?" I said, shaking off the start she given me.

"I got everything ready like you said." She pointed at a dark blur beside her feet. Her gripsack, and a pile of other things that must've been mine.

"That's good. Now, go on inside and make breakfast like always." I tried to step around her, but she clutched at me. Her fingernails cut into my arm like needles.

"You said we were going when you got back."

"I've had time to think it through. We gotta let Mister Markin see us." I turned her towards the door. "Mister Terry owes me for four days. I'll go collect, then come back saying you've had a letter from your folks, hailing you back on some family business, and we gotta leave right away."

I shoved her inside the door, and she went. Then I hauled all our belongings out to the wagon. I hitched up Sassy. It wouldn't hurt her to stand in harness a while, however long this was going to take us. My plan seemed as sensible as any Jack would've come up with. Fact is, the way I had hit upon it quick as a thought made me give a long pondering out by the barn door. I didn't know much about praying, hadn't had any experience at it, but it seemed like something or somebody was watching out for me just then.

"Jack?" I whispered. "Is that you?" then felt plumb foolhardy hearing my voice echo back at me in the quiet. Jack wasn't hardly the angel type, and since I didn't believe in spooks, I figured it must just be my blood creeping, after everything with the Tennessean, making me think such useless thoughts.

When I got back to the kitchen, Lily was hovering in the middle of the room, staring at the stove like she'd forgot what it was for. She had a lamp going, bright enough for me to see the strawberry on her cheekbone. It didn't have the look of anything but a man's handprint to me, and I couldn't think of one damned excuse we could give for it to Mr. Markin. When I touched the bruise with my thumb, she sucked in her breath but she didn't move.

"Did you get that fella's things packed up, too?" I said and she shook her head, a look of dread coming to her eyes. "We're gonna have to do it. Otherwise, Markin'll be wondering how come him to leave without taking his things with him. Where's some writing paper?"

She pointed towards the front room, where Markin's

desk sat behind the registration counter. She brought the lamp, and I sat down to dip the quill into the ink-well. I tore off a scrap of Markin's stationery, wrote GONE TO TERLINWAH TO HUNT SILVER. It took me a while. I wasn't sure how to spell the town's name, but then I figured the Tennessean probably couldn't spell any better.

I folded the note, not bothering to wait for the ink to dry. "We'll leave this on his bed, with the four-bits he owes on the room. Won't be no reason for Markin to think nothing fishy that way. There's lots of men going out mining for silver."

I started to explain to her about the fob watch I'd won off just such a man, but she was giving me such a dim-witted look I didn't go into it all right then.

Markin's quarters were situated right above the front room. I heard him moving around up there, and we both looked towards the ceiling. I closed his desk as quiet as I could.

"Do like I said, now." I shoved the note and a few coins from my shirt pocket into her hand. "Pack every-thing he owned, and leave this on the bed. I'll keep the old man busy for a spell."

She took the lamp towards the rooms underneath the stairs, and I went back into the kitchen, like I was after some early morning coffee. Daybreak had begun to light the windows.

The kettle was on the stove, but there wasn't any

water in it. Coffee beans were in a sack up high on the shelf. I considered dumping a few in the grinder to make myself look busy, but then I thought it would probably seem more suspicious for Markin to find me at the stove than if I just sat down by the table to wait. I gripped my forehead, rubbed my eyes, mussied up my hair. Yawned. I felt like a butter churn inside.

Markin stomped into the kitchen, squinted at me in the light from his bed candle. "What are you doing sitting here in the dark?" he shouted.

"Just roused," I grunted. "I knocked on Lily's door to let her know I was up and hungry."

"She needs her rest," he said, not as loud now, but like he was shaming me for slave-driving her.

He set his candle down on the table and reached for the lantern hanging by its bale above the stove. When he struck the wick, the light turned the kitchen yellow.

"I suppose you're wanting your coffee?" he hollered at me.

"A slab of bacon'd be nice, too," I hollered back.

He gave me a sour look, so I thought I'd done a fine job of sounding cranky. I huffed a few breaths of impatience, glared towards the direction Lily would be coming. Any minute now. I wished she'd hurry. I was ready to get this all over with, and in no mood to jabber with Markin alone.

"The bacon I'll leave for your *sister* to cook," he said, as usual putting more on the word *sister* than he needed to. I'd stopped trying to set him straight. "But I can brew coffee as well as any female." He poured beans from the sack into the grinder, and whirled the lever. The racket of it jolted my spine.

I thought about sitting through breakfast with the other boarders, just as if nothing any different had happened already today. Panic sat on me for a minute like it had down at the river—made me feel pukey and like I might need to rush outside for some air. What was stalling her? How many belongings could a Tennessee drifter have to gather up?

I looked down at my hands while Markin talked about the hot weather and how ready he was for fall to set in. A line of blood had rolled out of my shirt and dried onto my wrist. I used spit to wipe it off, then noticed my shirt was matted with it and stuck to my elbow where I'd taken the knife. I put my arm down under the table before the old innkeeper noticed, too.

Footsteps came from the center room, and then she appeared in the kitchen doorway. Her face was pasty white, from fear, I thought at first, till I realized she'd smeared something on herself, some kind of cream or salve, to cover up the bruise welting on her cheek. She looked at me and then at Markin, her eyes wide and glowing. She braced herself in the doorjamb. She had the Tennessean's grease-stained carpetbag clutched in her left hand.

"I just got a letter from my papa," she blurted. "My baby sister's sick and dying. I gotta go home right now."

I frowned at her, shook my head trying to tell her it was too soon. But she'd already said it all, and Markin had heard. He moved away from the stove where the coffee kettle steamed, headed towards her, and him going over to comfort her made tears spring to her eyes. They slid shiny and quick down her face, streaking the white cream. She dropped the carpetbag at her feet.

"Oh, my deary," Mr. Markin said, shaking a handkerchief out from the pocket of his morning coat. "This is terrible news."

He glanced back at me like I should be doing something besides sitting there. I got to my feet. I looked up at the shelf clock on the cupboard. The old man didn't seem to see nothing unusual about Lily's getting a letter at five-thirty in the morning.

She was sobbing into Markin's handkerchief, and though I knew it was no pretend cry, she couldn't have played it any better. Her misery kept the innkeeper's mind off the fact that her story didn't make much sense.

I took ahold of her trembling shoulders, bent for the carpetbag, and veered her towards the kitchen door, all at the same time. "We'll have to get going then," I said. "We got four hard days to McDade." I made sure Markin heard our destination, just in case Tennessee floated up before he got down river good. McDade was in the opposite direction from Mexico.

Markin grabbed the sack of coffee beans off the shelf above the stove. "Take this," he said. "You'll need it on the trip. And take fodder for your animals. There's plenty stacked up in the east corner of the barn." I knew where everything was. I'd already thrown some in the wagon, but I thanked him anyhow.

Lily lifted the coffee sack out of his hand, and I was busy holding open the door. He said, "That's a nasty cut you have there on your arm." He tried to reach for it, but I swiveled away. Me and Lily's eyes met.

"Got it at Mister Terry's yesterday. Backed right into a trestle stacked with iron rods. Reckon it broke open again in my sleep." I smiled, switched the carpetbag over to that hand, and sort of held it behind me so he'd think the wound wasn't as bad as it looked, though I could feel the fever burning in it.

Markin didn't say anything more. He stood there kind of quiet, though, which wasn't too usual for him. He let us go on out the door and down the four porch steps.

"You'll be back?" he called as we aimed ourselves across the well yard.

I hollered, "Soon as we can," real friendly at him. I thought he seemed more suspicious now, like things were starting to dawn on him. Maybe he'd recognized the carpetbag, or wondered where the rest of our things were at. Or maybe I'd talked just a little too long about the cut on my arm. I thought we'd get lucky if he didn't follow us to the barn where he'd see the wagon already loaded and ready.

To Lily, I whispered, "How the hell'd you get a letter at this hour of the morning?"

"I couldn't think what else to do," she said. "I found this."

She reached into her skirt pocket and came out with the Tennessean's big knife. It was spanking clean. Looked brand new. It struck me what a chore that scrubbing had been for her.

I grabbed the knife from her hand and stuffed it, blade down, inside the waist of my britches.

The four miles till we crossed the river seemed to take nine hours. Even though it wasn't the same spot where I'd dumped Tennessee, I strained my neck out to see over the bridge into the water. Dew had all the grass along the banks glistening white.

When I looked back at Lily, she had her hands folded in her lap, eyes straight ahead. The bruise on her face seemed to grow darker by the second, even underneath the white salve she'd smeared on so careful.

"From here on"—I cleared my throat—"if anybody asks us, you're my wife. Old man Markin thought it anyhow, and I don't reckon Shot'd mind so long as it keeps you outta harm. It'll make things a whole lot easier to explain." I snapped the lines down and the mule paced up. "A man's got a right to keep his woman in line if needs be. Could be you was acting up and I smacked you one. Long as folks think you're my wife, ain't nobody gonna ask questions about your face being marked up."

Lily's hand went to her cheekbone, and she turned her head away from me. She wasn't talking, though, so I had my thoughts to myself. They weren't happy thoughts. By all rights I should've been on my way to the Diamond M, not here in this wagon, jouncing over the broken path that was supposed to be a road. So much for a fresh start in San Antonio. So much for a new life with a future to it. Here I was all over again, with blood on my hands and slap in the middle of trouble.

I didn't seem able to get control of things. I never had much experience at it, since Jack had always seen to that end for me. And I kept on thinking what would Jack've done different, and the best I could come up with was he would've never got himself mixed up in this kind of situation in the first place. He'd have figured some way to look after Lily's needs without having her under-foot all the time, just like I'd planned from the outset and never done. I'd had too many pent-up guilty feelings where Shot was concerned, about him coming to rescue me and getting arrested himself for the effort, and about him going to the pen and me going scot-free.

Daylight burned down full-bore when we stopped the first time to water the mule and Mollie. Lily climbed right on down from the wagon like she was planning to head to the bushes. She didn't, though. She just fol-lowed along behind me as I went about checking the wheels and the harness, while I pulled the blinders from Sassy's head. I took both animals down to water at a little creek, and staked them there so they wouldn't wander off. When I turned around from doing that, Lily was hovering so close, I nearly knocked her backwards.

It perturbed me some, her dogging my heels so close. And I started to ask her was she hungry or something, but then figured that would be an ignorant question. We'd got out of town in too big a hurry to stock up on any provisions, save Markin's bag of coffee beans and the sack of feed corn from the barn. I reckoned her belly to be about as empty as mine was by then, and when I looked down at her, she looked back at me with her big, bewildered, upturned eyes. Then she stepped out of my way.

"We'll let Shot know where we're bound," I said, in case that was what was eating at her, "at the next town we come to. He ain't going no place for a while yet, anyhow."

She nodded, and moved a streak of hair that had blown into her face. She had a bead of sweat above her lip. "I got a needle and some thread if you want me to sew up your elbow."

I checked my wound again. It was still throbbing, and the shirt sleeve was bloody, but wasn't none of it fresh. "I reckon it's scabbing up," I said.

"Could get infectious."

I followed her back to the wagon and waited while she dug around in her clutch. I wasn't one bit anxious to have her poking me with no needle, but it seemed she needed something to do, so I let her. I tried not to flinch when she pulled the thread through, but it was near to impossible. I muttered a few goddamns which she must've not heard since she didn't correct me, and pretty soon it was over.

I reached to put my shirt back on and caught her staring at the old bullet holes in my arm, the ones from Mr. Milton's scattergun. Shot had taken eleven pieces of lead from me there, and they had left behind a kind of star pattern of deep, puckered, dark-red dents in my flesh. The holes looked worse than they felt. Oh, sometimes I ached, whenever it rained or got too humid. Nothing like this stitched-up elbow cut was paining me now, though.

"You oughta have on a hat or something," I said. "You'll blister in this sun."

She didn't answer, just looked down at her feet like she was ashamed for having come off without a head covering of some kind, or for having stared too long at the holes in my arm. I pulled my shirt on over my head.

I unlaced my saddle pouch, and fished for the bandanna I'd worn busting ponies for Castaneda. I shook it out one-handed, folded it into a V-shape, and palmed it onto her head. She took the two ends and knotted them underneath her chin. And I swear, wearing that scarf, and with her sad eyes, she could've been an immigrant girl just come off the boat.

I helped her up into the buckboard, led the animals

back to the wagon, and we got under way again. About a mile or two down the road, Lily said, "Thank you."

I wasn't sure exactly for what, the head scarf or something else. But I said, "You bet," and didn't mention it again.

We slept the first night in a lot behind a wayside store. It was pure luck we found the place when we did, because both of us were near starving and no game to be seen from the road. The store was also a post office, and there was a writing desk over under the window all set up with a quill pen and ink well. But Lily refused to go over there and sit down to write Shot, so I put the envelope and sheet of paper I'd planned to buy back up on the shelf. I figured I'd let her decide when the time was right.

The storekeeper sold us some meal, and he told me I could have the mean old yellow rooster in his house yard if I could catch him. Hunger will give you a cunning you never knew you had. I leaned on the yard fence, and watched the yellow cock strut around pecking at the other birds, fanning his tail. He was a big one, and likely tough and stringy as rawhide, but my stomach was grumbling, and it was a free meal after all.

I hiked over the fence, landed crooked on my ankle so's a pain shot up to the knee on my bad leg, and I snuck up behind the devil rooster. He caught me coming out of the corner of his beady eye, and flew at me with his talons open. I kicked him senseless, then wrenched his neck and head plumb off. The body darted this way and that, blood pumping like a spring from the hole where his neck had been, before the death rattle finally plopped him in the dirt.

Lily plucked the feathers but she wouldn't touch the bone-handled knife, so I had to cut the rooster into pieces and build the fire. While she fried the meat, I whittled the scabbard off the Tennessean's belt. It was the only thing from his carpetbag worth saving—that and an old shirt I'd already stripped into rags to bind up my hands for the harness lines, since I didn't own driving gloves. I fashioned the knife scabbard to fit down inside my right boot. Later, I slept with it there, and with my .45 and the shotgun beside me on the ground.

I dreamed of Pa, out in the pasture back home. He had this old bay mare he used to ride, and he was on her. Just out there in the pasture, near the trees where he once shot a yellow panther that had tore up some of the hogs. And Jack was with him, and me, and he was showing us something, an old cedar stump sprouting limbs ever which way. It was good to see Jack.

"Before you know it, it'll take you over," Pa said to us, and that was all. Nothing else. Just Pa, looking young on his bay horse out in the pasture. And me. And Jack. The three of us out there together, just as clear as daylight. It jarred me awake.

I laid there dazed, blinking up at the moonless sky,

and wondered what in hell had brought Pa's face to my mind. I never thought of him much, and if I did it was mostly with relief that he was gone—sort of how you'd feel after neck-yoking fresh water from a creek a mile away—the tingling relief all up and down your spine and in your shoulders. Pa'd been a hard man to have a fondness for, yet that's just what I'd felt seeing him in the dream.

I rolled over on my bedroll, still pondering the queerness of it, the night sounds ringing in my ears, and I about rolled into her, could've mashed her flat just trying to get settled on the hard ground. I sat up; rubbed at my eyes. It was her, sure enough, wound up tight in the wagon blanket, stretched out in the dirt not two feet from me.

I started to reach over and shake her awake, make her get back up in the wagonbed. But then I realized it didn't make any real difference to me where she slept. If she wanted to chance ticks and scorpions out here on the ground, it wasn't none of my business. Maybe it got hot in the wagon. Maybe the breeze wouldn't reach down past the side boards.

But I knew that wasn't the reason she was down here on the ground with me. She was plain scared, and just as soon as that thought popped in my head, the next one to follow was of the Tennessean going limp in my arms, his blood, warm as piss, soaking over my hand.

I moved my bedroll over about ten feet, took my .45

and the shotgun with me, and I laid there with my eyes wide open. I thought about Pa some, and then about Jack and Az, watching them get cut down and me not being able to stop it; and about Lily and the dead Tennessean, and that there wasn't nothing I could've done to stop that either. And yet there she was, pulling her blanket down out of the wagon to sleep near me, thinking I was somehow fit to be a caretaker.

From that store all the way to Oakville, we had no trouble finding food. Bobwhites were on the move, what with all the wild grass gone to seed down south. I bagged us a mess every day for our supper. I had to hunt on foot, though, for Mollie had gone funny about gunfire. The first time I took a shot from her back, she'd jumped clear off the ground with all fours, and pitched me flat. It took nearly two hours for me to catch up to her again, after she'd run herself down. I reckon she'd just got out of the hunting habit with her new life of leisure these months away from Shot.

At Oakville, we stayed at a hotel so new the walls leaked sap. Alone, I wouldn't have spent the two dollars the room cost me, but Lily looked peaked and worn out with the wagon. Her cheeks and nose were sunburnt, and she'd gotten kind of dirty without a place to wash good. But we weren't in the money enough, not even with the inheritance from Mr. Tennessee, to afford to buy two rooms. So I checked us in as Mr. and Mrs. Beatty.

It wasn't an outright lie. And I reckoned Shot wouldn't mind. Not if it kept her safer. I gave her the bed while I took the floor, sleeping on my thin saddle roll.

During the night a September rain sprang up, with lightning and thunder that shuddered the sappy walls. I woke up once long enough to feel grateful for the roof over my head, and to move my arm so it felt more comfortable. I guess Lily heard me stirring.

"Haywood?" she said.

Her voice came out so light, I thought at first she'd got mixed up, somehow, in the dream I'd been having. A good dream it was too, of riding herd on the open range. But some place with lots of trees like back at McDade. And I still had Ben and he was just as soft-jawed and easy on the backside as I remembered. And Jack was in this dream too, I'm pretty sure. Or somebody that looked just like him.

She said my name again. "Haywood?"

"It's just a storm," I muttered without opening my eyes. "It'll pass."

Another big crack of thunder came, beat a hard lick against the window. Might've been hail with it.

"It's sure loud, though," she said. "Could be a cyclone coming. You hear about them all the time, popping up out of nowhere. Scattering houses and things to bits."

It was the most she'd said all at once in three days. I rolled over and saw her silhouette in the lightning flashes. She was sitting up on the bed, facing towards our one window.

"Won't be no cyclone." I shifted again, trying for some comfort on the hard floor. "Anyway, you can hear them coming before they hit. Sound like a runaway train."

That shut her up for a second, but then her breath took in with the next crash. "My mama used to say thunder is God's drums," she said, quivery, but louder. "And lightning is his sword for fighting with the devil. Do you believe in God?" I knew then I wouldn't get no sleep till this storm passed.

Why was it, I wondered, females had to get so damned fitful in bad weather? I once knew a whore over at Caldwell that couldn't get her work done proper for all her screaming and carrying on in a thunderstorm. Fellows even took to calling her Old Boom-Boom on account of it.

A yawn came over me and my eyes closed again. "Clouds," I said. I only wanted peace and silence. "Clouds get full of rain, and thunder's the racket they make emptying out. That's all there is to it."

"But God? Do you think he's up there?"

"How the hell should I know?"

"I used to believe in God, but I don't know anymore. Too many bad things happen to people for God to be watching over us like the preachers say."

"Maybe he tries best he can, but there's just too much going on for him now. Or maybe he's got bad helpers and they ain't doing *their* job right." I shifted on my pallet again. The floor was feeling awful hard to me now that I was awake. "I don't know. I don't ever think much about God."

Rain kept spitting at the window, but slower now. The lightning wasn't so fierce or often. Sleep almost grabbed ahold of me and pulled me under before she spoke again.

"I gave him an extra helping of peach pudding at supper." Her voice came soft and with a rumble of thunder, far off now. "He said he never tasted such sweet peaches. Said they didn't grow them like that where he came from. I'd picked a whole bushel basket full that afternoon just to keep the birds from getting to them. There was too much pudding. But I told Mister Markin I could get rid of it all."

I didn't know what to say. I remembered eating the pudding, too, and it had tasted good. But the Diamond M had been on my mind, and leaving come morning. I hadn't much noticed the Tennessee fellow sitting at the table, or him taking seconds. I tried not to think about him on top of her, her white foot poking out from under him. I stared at the black wall in front of me.

"It ain't your fault," I said.

"I shouldn't of been nice to him. I was just trying to get rid of all that pudding."

The darkness wavered in front of my eyes. I felt again his blood pouring over my hand, thought about him washing down the river. Maybe he was in the Gulf of Mexico by now. I flopped over, pushed in the saddlebag to make a crevice for my head.

"I don't want Marion to know," she said. She sounded calm, bossy almost. It came as a relief to me. "I want your word you won't never tell him about it."

"All right."

It wasn't a hard promise to make. Shot would've probably blamed me for it, anyhow. I was supposed to be taking care of her for him. Instead I was busy making plans to trail a herd to the Panhandle. I wished like hell that was where I was, too. Even with the rain pattering outside, and the hard work it would've meant, the long miles.

In a minute, I heard her breath come again, this time ragged and wet-sounding. I knew she was probably weeping, trying not to sob out loud, keeping it to herself, which was good. There wasn't any use in us talking it to death. What happened happened, and there was no changing it now.

"Go to sleep," I mumbled, and she made a sound like "Uh-huh."

In the morning, a group of cowhands, lashing and ya-ing a herd of cattle through the center of town, woke us.

Three days out of Oakville, headed down the Matamoros road, Lily got her first cramp. It hit her sudden and hard. I knew because she reached out and clamped down on my forearm, and I saw by her face something was wrong. She told me what.

We were out in the middle of nowhere, just brush thickets along both sides of the trail, someplace east of the Nueces because we'd had trouble crossing that river the morning before. I said, "Good godamighty, girl. You can't be having no baby right here. It ain't a good time."

She looked scared; I felt a little scared myself. She nodded and I made her give me a sworn promise she wouldn't be having any more cramps till we got someplace around other folks, hopefully womenfolks. I didn't rightly know which way to head for that. I kept on the road going south. For more than an hour, she didn't say again if she was having pain, but I heard each time she sucked in her breath. It seemed she did it more and more regular.

I knew we must be getting close to San Patricio, since we'd already passed the ten-mile marker a while back. It was the town I'd figured on stopping in for the night, anyhow. They'd surely have a doctor there. But I hadn't been this far south before, and so I wasn't familiar with any landmarks that would tell me how much farther we had yet to go. We went down into a hollow and then over a creek bed running with just a few inches of water, but the ride was rough.

She clutched my shoulder this time and said, "Woody . . . ," which she hadn't ever called me before, but which I figured she'd got from Shot's letters, since he'd decided that was my name from now on. Cattle were grazing in the creek bottom, so I hoped there'd be people somewhere close by, too. "I think I better stop," she said. Her voice sounded echo-y and solemn.

I thought about everything I knew on the subject of birthing, and it didn't take me long. I'd seen cows drop calves, and I'd helped Pa foal his old bay mare, but that wasn't the same as a live human baby. I didn't think I'd have the stomach for it. My throat dried up and I popped the lines on the mule to go faster.

"Woody," she said again, and she was leaning backwards, stretching her legs out straight before her.

"It ain't far now," I said, keeping my voice stern.

"I can't go on!" she hollered at me. She was panting breath, clawing at the seat underneath her, and leaning back like she was going to slide off onto the floor boards. "You gotta stop. Now!"

I thought about Shot lazing away at the prison back at Huntsville, and me here with his wife, his baby coming on. I couldn't remember ever feeling such hand-wringing helplessness. I started shaking all over like with convulsions, and at the same time, hollered out at the mule to whoa down.

Sweat was dripping off Lily's face, more than it should've been, even in the September heat. She was still hunkered down, panting through her mouth.

"I don't know what to do," I said.

"I gotta lay down."

I started trying to help her up, to get her into the wagonbed. The mule turned her head back at us, like she was wondering why in the hell I'd stopped at this place. Mollie blew and nickered. Lily grabbed ahold of both my arms and almost pulled me down on top of her.

"Lemme get on the ground," I said. "And then you scooch to the edge and maybe I can carry you around to the back."

"I gotta rest," she breathed. "Oh my . . ."

I jumped off the wagon, stepped over the wagon shavs, and reached up at the seat on her side. "Can you lean towards me?"

She looked at me, her eyes red and watery, bugging out of her face. She shook her head. "I don't think so."

And then I thought I heard something—something like laughter or maybe shrieking. My ears perked up. My spine straightened. A hawk flapped up from the brush with something dead, or soon to be, dangling in its jaws. Lily groaned again, and I kept listening.

It was for sure laughter. Coming from just up over the rise. I took my pistol off my belt. I wasn't thinking of nothing except I needed help. And fast. I cocked back the hammer and fired once straight up in the air.

Down in the draw like we were, and with the creek to carry the sound, the pistol-shot boomed like a cannon. Mollie reared against her rope, busted off the back board of the wagon and the wheels lurched. Lily floundered on the high-seat. Sassy kicked backwards first, brayed, then took off like an arrow, straight up out of that hollow. I yelled at the top of my lungs but that godforsaken mule kept right on running. I could see Lily bouncing around, could feel her misery, or close to it.

I bounded after Mollie, who'd already wheeled around, headed back to the shallow water in the creek. The herd of cattle I'd seen before came stampeding straight at me. Luckily, it wasn't a big herd, maybe a dozen.

For half a second, I hesitated, confused. Then I started hollering, running after the wagon, and running wasn't my best talent with my gimped-up leg. I didn't seem to make any headway, and the goddamned mule wouldn't slow down. I heard a moaning scream that I knew came from Lily. I stumbled over a gopher hole and fell flat, skinning my hands and face, and tearing bigger holes in my britches. And I figured it was no use then. Lily and her baby were done for, and I'd have Shot to answer to for my poor caretaking of his family.

When I pulled myself up off the ground, I saw that a gang of Mexicans—men, women, and children—had swarmed down over the rise, and two of them got hold of the mule. They were yelling and whistling, but they stopped the wagon. I started running again, more crippled up than ever. Before I got there, they'd already pulled Lily down and were carrying her off someplace, just beyond my sight.

"Hey!" I shouted, hobbling as fast as I could. "Hey, now! Where're you going with her?!" I didn't even have my pistol with me. I guess I'd dropped it when Mollie jumped.

I couldn't think of any worse jam to be in than we were now—Lily's baby coming, the wagon broke up, Mollie strayed off, and kidnapped by Mexicans. Two little ones were still with the wagon, unhitching the mule, which I reckoned they planned to steal.

"Hey!" I waved my arms to try and scare them off. They jabbered something at me in Mexican, and kept on with what they were doing.

I snatched the bone-handled knife up from my boot and held it out, threatening. I figured I'd have to fight our way out of this mess I'd gotten us into.

The one unhitching the mule nodded at the other

one. They were little, but full-grown men. The smallest one came towards me. I jabbed the knife in his direction. He held up his hands.

"No! No, *señor*," he said and I understood that much.

"Take your hands off that mule," I said, wanting to get close enough so's I could force an armhold on the little fellow. I aimed to use him as bait to get Lily back.

He smiled at me, pushed his hands palm out. "*Mi amigo*," he said, and then some other Mexican stuff I didn't catch. "*Amigo, sí?*" He smiled so broad all his teeth showed. They were fairly white teeth for a Mexican, and glinted the sun back at me.

I glanced up the rise. I could see the tops of some thatched-roof huts up there, and still heard all the jabbering going on. My leg and face where I'd scraped them were paining. Behind me came some slow hoofbeats, and when I looked, Mollie was nosing my way, her rope and a stick—all that was left of the wagon gate—dragging behind her.

"Goddamned your hide," I said to her.

"*Sí*. Goddamn," the little Mexican in front of me added. He kept grinning.

I stuck the knife back inside my boot.

The jug that kept coming past me had some kind of clear-colored liquor in it that tasted a lot like the busthead Pa used to make from molasses and homegrown tobacco. This brew fuzzed up more of a head, though, and had an after-sting like chili peppers. I figured that it was made from the tiny red peppers that grew wild along the waterways.

Lily was having her baby, and I was getting drunk. Some of the women had her squirreled away inside one of the huts, but now and then we heard her, the group of us men out by the fire, wailing and screaming like a starved coyote. One fat mamacita kept coming out to scold the group of us, always in words I couldn't understand. Once, she brought us some goat meat wrapped up in flat brown tortillas.

Ruben, the one who'd talked me out of knifing him down by the wagon, slapped me on the back, gave me another one of his wide greaser grins, and bade me with a wave to drink up, to swill big. He tilted up the bottom of the jug till it dribbled out my mouth corners and speckled my shirt. They all got a laugh out of that, and my mouth was on fire, a fire only more liquor could quench.

The world was already bobbing—the flames that licked up from the fire, the stars spattered all over the sky. It was all I could do to hold my head upright. The jug came back around to me, and while I was slugging back another gulp or so, I heard the coyote wail again.

We all looked, the eight of us around the fire, Mexican and white, towards the fat lady's hut, our faces drawn in, almost wondrous at a thing couldn't any of us know or understand. Then Ruben yanked the jug from my hand, grinned. He upended the crock at his mouth and the others let out a hoot. Three of them started singing, clapping. One had a guitar with two strings missing. The music, the clapping and yelling, drowned out the suffering pain across the camp.

The drunker ones got up to dance on the other side of the fire. They hooked arms and sang, all in words I couldn't decipher. I'd always had a pretty fair singing voice, and I tried to hum along. My throat took to hurting, and the night got deeper. The moon came out, and bobbed around up there with the stars. I laid back on the ground. Ruben and his brothers' singing filled my head. I didn't know where I was, or care. Texas, but it might as well have been Mexico.

The next thing I knew, somebody was punching me on the shoulder. I was laid on my side, a scratchy blanket I didn't remember thrown over me. Everything, except for a nightbird somewhere and the crickets, was silent. Fingers jabbed into my shoulderblade from behind.

It was the mamacita frowning at me. Her fingers pecked at my back. She chattered something. I blinked to try to get her in focus.

"Huh?"

It wasn't yet daybreak, but I could see her shape, sort of squatting beside me, holding out some kind of food at me. A hunk of bread. I bit in and spit oozed off my tongue at the sweetness of it.

She started rolling out words at me, fast and urgent.

But anything said in Mexican sounded urgent to me. My neck was stiff and aching. I shook my head and laid back down. She punched her fingers into me again.

She rose, jabbering at me, then shook her finger at Ruben when he sat up from under his blanket three feet from me. He was bleary and dark, like a shadow even so close. The woman pounced on her feet, looking huffed about something. I tried to raise, but my head hammered.

"*Es una niña*," Ruben said to me. He rubbed his eyes. "*Niña*," again with more force. He made his arms into a cradle, rocked them side to side, and grinned.

I threw off the blanket, suddenly realizing I hadn't heard the coyote in so long I'd forgotten. I stuffed the rest of the sweet bread into my mouth as I started for the hut. The fat woman came behind me, grumbling like a crotchety hen.

A girl I hadn't seen before stood right inside the door of the hut, holding a bundle of something in her arms. The bundle squeaked and wiggled, and a wrinkled pink arm came out of the swaddling. The girl smiled at me. She was beautiful, black eyes, smooth face, hair that fell in a velvet cloud to her waist. She showed me the baby but I barely saw. I was too busy taking in the girl's face. I swallowed the wad of sweet bread.

The fat woman noticed where I was staring and gave me a shove towards a low doorway, slung across with a dark red curtain. I had to lean to go under it. Lily was in there, lying white and still on a mat near the wall. There was a smell I recognized, of blood and wounds and suffering. Her head rolled towards me, but even in the dim candlelight, I didn't think she saw me.

The mamacita's hands pressed on my back. I stepped forward. I wasn't sure what to say or do. I leaned myself against the wall to steady my balance, and looked down at Lily on her pallet.

"Well, you sure enough done it," I said. "It's a right handsome baby."

"They won't let me have her." Lily's voice came dry and whispery.

I glanced at the fat woman standing in the doorway. She nodded at Lily and beamed in my direction. I nodded back, smiled. I was still feeling a little woozy.

"Maybe they think you're too weak yet," I said.

"Tell her I want to hold my baby."

"I don't speak meskin."

"What if they mean to keep her?" Lily said, a little louder now. I saw the worry on her face.

"They ain't gonna do that."

"How do you know?"

"Cause they don't mean us ill. They helped us." Surely she knew that. But the scared wasn't leaving her eyes. So I went back through the dark curtain, and the beautiful girl still had the baby, holding her in a chair now. The older woman followed me and both of them watched me lift the baby out of the señorita's lap.

"I'll just take this," I said.

It was a tiny, tender baby, and she made a grunting noise that made me afraid I was squashing her. I tried to hold her lightly. She screwed up her face at me and opened wide her unseeing eyes. I felt something inside me stop. I don't know what it was exactly. But it was that baby looking so clear at me that caused it, like she recognized me as her uncle. I brought her to my neck and held her there like a fragile piece of crystal glass. There wasn't just Lily to take care of now.

"Gra-shus," I said to the two women, and repeated it several times. It was about the only Mexican word I knew.

I tiptoed—I'm not sure why, but it felt like I ought to tiptoe—with the baby through the curtain and into the room where Lily laid. I knelt down and wedged the soft bundle into her arms. The fat woman and the pretty one both peeked through the curtain at us. They were smiling.

"There you go," I said. "See? I don't think they was planning on stealing her."

Lily looked at the women, gave them a weak smile, then stroked her finger over the baby's tiny cheek. "Isn't she beautiful?"

I sat back on my heels and cocked my head at the baby, trying to decide how to answer that. She made little squirming noises and squenched up her eyes. She looked like an Indian she was so red. Didn't have no hair to speak of. Ears seemed kind of big and flapping out. I shook my head. "She surely is," I lied.

"Her name's gonna be Emmaline. That was my mama's name. You think Marion'll like it?"

"Oh sure." I glanced back at the women. They were both still watching us.

"She needs a middle name, too. Something pretty as she is. Haywood?"

I looked down at Lily. "I don't know. I ain't no good at that sort of thing."

"What was your mama's name? Yours and Marion's?"

"I didn't ever know her."

"Not even her name?"

"Eliza," I said, thinking back to the faded tombstone planted behind the house at McDade, there beside where we'd laid Pa three years ago. "ELIZA ADELLE BEATTY Loving Mother," it said. She died the day Shot was born.

"Emmaline Eliza." Lily pressed her lips against the tiny, fuzzed head. "How does that sound?"

"Fine. It sounds just fine." I looked again at the two women in the doorway, wondering how godawful it would be for me to leave Lily and this baby here a while. Just till I figured out something else. What the hell was I going to do with a mother and a newborn babe?

Before I left, I gave all the Tennessean's greenbacks to Ruben. There were seventeen of them, all dollar bills. The hard cash—the gold and silver—I kept for myself, as I'd always preferred coin to paper. I liked the way it felt jangling inside my pockets. And, too, there was a little more of it—twenty in silver, ten in gold. I reckoned I'd need it for my trip. There wasn't any way of telling how many more days I'd be to Matamoros.

I tried explaining to Ruben that the money was for Lily and her baby's care till I could get to Mexico and find work of some sort. I told him I'd send more when I could. He grinned and nodded and swatted me on my back, said, "*Sí, sí*, Mexico," but I don't think he savvied any of the rest of my English. I left the wagon and mule with him for safekeeping too, and I'm pretty sure he thought I was giving him a gift.

Just as the sun was breaking through the low morning clouds, I set out. It wasn't no time till I struck the town of San Patricio, and from there down to San Margarita's Crossing on the Nueces River.

I knew I should've been feeling guilty for sneaking off, but instead, aside from a sick head left over from last night's binge with the chili pepper liquor, I felt as free as the dust from the road blowing in my face. This was how it ought to of been from the start: me on my own and Lily in some safe spot with other womenfolk around her. It didn't occur to me just then that womenfolk who didn't understand one word she said might not of been such a comfort to her. I had my mind on Mexico.

The river was booming from the wet weather further up country, and the ferry was out so I had to wait. Standing there on the north bank, I sang a piece of one of the songs from last night with Ruben and his buddies. It went something like "Hi, yi, yi, yi. Quon toe doe nochy." Course, I was pretty sure I wasn't singing no real Mexican because when the dark-skinned ferryman hove his raft to the shore, he peered out from underneath his sombrero with a queer look my way.

"*Tres centavos* to cross, *señor*," the ferryman hollered at me. "*Dos* for the mare." He held the raft at the bank.

I led Mollie aboard and searched my pockets for the fare. I handed over two bits, which from the sudden respect that came to his weather-beaten face was more than I owed. He jabbered something at a little boy of about nine or ten, in tattered britches and dusty bare feet. The boy jumped up from his perch at the end of the raft and came over with a curry to brush Mollie's coat.

The ferryman sang as he poled us across the river, the same song I'd been trying to sing on the bank. It still sounded like "Quon toe doe nochy" to me. But I reckoned right then, if I was to be living in Old Mexico from now on, I'd best start to learn the language.

"*Buenos suerte,*" the old Mexican called as I lighted onto the south bank. It was a long time before I understood he'd been wishing me good luck.

The country changed quick to dust and alkali, with thick stickery brush on either side of the road. I'd moved into the chaparral.

At first it didn't mean much to me, except it was different to look at than what I was used to seeing. And I was awful grateful for the good hat on my head. It did occur to me that there wasn't much point in going all the way to Mexico when there was country this lonesome right here in Texas. If somehow Tennessee's corpse had turned up and the deed had some way been pinned on me, I doubted anybody would come looking for me in this wilderness. And even if they did, they'd never find me among the ocotillo and prickly pear, the mesquite and the cat's claw. I traveled along thinking all this, feeling freer by the second. If I'd had some whiskey I'd have stopped to celebrate right where I was, which was nowhere, smack in the middle of nowhere.

I laughed out loud, then laughed some more, and felt the wind at my back and smelled the dust and thought about that whiskey. At the next settlement, by damned, I'd sure enough stop. Rent me a room and a bottle, maybe a woman. She'd probably be Mexican but that was all right. Especially if she looked anything like the girl at the hut back there holding Lily's baby.

Jack had always been apt to like a girl with some exotic blood in her, and I could see why. When you're riding along with nobody to talk to, your mind gets to wandering off, and for so long mine kept going back to that girl, how she looked in the lamplight, the shine of her coal black hair hanging down. I didn't even know her name. I'd assumed she belonged to Ruben, but she might've been his sister or some other kin.

The longer I thought about her, the randier I felt. I got to sweating so hard, my shirt and hair were as soggy as if I'd been dunked under water. And I started to smell just like the Mexican liquor I drank last night. It might as well have been seeping, unchanged, right through my skin. My head pounded.

A few miles past the river, I came to a crossroads, one turning west, the other continuing south. There wasn't a marker, and no way to tell from the size of either road which way I should aim.

At one time, I'd had a map of Texas. Got it back in San Antonio at Mr. Terry's. He'd had a whole stack of them, all with POE TERRY'S IRON WORKS AND TIN SHOP printed on them. And I'd taken one and studied it some, though mostly the route up through the Panhandle that I figured I'd be heading with the Diamond M herd. The map must've got left back at Markin's place.

Try as I might, I couldn't recollect how the road to Old Mexico came through right here in this spot where I stood. Could've been westerly. But could've been south, too, though I was afraid heading south might lead me to Corpus Christi where I would stall out at the Gulf of Mexico. Without a map or a compass, I was as lost as a jackass in a pig wallow. I rose up in the stirrups and gazed south first, then west.

That's when I noticed a squat little building set back among some switch mesquites. There was a sign with the word GROCERY hand-painted on a board looked like it had been ripped off the side of an old barn. Now in Texas anyway, "grocery" usually meant a whiskey barrel inside, or at the least, a beer keg. In fact, a lot of times "grocery" was just a nicer way of saying "saloon." Especially if there were many God-fearing, Bible-folk around.

Reading that hand-painted sign, I decided I could use a drink. A hair of the dog that bit me, so to speak. It was the best way I knew of to end a hangover. Watching my own pa had taught me that trick. Pa never suffered hangovers, since he never sobered up. The inside of my mouth felt like a cotton patch had been planted in there.

I looped Mollie to one of the stouter mesquites, far enough away from two other horses already tied up outside, so's she wouldn't get into a fight over the few lonely sprigs of curly grass shooting up through the bare dirt. I left her enough rope so she could nibble.

A pissy smell came from round the side of the building, and I glanced back there at a water trough scooped out of a log that had been being used for a privy. That made me feel pretty certain I'd find what I was after in this "grocery." A privy that stinking had to mean liquor inside. I tipped back my hat, stepped through the open doorway and into the dim store.

Even in the forenoon, with the sun leaning on the bright side, the place was lantern lit, there being only one small, dust-caked window at the west end. The place smelled of spit-out tobacco juice and sour mash. There wasn't a floor, nor much of a roof. Cowhides had been stretched over leak holes and nailed without any worry as to neatness, and water, left over from the morning's dew, dripped through the leather, making little craters in the dirt floor below.

Three turned-over goods boxes served as tables, and at the furthest one, two fellows were humped over a checkerboard. The counter at the rear of the room was broke down on one side and cantering to the left. And sure enough, right behind the counter, on a ledge nailed into the wall, stood two bottles of liquor and a crock jug. And underneath the ledge, a man was slumped in a chair asleep, his snores drowning out the clink of checker pieces. He had a long, red beard spread out from his chin to his breastbone. It was hot inside, too hot for any sober man to be sleeping so sound. I cleared my throat.

The checker players glanced up from their game. It was too dim to make out much about their faces, and I didn't look for long, anyhow. I let out a half-smile so they'd know I was friendly, though in truth a smile didn't really mean much. I'd seen Az smile as he cocked his hammer against some poor fool's temple.

My .45 was hanging on my belt, and I reckon they both saw it there. I scanned the one shelf of rusted-up canned goods near the door, pretending that was what I'd come inside after.

"Got a customer, Lige," the one with his back to me said, and the man with the long beard stirred awake.

I scratched at my mustache and glanced towards the old man waking up in his chair. "Well, mainly I come in to ask which one of these here roads outside I take to get to Matamoros," I said, keeping my voice calm and business. "But I wouldn't refuse something to drink, if you got it."

The checker player with his back to me turned himself all the way around. Then he stood up from the nail keg he'd been squatting on, and I almost wiped my eyes. I couldn't believe what I was seeing.

"Hillie?" I blinked; squinted. "Hillie Sullivan?"

It was him all right. He was about three-fourths lit up already, judging by the way he grinned and braced himself for balance against the goods box. He leaned back his head and let out a laugh that I swear shook the leather flaps on the ceiling. Wet drops rained down. Then he looked towards the old man who had stood up back of the counter.

"Pour my friend a drink, Lige," Hillie said, and his voice sounded so familiar to me then, I couldn't imagine how I'd missed it before.

He came over to me and gave my hand a shaking that nearly raised me out of my boots. I didn't mind the shaking, but he had a case of horseradish BO that like to have gagged me. I figured then he'd been inside this place drinking for quite a while.

"What the hell are you doing here?" he said, and his breath smelled as foul as his armpits.

"I might ask you the same question," I said. "Why ain't you on your way to the Panhandle?"

"Got fed up with that chili-belly Castaneda," he said, still grinning wide and goosey. "Went to him asking for a simple little advance on my pay. All I wanted was enough for one night before we headed out. I wasn't planning no big jag or nothing. And that half-breed sonofabitch told me he had me figured to be about ten months in the hole already, and he wasn't gonna bankroll me no night out on the town come hell nor high water. And I said to him I didn't know about high water, but he was sure as shit about to get some hell. And I took my hat off and I slapped him in the face with it right there in front of the whole damn outfit."

The old man behind the bar held out two ponies of beer at us. Hillie handed me mine and I dripped some on my sleeve bringing it up to my lips. It tasted bitter and good.

"And then what happened?" I said, feeling glad— no, more than glad—overjoyed, now that the shock was past, at finding somebody I actually knew down here in this wilderness.

"Castaneda booted his ass up to his shoulder," the other checker player piped in; loud.

Hillie nodded. "I got fired. You remember Kip Sanderson, don't you?"

I didn't, but I shook Sanderson's hand like I did. He had flaming red hair, and the worst teeth of anybody I'd ever seen—black and snaggled, a few gone and just holes where they'd been. Looking at his mouth caused me to run my tongue around my own teeth. They seemed all right, though I couldn't recall when the last time had been that I'd picked them clean. Didn't want to end up like Pa, who didn't have one tooth in his head by the time he died. Course, Pa hadn't needed any teeth. They just got in the way of his whiskey drinking.

They rolled up another keg for me to sit on, and Hillie scraped the checkers into a pile. Sanderson hollered at the old man behind the bar to bring over a jug to chase down the beers. I gathered from the way they were all gleaming, it was something they'd done a few times this morning already.

So, before we ever got onto any more small talk, we had three or four more beers with whiskey chasers, all of us sitting around the upturned goods box. Ever since I'd known him, Hillie had enjoyed a drink, and this Sanderson sure seemed to like it, too. Myself, I had a hangover to cure.

They told me they both came from down around this country, though Hillie said he hadn't had any kin in the brush for years. There were some ranchmen they still knew, though, and that was what him and Kip were doing hanging around this bar. Some important fellow named McGloin was rounding up hands to herd some horses to Louisiana, and they were all supposed to meet here to final up matters.

"But that was day before yesterday." Hillie laughed and glanced around at old Lige, who had recommenced his snoring over in his chair. "We been trying to reckon how much longer the old man's gonna extend his hospitality."

"You just been sitting here for two days?" I said.

Kip patted his shirt pocket. "We've been playing the same four bits back and forth so he wouldn't get the idea we're busted. Told him McGloin would make good on us, so he's been pouring freely."

"It's mostly just corn juice, anyhow," Hillie said.

"Here. Have some more." Kip filled my glass again, and the red liquor swirled up the sides and over onto the goods box. It got quiet for a minute, save for old Lige's snores, while we drank.

"What's in Mexico?" Hillie said, sounding sleepy himself. "You kill somebody?"

The question came so matter-of-fact, it stunned me. I'd had my glass on my way to my mouth, and I almost spilled it down the front of my shirt. By then, I'd plumb forgot all about Mexico, about Lily and her new babe, about nearly everything but that my headache was gone. Seemed like with Hillie's question, all that murky business came back on me hard.

I'd already gone well past the dog's hair I'd stepped in for. Things were weaving on me. Hillie's dark face turned into four—four beak noses, four pointy chins, and about twelve eyes.

I set down my glass. He kept staring at me so intent, it made me shudder. I said, "Somebody told me they're finding silver in Mexico."

"They keep on saying that, but mostly it's a lot of horseshit. Spaniards cleaned all that out years ago."

I sloshed the whiskey around my glass. "Maybe so. But I sure as hell ain't got nothing keeping me here."

"Ain't it the truth. To Mexico." Kip held his glass up like for a toast.

Hillie and me did the same with ours. We all drained them at once, and it was back to jolly again.

Kip slammed his empty down so hard, I was surprised it didn't break. "Hilbert, my friend," he said, "what say we show this man the way to Old Mexico? And while we got Lige over there nodding, we can slip on out with a IOU."

I sort of laughed, since it sounded like Kip had meant it as a joke. But then he stood up and went behind the counter after their saddlebags, dodging careful around the snoring old-timer.

"He need killing?" Hillie said, rising from the nail keg beside me.

"Huh?"

"The reason you're high-tailing it to the border." He looked down at me and so I stood up, too. I never was comfortable with getting looked down on. "I knowed it the first day I ran into you," he said, "that you weren't no goddamned waddie. No hard-assed horsebreaker either, though you *was* pretty damned game for it. Then I seen you in town smithing and I figured that was the true cloth you probably come from, but now I ain't so sure. You look like a man running from something, Beatty. You got the smell of it on you. And I take it to be either the law or a woman."

"A man can't just wanna head down to Mexico for the hell of it?" I tried to make a laugh, but it came off sort of screechy.

He shrugged, but I could see he wasn't buying it. I wanted to say more. I just never could put my mouth around a long-winded brag the way Jack used to could do. I hadn't inherited the knack. Fact is, I'd about decided I hadn't got much of any Beatty traits past maybe Pa's thirst. I sure didn't have Azberry's taste for revenge, else I'd have been over at McDade the first day they let me out of jail, making Mr. Milton and Tom Bishop pay the debt they owed me. Or I'd have tracked down Jeff Fitzpatrick and made him pay. Or maybe done both and to hell with the consequences. You'd have never seen Az quivering over a little jail time. And you'd have never seen Jack standing here like me, blinking at Hillie Sullivan, trying to think up some good way to get the subject changed. Hell, Jack would've been proud to talk about the Tennessean, and in the telling, he'd have made Hillie's eyes go wide with respect.

Kip came over with their saddlebags and tossed Hillie a roll of bills. "Divided equal. Eight bucks apiece."

Hillie chuckled and stuffed the greenbacks into his vest. "He'll be madder'n a wet hornet when he wakes up."

Kip said to me, "Hope you understand why we ain't divvying out with you, partner. Since you just got here and all."

I looked towards the snoring old man. His eyebrows fluttered at a flying bug that lighted on his forehead, but he didn't wake up. "You robbed him?" I said, and got a sick feeling in the pit of my gut.

"Hell no. He ain't robbed. I left a IOU in his drawer." Kip nodded at the counter.

Hillie said, "That old fart. It'd serve him right. Passing off his homemade squeezings as quality whiskey."

We went out to our horses. More of the day had got away than I'd realized. The sun blazed down, blinded me after the inside darkness. I started to go back in and check the cash drawer, just for my own peace of mind. It struck me that I had truly had enough of that kind of life and didn't want any more. But I didn't want to seem a coward either. I left it go with just a glance back through the open doorway. Old Lige's snore wandered out to mix with the heat and the wind in the trees.

Mollie wouldn't stand for me. She wasn't of a mind to have no drunkard astraddle her, and she kept rubbing into the mesquites. I had to go up on her off-side, and that got her mad enough she liked to've dumped me once I was aboard.

Hillie and Kip Sanderson had already started on the west road without me, so I had to run to catch up. "What about your horse herd, and your big cattleman friend?" I said to them when I got Mollie up even with their horses.

They were talking to each other about something else, and didn't either one of them answer my question. I didn't press for one. I was too drunk and glad to be in familiar company right then to care.

10

e ended up in a place I thought was
said "Ban Katy" from the way Kip Sanderson pro-
nounced it, but which turned out to spell Banquete when
I saw the welcoming sign outside town. There were some
horse races going on and the townfolk, women and children as well as men, had all turned out for it. I still had
all my money, so right away I got in on the gambling. I
bet my whole caboodle on a wild-eyed Indian bay. She
came in like a streak of lightning, so I had money for the
next match and the next, and for some of the ten-cent
tequila they were selling out on the street off a wagon
gate. The ride into town had nearly sobered me up. It
didn't take long to fix that situation.

The races were right down the main street, for one

quarter mile and no more. After the fourth match—and with me riding high on my winnings—it struck me that at the distance of one quarter mile, Mollie could go right with the best of them. She might be butch and no good for breeding, but she could sure as hell run. So I stumbled back around to where I'd left her tied to the back of a general notions store, and I had a talk with her.

I poked my face right up to hers and looked straight into all four eyes wavering back at me, and said, "Now, I know you ain't never warmed to me all that good, but I'm asking just one favor of you. To trot out there and show all them folks what you're made of. And you don't have to do it for me if you don't want to. Think of it as a thing of self pride, if you like."

I got her untied and showed her the wad of money I had in my vest pocket. About sixty-two dollars by then. "I'm gonna stake you with this," I said, hoping I wouldn't need more. "If you win, you got a bucketful of oats and sweet corn coming to you."

She didn't much want to go with me. I guess the eleven-mile ride to this town had her tired out. But she came finally, and didn't step on me the two times I fell down in front of her. My brain was sort of going faster than my feet. Or else it was the other way around. Anyhow, I kept talking to her the way Shot always had done, telling her how we would be sitting pretty, high on the hog, and all she had to do was go her best gait just to the end of that main street.

Now, I know there's some horses that understand English, though I wasn't at all sure Mollie was one of them. Jack had a gelding once, Old Suet, that you could ask a question to and he'd nod his whole head up and down. Of course he could only answer yes. Jack never did teach him no. Said *no* was a word ought not be in a horse's vocabulary. Walking along there leading Mollie, I got to wishing she'd nod like Old Suet, or even shake her head no, just so's I could be sure she was at least hearing me.

The stakeholder was sitting on a platform, which, up close, I saw was really just an unharnessed buckboard. I'd lost track of Kip and Hillie in the crowd of people. But they turned up just as I got to the stake man. Hillie grabbed me by the shoulder. He liked to have yanked my neck out of socket.

"What're you up to?" he said, and I gave him a quick look at the roll I'd hoarded in my pocket.

"Staking Mollie on this race," I answered.

He nodded and gave Mollie a pat on her nose. He was gleaming all over by now, like a Christmas tree lit with candles. And his BO had got lost in the crowd around us.

"Which horse are you matching her against?" Kip asked me, and I shrugged. It didn't matter to me.

I put my arm up over Mollie's withers. "We had a talk," I said.

"You have a jockey picked out, then?" Kip said, and

it kind of made me cross him asking so many sensible questions. Hillie didn't seem to think there was nothing wrong with my plan. He was running his hands down Mollie's flanks, and her legs. Any fool could see Mollie was a winner. She had a broad backside, and big old muscles down her hips.

"*I'm* riding her," I said.

"You think that's a good idea?"

I was just about to say for Kip to keep his nose out of it, but then Hillie raised up and looked at me over the top of Mollie's back. He had red cobwebs streaking his eyes.

"Let's get this saddle off her," Hillie said. "We'll find you some little meskin boy to ride her."

"I can ride bareback," I said, holding onto Mollie even firmer, mostly due to the fact that she was steadier on her feet than I was on mine.

"You also weigh, what? About a hundred seventy, eighty pounds?" This was Kip again, sizing me up.

I straightened. "About that." I felt like he was accusing me of something. "What of it?"

They weren't either of them paying me any mind. Kip walked off into the crowd and Hillie got Mollie's saddle a-loose. He humped it up over his shoulder and hollered at the stake holder. "We want the Old Squaw," he said. "This paint mare here against her."

The man went to scribbling down something, and held out his hand. "Your stake?"

I *was* listening, sort of, but a group of schoolboys betting pennies on who could spit the farthest had caught my attention. The crowd had already moved back to give them room, and so as not to get spewed, and some of the boys betting were chewing up wads of tobacco in their cheeks, looking green I thought, but spitting some whopping distances. This whole town had caught the betting fever, even children. I'd been in some rowdy towns in my time, but I'd never seen such a hellabaloo as was going on here this day.

Hillie slapped the back of his hand into my chest. "Give the man your roll," he said, and so I came back to my senses some, dug in my pocket, and brought out the wad.

The man took every bit, then hollered out at the crowd through a cone: "We have another challenger! The stake is this paint mare and sixty-two dollars in cash!"

Hillie started pushing me away from the buckboard platform, and Kip reappeared with his hand locked around the neck of a skinny, little slanty-eyed Mexican boy about twelve. He had a pair of big-roweled spurs strapped around his bare feet. Kip rattled something off at him, and I swear Kip sounded as much like a Mexican as anybody I'd ever heard. It stunned me, him knowing the language so good, and I stood there, staring at him with my mouth flung open, watching as he gave the little boy a boost onto Mollie's back.

The boy grabbed her reins and a handful of her mane, and before I could holler, "Don't you mark her, you little sonofabitch!" the Mexican kid stuck his spurs into her side.

It was the wild, Indian bay we were matched against, the one hadn't any of the other horses yet beat, and nobody was wasting time getting the thing set. Hillie drug me along, and I fought at him. I didn't feel in control of things anymore, and I kept saying to him, "Lemme go, goddammit."

We got up on the gallery in front of the notions store just as the starter was raising his pistol. The bay was agitated, steaming sweat and frothing. Mollie had her ears pinned flat on her head, eyes flared wide open. When the pistol fired, she did her straight-up jump, and started trying to buck the little, spurring Mexican off her back. While she was jumping around doing that, the bay dashed down the town street, won the race and every cent I had in my pocket. I plumb forgot all about Mollie going gun shy.

I threw my hat down at my feet and grabbed Hillie's shirt with both hands. "Goddamn you!" I said. "You should've let *me* ride her."

Hillie just laughed in my face, and took both my fists off him. "You win some, you lose some," he said, and he reached down to pick up my hat. Somebody had already walked over it, and the crown was crushed flat, the snake band creased and crumbling. He stuck it on my head anyway. "Let's get a drink. I'll buy." And he seemed to think that was a funny joke, too.

I left Hillie standing there, and pushed through the

street over towards Mollie. A man in skin britches had a rope on her neck, and he was trying to pull her. She was fighting hard against him, rearing and screaming like a banshee. The little Mexican boy with the big spurs had disappeared.

"Hey!" I yelled at the fellow in buckskin. "You let go of my horse!"

He ignored me, so I hollered louder. That time he heard and looked my way. "*Was* your horse, you mean, don't you?" he said. "You lost her." He gave her head a hard yank and two other fellows came over to help him with her.

I walked faster. "No! That ain't the way it was! You got my sixty-two dollars! That horse is mine!"

"Check for yourself," the man said and pointed towards the stakeholder's platform.

"I never bet my horse!"

Mollie had just about tuckered down. She let them start leading her off, but she raised her head at me, gave me as put-out a look as I ever got from a horse.

"Let her go!" I shouted and reached for my pistol. Then I remembered Hillie had made me take it off before we hit town. The .45 was packed in my saddle pocket, and a good thing too. I was in the right temper to have used it just then. The man in buckskin and his two helpers kept leading Mollie off like I wasn't there.

Just as I was about to bend for the knife in my boot, Hillie and Kip caught me up, one on each of my arms.

They pretty near carried me off the street and into a saloon.

Kip said, "I thought he wasn't one to fly off."

"The stake was a hundred dollars," Hillie said to me. "I had to put your horse up to make the bet."

"You done that? Without telling me?" I slung Hillie off, rared back my fist, and punched him a good lick in the face. Kip pulled me backwards, and the men inside the saloon ganged up around us, eager, already placing bets. Mostly against me, I reckon, since it was two on one.

Hillie stood up straight, rubbing at his chin. The gleam in his bloodshot eyes was replaced with murder. He grinned, worked his jaw back and forth to see if it was broke. It wasn't.

Kip had both my arms pinned behind me, so just as Hillie doubled his fist to wallop me, I kicked out with my good leg. My boot heel caught Hillie in the gut, doubled him up. Then I chopped my elbow into Kip's ribs and got loose. All those years of rastling my brothers, sometimes for fun and sometimes not, had taught me a few things.

The crowd around started yelling louder, thinking they had them a scrappy underdog to root on, but I wasn't drunk no more. Nor was I out to start a barroom brawl, either. All I wanted was Mollie back. I *needed* her back. A man without a horse ain't no kind of man at all, and I was feeling near desperate to find her before the man in the skin britches got away too far with her.

The crowd, though, wouldn't let me pass through to the doors. There was all kind of back-slapping and shoving going on, and getting rougher by the second. I made a try at bulldozing my way through, head first, since my hat was already lost someplace underfoot.

And then all hell broke loose inside me. I don't know where it came from or how long it had been down there waiting to come up. But it did. Like an ugly, pussing boil.

I grabbed the man nearest to me. Don't even know who he was, because it wasn't me, see. Not really me. I felt about like I had back last Christmas Day when everything started happening so fast. Back when my life changed. After we'd all gone to Mr. Milton's store to convince him I hadn't had a thing to do with killing that Lee County deputy sheriff, that Bose Heffington I'd carried out of town draped cross old Ben's back. And that neither had our cousins, Thad and Wright McLemore, killed him, nor Henry Pfeiffer either, the three Mr. Milton and his mob had already lynched the night before. The same mob that had come calling for me.

Jack didn't even take his pistols along when we went up to Milton's store that Christmas morning. Said he wouldn't need them since we weren't looking to start trouble, just to set the record straight. I thought Az was right with us in that store. I didn't realize he'd stopped outside to speak to Tom Bishop. Somebody at my trial said Az told Tom to get out of town before sundown, but I know Az never said nothing that poetic. Probably Az saw Tom Bishop sitting out on that store gallery and called him a chicken-shit sonofabitch or something, cause we all knew Tom Bishop was Mr. Milton's right-hand man, and Tom knew we all knew it, too.

Most everybody back at McDade was afraid to fist-fight with Az lest he throttle them to death with his big, hammer fists. Tom Bishop was a little man, hardly much over five feet, so I reckon Tom pulled his gun out and shot Az cold-blooded, but I'll never know for sure. I was there, but I didn't see it. I was looking, but it didn't make sense.

It wasn't me there out on the street that day, firing wild at everybody around me, watching Az fall, and then Jack, too, without his pistols even on him. His head got blown apart. Blood and brains soaking into the street. So much blood . . . like a river streaming into the wagon ruts and potholes. . . .

Just like it ain't me here in this barroom, whipping the living shit out of somebody I ain't ever laid eyes on. Whanging his face into a table and him gushing blood from his mouth and his nose. Like Az did. Like Jack.

Somebody with a ball bat, or a rifle butt, hit me between the shoulderblades. Put out my lights. It felt like sinking into a badger hole. I barely knew when my head hit the floor, except I think I might have heard it.

11

A fly, big as a hornet, kept buzzing my face. When it popped me on the eyebrow, I slapped my own head, and woke myself up. My eyes opened. They burned hot and watered up.

The place I was in was some kind of shanty. Hell, it wasn't even fine enough to call a shanty. No bigger than a corncrib. Only two walls were whole. The other two were of rusted roofing tin, nailed up slapdash and not even fitted flush with the wooden walls. A door-sized hole was cut for going in and out, and another half the size, only sideways, was for letting in light and air. Also rain, because in spots where the floor was broken, a good stand of grass grew. And both these openings, the door hole and the window hole, were covered with pieces of two-inch strap metal, top to bottom and side to side. The whole thing wasn't more than four by nine.

Outside, somebody hacked, coughing like from a bad cigar or the croup. I raised up off my bed, or rather the boards tacked down to make a bed, and when I did, all the tequila, whiskey, beer, and no telling what other manner of rotgut, came surging as hard as a flood. I got to all fours, but no farther, before it flew out of me. I thought I'd die choking, and it just kept coming out, heaving me forward and burning my tonsils.

While I was down there puking into one of the holes in the floor, it came to me that I was in jail again, sure as hell, and that this was no dream. That I might have killed another man last night, bashed his head in for him, and for no reason except I'd gone out of my mind and he'd been the one closest to me.

When I finally stopped retching, I sat back on my haunches. I didn't feel too alive right then myself. I hurt all over, especially between the shoulderblades and behind my neck. The stitches Lily had put in my elbow were all busted out, the knife-cut there reopened and bloody. The knuckles on my right hand oozed and throbbed. I couldn't make a fist. And I was sweating like a pig, even though plenty of air came into the little box they had me in.

My boots were gone from my feet, and I had a ball

and chain shackled to my ankle, my right one so's the weight was going to give my leg fits dragging it around. I wiped my mouth on my sleeve. I still had my shirt, the blue checkered one I'd bought in San Antonio, my britches and my galluses; but everything else—my hat, my vest, my leggins, my boots, the knife, my gun and gun belt—was all gone.

The horse fly that had stung me awake, and some of his pals, buzzed in to light in the slop I'd spilled down the floor hole. The sight of them swarming gagged me, but nothing more came up. My ribs pained, gut muscles ached. I gasped for my breath.

The dry, raspy cough from outside came again, closer now. Then a voice said, "Top of the morning to you, Beatty."

A glob of thick slobber fell out of my mouth. I raised my face, slow and easy, and looked into the eyes of a man I'd never met. He had a mule face, light curly hair, and clean-shaven cheeks. And he was wearing my vest, with a hammered star pinned to the lapel. I couldn't read any words written on the badge.

He grinned wide at me, wiped a rag over his mouth, and motioned at somebody standing out of my line of vision. "Don't he kinda remind you of something, Huck," he said, "spraddled there over his soup? Maybe like a baby calf ain't yet found his legs good."

Another fellow peered around the edge of the door

hole. He was dark like a Mexican, only different some-how, and he didn't say nothing, nor did the expression on his face change in any way. He just looked bored by me and my predicament.

The one with the badge laughed, and it turned into another fit of hacking. This time he didn't bother with his rag, but just spit what he brought up onto the ground behind him. "I don't believe he remembers me, Huck. No. I surely don't think he does."

"Where the hell am I?" Even speaking hurt my throat. I tried to swallow; it was dangerous. My guts were empty but they still whirled.

"Banquete. It's near to hell. But it's still Texas." He laughed again. "Get him some water, Huck." The other one disappeared.

I pulled myself up onto the bed. The ball attached to my foot rolled around, and nearly off into the hole in the floor. I bent to catch it. It weighed at least ten pounds, maybe fifteen. "This a jail?"

"Yep. I know it ain't much, but it's the best we can do you for now. And don't get the idea you can get out. Ol' Huck here'll be watching ever second to see that you don't."

"You the sheriff?"

He put his hands on his hips, shook his head, spit. "City marshal. You'll get to know the sheriff soon's we can get you down to Corpus Christi. You're gonna like it down there. They got a real fine jail. Steel walls and floors. No windows. Real fine place." The smile never left his face. I didn't much like looking at it.

"What're my charges?" I set my mouth, ready for the worst, flexing my right hand. The knuckles were swollen so tight they felt ready to pop. I had speckles of blood on the front of my shirt.

"Public drunkenness. Assault. For now. Depends on how Mister Meriweather fares. You 'member him, don't cha? Feller 'bout yea-high." He held his hand at chest level and the marshal wasn't a particularly tall man.

I shut my eyes and leaned my head against the wall. Least I hadn't killed him. At least that.

"Here's you some water," the marshal said. "Just shove her in under there, Huck."

I cornered my eyes at them. The stone-faced Mexican, or whatever the hell he was, used the muzzle end of a rifle to slide the tin cup of water under the metal straps across the door. I didn't doubt but that the gun was loaded, and if it had gone off, I would've been in line to take the blast. At that moment, I didn't much care.

"Oh yeah," the marshal said, "thanks for the vest. Right good made. Ain't hardly been wore."

Every time I saw the marshal after that, it seemed to me he had something else of mine. And he was mouthy about it, too, making a big show one day of flipping out the fob watch I'd won off the San Augustine gambler back at San Antonio. Another time, he came by my cage humping my saddle, or rather Shot's saddle. A good one it was too, a high-tree Gallatin with a full-tooled skirt. I knew Shot had given fifty dollars for it, and prized it, keeping it oiled and supple, adding pretty silver conchos to decorate the tie strings and cinches. Though without Mollie to wear it, that saddle wasn't going to do neither him nor me much good. Losing her was causing me about as much misery as anything.

After a while, I did get to wondering when I would have a hearing, or get sent to Corpus Christi, or meet a lawyer, or something. It seemed almost like the marshal just liked having a prisoner in his jail to torment, especially after the Meriweather fellow lived and got well, even came by to spit on me one day, which he did fairly easy with the gap I'd knocked in his teeth. He was a small man, one third my height and half my bulk. I had blacked both his eyes, busted his jawbone, and turned his nose to pulp and plum jelly.

Seeing the damage I'd wrought haunted me. I dreamed about it. Dreamed about the Tennessean, too. Dreamed a lot about him. And sometimes, in my dreams, he wouldn't die when I killed him, and sometimes, when he got up, his face had turned into Tom Bishop's, or somebody else I'd known in my lifetime. Once he was Azberry, and he pulled a gun on me so I had to kill him again anyway. And once it was me on the bed underneath Tennessee, and that time I castrated him with his knife and left him to bleed to death.

Lily was hardly ever in any of these nightmares, except for the one dream I had where I let her shoot that pistol of hers, right into his belly where she'd been aiming it. But the bullet went all the way through him, just like I knew it would, and got me in the guts, too.

Sitting alone in that skinny jail cell, with hardly enough room to even turn around, gave me plenty of time for thinking. It's what stewing in jail was supposed to do, I reckon, give a fellow time to reflect on things, like where his life went wrong, and how he'd come to be the kind of man he was. I'd spent six of the last nine months locked up, but I hadn't learned a damned thing. Had come out cock-sure and thinking the world owed me a favor. There was a nasty pattern starting to form to my misfortunes, that I knew I had better change.

I started planning what I'd do when I got out, where I'd go. And it wouldn't be Mexico. If I couldn't get along in South Texas without getting in trouble and landing myself in jail, then I sure as hell wasn't going someplace where I didn't speak the language.

I even thought I might go on ahead up to Parker County and see about what kind of farming work it was Wash Jones's brother had to offer. Probably should have gone up there just as soon as old Wash spoke about it, calling me a good man, like I had it in me to make something of myself. But I'd had my fool sights set on San Antonio and cowboying, and on getting shed of Lily the first chance I got.

Well, now I'd got rid of her and here I sat in jail again, waiting for nothing, because it was damned sure certain Hillie and Kip weren't coming to try to help set me square. I wouldn't have even been surprised to find out they'd in some way ended up with Mollie themselves, or been working partners with the man in buckskin at the races.

I had sunk mighty low this time, sitting there hour after hour, with hardly a breath of air, slurping hasty pudding three times a day from a crusted bowl, getting eat up by skeeters at night, and hoping I didn't die of rickets or dysentery before somebody who maybe cared found out I was in here. I couldn't for the life of me think who that somebody might be.

Huck, my jail guard, turned out to be an all right fellow, though he never smiled nor talked much. His last name was Featherstone, and he was part Tonkawa and part French, was why he looked different than a Mexican. Though he could speak Mexican, and English, too, about as clear as me or anybody. He just didn't do it much, is all. But he gave me a board to lay over the shit hole in the floor of my cell, and he gave me something to smoke now and then, and he let me write a letter, though all these things he did when there wasn't anybody else around to see him do it.

I wrote this letter:

Dear Lily,

They have give me this tiny scrap of paper to pencil you a note so I will have to keep this short. I am in jail in Banketty. Dont have enouff space to go into how I got here, just to say I hope to get out soon. I did not kill nobody so it shouldnt take long. As soon as I am free I will come back to get you and keep my promise to Shot. Should never have left. Hope this letter finds you.

Haywood Beatty

And I wrote on the outside of the envelope LILY DELONY, then had to scratch out DeLony and write in Beatty. I kept forgetting she had my same last name. I wrote SAN PATRICIO TEXAS and, underneath that, scrawled "The Mexican camp north east of town." I hoped it was enough to reach her.

I lost so much weight in that stinking jail, it got so's my galluses were all that held my britches up. I kept a case of the trots, and got dizzy any time I had to move around. The shackle on my ankle had worn through my sock and cut into my flesh, and the weight of the ball worked on the old bullet hole in my leg till it ached day and night like the bone was coming unhinged. There wasn't much feeling in my toes anymore.

After nearly two months, I finally told the marshal he couldn't keep me like this. I knew from old Wash Jones about habeus corpus, and since Meriweather hadn't died, they had ought to charge me with drunkenness or whatever, and just access me a fine.

"A fine?" The marshal hacked out another of his consumptive coughs. Sometimes I saw blood in the wads of spit he flung to the ground. The thought had come to me that he knew he was dying and was taking it out on me.

"Yeah. A fine," I said. "Public drunkenness carries a fine of about fifteen dollars and thirty days. I've already give you the time, so fine me."

"How would you pay a fine, Beatty?"

"With that vest of mine, and that saddle of mine, and everything else of mine you've took."

I noticed Huck watching the marshal close, but nothing I said seemed to make a hill of beans. The marshal said, "You ain't no judge or no jury, Beatty. It'll be up to the court in Corpus Christi to decide."

"Then send me there!" I hollered at him as he walked away from my cage. "Send me there!" I hollered again, and tried to rattle the strap metal off the door hole.

My strength was leaving me. I shook all the time— couldn't keep the mush on my spoon, and sloshed the coffee out of my cup. But still the marshal didn't make any effort to change my situation. And then he stopped coming around at all. After a week without a sign of the marshal, I started thinking about trying to escape.

The holes in the floor weren't man-sized, but I figured I could rip up some of the more rotten boards and have me a look, see if I could shimmy out through all the muck steaming underneath there. I wasn't going to get any stronger just sitting here.

Sometimes Huck stepped away to the scrub brush to relieve himself, and sometimes he dozed over in the shade of a live oak motte. If I could get loose while he snoozed, I might could steal away. I'd still have the damnable ball and chain slowing me down, but I didn't reflect on that for long. If I had to crawl, I was determined to get out of this place before I died here.

I waited till Huck had gone off to the woods before I pulled up the first board. The ripping and tearing it made brought him on the run. He had his rifle cocked and ready. He said to me, "Don't start acting reckless now, Beatty."

I held the board in my hand, splintered end out, threatening so he'd know I'd gone past recklessness. I was pure desperate. The stink came putrid from underneath the shack.

"I ain't got no other choice, Huck. I've been sitting here almost two months trying to be good, and it ain't got me nowhere. Your marshal don't ever intend to take me for a trial and you know it."

Huck lowered the rifle barrel, and looked around us, like to make sure we were alone. "He's planning to let you go."

"When?" I moved closer to the strapped-over door and Huck stepped back. I reckon I smelled as foul as the floor hole behind me.

"Pretty soon. He's just making a show of it for old lady Meriweather. She about owns this town and that was her only son you manhandled at Cluney's saloon."

"But he ain't dead. I know I had no business roughing him up, but—"

"You're lucky you didn't get mobbed for it. You can thank the marshal for that. You would've been if he hadn't brought you out here."

His black gaze stayed on me a moment, then he leaned his rifle against the outside wall. He went around the corner out of my sight, but he left the rifle there. I craved it, petted and stroked it with my eyes.

"You don't understand how things has been in Banquete in the past," Huck said, his voice coming to me from somewhere around the corner. "We've been known as lawless. The devil's line. Sheriffs' demarcation."

The rifle stood about four feet from me. I thought if I could knock it down somehow, so it would fall my way, I might could pull it through the crack under the door where they pushed in all my food.

I crouched to my knees. It hurt my right leg something awful to do that. With the broken board, I reached for the rifle. My arm wouldn't fit under the door. I could only flick my wrist back and forth. The board sawed in the dirt.

"We had the reputation as the place where the law stops," Huck's voice said. "The marshal has been trying to change all that."

He came back around the corner and saw what I was doing. He put his foot down on the board and I drew back my hand. The strapping on the door bottom scraped the hide off my knuckles. I raised up and saw he had a string of keys he was picking through.

"I can't let you have the rifle," he said, sounding dead calm.

My heart leaped when he started fitting keys into the padlock holding me in there, trying to find one to fit. I sucked blood off the back of my hand watching him.

"Are you meaning to let me go?" I said, not believing, afraid it was just him taunting me like the marshal all the time did.

"I reckon you've served your time. Can't have you tearing up my calaboose."

The padlock snapped and he swung the door open wide. He led me out, barefooted, to a bench, and he gave me the key to unlock the shackle on my foot. He stood back and kept the rifle aimed on me, like he thought I might try something. But I was too weak and sick and glad to get loose to do anything dumb like that.

He gave me my boots—my jingle-bob spurs were

gone—and he handed me a creased-up, dirty envelope. On the outside it said:

Lily ~~DeLony~~ Beatty
San Patricio Texas
The Mexican camp north east of town

When I looked back at him, he shrugged. "I felt pity for you."

I wadded up the letter, shoved it and my hand into my empty pocket.

12

If it had been any further to San Patricio, I'd have never made it walking. My feet weren't used to my boots anymore, and I blistered before I'd gone the first mile. My legs were weak, my innards soured, and my head so light, I tramped most the way seeing visions before my eyes. Twice when I stepped off the road to let a traveler by, I thought it was Mollie hitched to the passing wagon. I stayed hunkered down quiet in the brush, though. I didn't know how much power Huck had acted with in setting me loose, and I sure as hell didn't want any stranger taking me back.

I had nothing—no horse, no money, no weapon to defend myself with nor to hunt for food. I didn't even have a hat, and I felt the sun baking my face. The heat of the sunshine and my sweat confused me. It had to be November by now, at least, yet the wind blowing didn't feel cold to me. Then I got to wondering if I'd lost track of more time than I knew, and winter had already been and gone without me realizing. Maybe it was coming spring already.

I was parched for thirst. The sun pelted me. Not one cloud in the sky. I got to thinking clouds were something I'd seen in a dream once, and not real. This couldn't be November. Must be July or August already. The road wavered in front of me. I swallowed up the last of my spit.

Sometime along toward evening, I passed the grocery at the crossroads where I'd met up with Hillie and Kip before. The building looked gruesome to me, with the door yawning open and the cowhides stretched over the roof. I could almost imagine it to be an animal hungry for flesh, swallowing everything in its path. I hurried my steps and I tripped on past without stopping, not even for a drink of water from the horse trough outside.

When I finally made San Margarita, I waded right out into the river, hip-deep, without one thought for cottonmouths. I drank and washed my face in the water, dipped my whole stinking body under. The ferryman and his boy came rushing over to me like they thought I was drowning myself. When the old man raised me up, I got a good look in his eyes. I think he might've remembered me.

"Do you need help, *señor*?" the young boy said in clear English.

I tried to answer, but I couldn't get my mouth to go around the words. Finally, as they were dragging me aboard their raft, sodden as a rag, I managed to mumble, "I can't pay," but I don't think either of them heard me. They were too busy jabbering to each other. About me, I reckon.

I found Lily in a nunnery, or rather she got found for me. I don't recollect much of the particulars. Fuzzy pictures in my head like dreams is all: of seeing old Ruben again and him knowing me; of the beautiful girl with the dark velvet hair; of a bumpy, spine-jarring wagon ride in the dead of night.

I'd caught a fever some way. Had chills so racking, the whole bed they put me in shook. The whole room shook. I thought for a while I was dreaming Lily, too. Her hands bathing my forehead, spooning food into me, the old gold ring Shot had put on her finger. She was skinny, her hair twirled around with braids. And the clothes she wore, so white and clean, I thought she might be an angel.

Thinking that brought on another thought of how Shot was going to sure enough kill me for letting Lily die, for leaving her with the Mexicans while I was off getting myself in trouble again. And his baby—I hadn't seen his baby anywhere in this white place, and I got afraid it had died, too. I guess I must've mumbled about it.

Seemed to me Shot's face was right up in front of mine, contrary, damning me with his eyes. And then Pa was there too, and he wasn't drunk but just as yellow and moldy as he'd been on his deathbed. And Jack's face came up and right as soon as he appeared to me, his skull cracked down the forehead, and I reached with my hands to hold it together. I knew if I let go, his head would fall apart like a busted melon.

"Hush now. Hush." Something soft patted my chest. "Woody? Do you hear me? Are you awake?"

I blinked, blinked again, and saw that it was Lily blurring in and out. My eyes felt like hard, dry stones poked into my sockets. My hand came up and touched hers where it laid on my chest. She was warm. Not dead.

"You were having nightmares," she said. "Do you know me? Woody? Do you hear me now?"

I tried to focus on the wall opposite my bed. A cross hung there, with a doll that was supposed to be Jesus nailed to it. Somebody had dripped red paint on the doll's hands and feet. It looked gory, and in the lamplight sort of unworldly, hanging lonely and small on that plain, white wall. There wasn't any wonder I'd been having bad dreams with such a thing staring me in the face.

"How'd you get set up here?" I said, and my voice came full of cobwebs and dust.

She backed away from me, clasped her hands together underneath her chin. "Thank you, Lord," she said, half under her breath, and the way she looked, so pious, and downright joyful even, made me feel like the guiltiest sinner that ever lived on God's earth.

I hadn't expected to find her happy to see me. Not after the way I'd left her. Though I had to admit, she seemed to have come out all right on her own. Better than I had fared for sure. Still, I had to wonder at a person that had such a forgiving nature as she seemed to have. Maybe she was just plain simple and didn't know any better.

Anyhow, she never said a word against me for leaving out on her, though she clearly was disappointed over the loss of Mollie. "We won't ever find another like her," she said in an almost mournful voice. And though I knew her words to be true, I was thinking more, just then, on getting a little farther away from Banquete.

She still had the light wagon and the mule. They had been the means of carrying her to the nunnery when she came down with childbirth fever at the camp. I hadn't just left her in the company of strangers, but *sick* and in the company of strangers. Which was how come them to bring her to the St. Joseph convent. They'd been afraid for her life, and the nuns ran a sort of hospital.

Emmaline Eliza had turned out fat and laughing. She had Shot's red hair growing all over her head, and blue eyes like mine. I didn't know where she'd got those eyes, but I took the credit for them. I reckoned she had some of my blood flowing inside her someplace. Lily said her eyes would turn brown directly.

One of the sisters put her in my lap the second day after I'd woken up from my fever. I was feeling strong enough to sit in an armchair, though getting there across the room had been more of a trial than I had expected. They thought maybe I'd had a case of malaria. Whatever it was it went awful hard on a person, left me with a hangover as thundering as if I'd been on a three-day binge.

"There's those of us that had come to doubt you really existed," said the nun, Sister Mary Kate. They were all Sister Mary something. This one was tall, and seemed to be the one in charge. Her robes swished when she moved. I wondered was it her and her nun friends or was it Lily who'd stripped me down to just the long-handle britches I'd woke up in? Somebody had put a bandage around my raw ankle, so's getting my socks on that morning hadn't been easy. They'd shaved my whiskers, too. Even my mustache was gone.

"Your wife said you'd be back to get her and here you are. Just like she said." Sister Kate had an Irish lilt in her voice. She smiled at me and Emmaline. "There's a resemblance."

I glanced across the room at where Lily was changing my bed. She put her finger to her lips, like to warn me of something. My niece strained her feet into my gut trying to stand on her board-stiff little legs. She laughed right in my face.

Lily quit with the bed-making and came rushing to my side. "You got to give her little head support," she said, showing me. But I had the feeling she was drawing the nun's attention away from talking to me, more than worrying over Em's wobbly head.

"She ain't got much of a neck, has she?" I said, as Lily took her out of my grasp.

"I guess you'll be leaving us soon. We'll all miss you so," Sister Kate said to Em, tweaking her fat cheek. The nun smiled at the three of us. "I'll be right down the hall if you need anything."

As soon as the nun left the room, Lily let out her breath. She took her eyes off the door and said, "It was just easier to let them think what they wanted to about who you are. Anyway, I suspect the Rosaleses already told them we was married-folk."

"Rosaleses?"

"The people you left me with." She put Emmaline against her shoulder and patted on her back. "The sisters have been real good to us, but I didn't know what they'd think if I said my husband was a jailbird."

For a second my instinct was to defend Shot, since I'd just recently been a jailbird myself, and since she was his legal wife and ought not to've been worrying over how a bunch of nuns might judge her. But I saw how nervous she was acting. She gave the baby a kiss on the forehead.

"I didn't want them believing Emmy was a woods colt. I just said you were off trailing cattle."

I nodded my head, cleared my throat, swooped my

hair back from my brow. "I *was* headed off to get work and then things just started happening. I regret I went and left you." I felt it needed to be said, though it made me uncomfortable to. I couldn't help but hearken back to something Jack used to tell me—that apologizing was a sure sign of weakness in a man.

"I found the letter you wrote to me in your pocket," she said, "smeared from the river, but I could still read it."

I felt a heat come to my cheeks. So it *had* been her that undressed me and not the nuns. I scratched at the razor burn pricking my neck, smoothed down the front placket of my freshly clean, striped shirt. "I seen you a-lying there pale as ash with your babe in your arms, and I lost my guts. I thought I had to get to Old Mexico, and you was holding me up."

She waved her hand in front of her face, but I wasn't sure if she was shushing me or just waving off a bothersome gnat. She sat down on the end of the bed. Little Em shrieked a laugh and started trying to stand against Lily's belly, what there was left of it, which wasn't much. Lily giggled. I couldn't help but smile either. Watching Em was about like watching a litter of newborn pups rastle each other.

"They made me let them baptize her a Catholic." Lily turned Em to face me. A string of drool had slid out of her mouth. She was in a grinning mood. She sent another big one my way. "You think Marion'll care?"

"No." I shook my head, certain of it. None of us ever cared anything much about religion, though Jack had made a stab at it once or twice when he was courting Estelle.

"I didn't know what else to do. They said that was all they required of me. That I keep my quarters clean, help with sick people, and let them baptize Emmy. Sprinkle her, really. I don't think she knows she's a Catholic."

"Or care." I waggled my finger and made a face at her before it struck me I was acting plain stupid. I sat straighter, tried to ignore Emmaline's grins. It wasn't so easy. She was cute as a pistol. I said, "She don't have to stay Catholic, does she? Can't you change it? Once we leave here?"

"Where're we going?"

"Remember Wash Jones," I said. She nodded. "Well, he's got a brother up in Parker County with some farmland he can't tend to. Told me about it before we left Bastrop, but it didn't much interest me then."

"It interests you now?"

"Might be worth a look." A thorn I'd got from hiding in the cat's claw on my eleven-mile trek was buried deep in my palm, and festering. I scraped at it till pus came. "I had a lot a time to think. And I realized Shot could of been doing me a favor and I just didn't see it clear." I looked up from the thorn. "See, I got a tendency to get into trouble. He knows that better than anybody. I mean, look at me. No sooner am I out of jail in Bastrop than I'm back in a fix down here. And I killed that man in San Antone. Nearly killed another one, too."

She jerked her head and waved her hand in front of her face again. I realized there wasn't any gnats bothering her, she just didn't want me talking at all about that business up in San Antonio. Her lips were pallid, she had them mashed together so tight.

"I ain't sorry for it," I said quick, so's she'd know I wasn't holding her to blame for anything. "A fella like that—he needed killing. And if it wasn't me, it would of been somebody some time. I don't want you thinking I'm one bit regretful."

She grasped her arms closer around baby Em's middle. She was still looking off, lifting her chin stiff, blinking a lot. "I ain't sorry either."

I kind of laughed. "I ain't hardly even thought of it again."

"Me neither."

We sat there for a while, both of us silent. Em wagged her arms up and down and babbled. From her apron pocket, Lily pulled out a play-pretty, and shook it at her. Em reached with her hands and feet, like a little monkey.

"I told Shot I'd look after you," I said, holding my voice quiet. "And I reckon it's my bounden duty to keep my promise to him. He *is* the only brother I got left."

"I don't care to be your duty," she said, and it was the first note of sass I'd heard come from her in a long while. She gazed at me, dry-eyed.

"Look. I ain't no good at words. But if you want to—and I wouldn't blame you if you didn't. But I figure if we stick together, you could help keep me out of any more trouble, and I can look after you and little Emmaline there like Shot wanted me to." I bent over my hand again, squeezed at the bedded-in thorn. I felt a bit pissyant saying all this. My face burned.

"I didn't expect you to remember her name."

I looked up and Lily was smiling at me. They both were. "She's my niece, ain't she? How many times you think I've been an uncle before? Course I remember her name."

"She's a good sleeper. Not one bit of trouble."

I sat there picking at my hand, wondering what else there was for me to say. I guess I could've told her what a hard trip it was going to be, if she decided to go with me. Parker County was ever bit of four hundred miles straight north. She didn't ask, though. She wasn't the talkingest person herself.

"Your elbow heal up all right?" she said, and it took me a second to remember what she was meaning.

I looked up at her and nodded. "Stitches popped right out."

She craned her neck a little, her eyes aimed towards my hand. "What you got there?"

I brushed my palm against my shirt. I could still feel the sticker buried in there. "Nothing much. A cockle-bur or something."

"Let me see." She laid little Em face down on the bed, and came to turn over my hand.

"Ain't nothing," I said.

"Well, I can get it out."

She went to a cupboard and lifted out a sewing bas-ket. Over on the bed, Em pushed and strained to raise herself onto her hands. She couldn't seem to get her backside up. She brought to my mind a big, old, clumsy turtle. I laughed. She looked my way and laughed back, losing her balance altogether. Her chin rocked down onto the bed. She sure had colored up and rounded out since the first time I'd seen her.

Lily swung another chair up next to mine. She held onto a needle. She grabbed my hand and turned it palm up. "Keep still now," she said. "This won't hurt but a tiny bit."

When the tip of that needle dug into my skin, I liked to've come right out of my britches. Again.

13

She still had the seventeen dollar bills I'd given to Ruben. Turned out the Rosaleses were superstitious people and believed that if they took money for her and Emmaline's keep, something bad would befall their family. It was the same reason they had brought gifts to the nunnery every week. Gifts for Em mostly, but some for Lily too. Betwixt the two of them, they had enough belongings now to fill two wagons. As it was, I worried Sassy might not could pull everything, though the mule surely didn't look any worse off than she ever did, even after spending two months penned up with a herd of milk goats.

Lily had three dresses, shawls, and underthings she thought she was keeping packed away from my eyes.

There were pillows and quilts, frilly things to throw on furniture, and the tiniest little towels I'd ever seen.

"Tea napkins," she said, snatching them out of my hands. Somebody had given her a trunk for it all, and she slammed the lid down before I could check what else was inside.

Then Em's share started coming out—little hand-made bonnets and booties and blankets and clothes. She had a turned-wood cradle with rocker sleds I had to knock off so's the thing would set level in the back of the wagon. We still had the lamp from Markin's kitchen, the skillet and coffee pot I'd bought us in Bastrop. The sisters gave us sacks of fodder to strap under the wagon, and one of the nanny goats to tie on behind.

"In case," one of them said of the nanny, and I didn't catch what she meant till we were off down the road a ways and Em started to fuss. We hadn't been out an hour and no amount of coddling on Lily's part could get the baby to shush. To be so little, she had a strong set of lights in her. I had to shout to make myself heard.

"What's the matter with her?"

"She's hungry!" Lily hollered back.

The wailing was making my head hurt. In truth, my head hadn't stopped hurting since I'd woke from my sick stupor. I was coming to believe it might be something else I'd have to learn to live with, alongside my aching arm and bad right leg.

"Why don't you feed her?" I yelled out.

"I can't! It's too rough a ride! She'll get the colic!"

I nodded at that. I knew all about colic. Old Ben had gotten colic eating green corn once, and we'd had to purge his stomach. It took me and Az and Jack, all three, to get the drench down him. A horse could die of colic. I wasn't sure about a baby, but I whoaed the mule.

I got out and tied the lines to the left wheel, then reached up a hand intending to help Lily out. But she didn't take my hand, just kept bouncing the baby on her shoulder. She said, "Can you get me that blanket out of her cradle?"

I went to the back and found the blanket, a ruffled thing of pink satin and outing. While I was back there, I decided I could stand to eat a bite myself. I brought the food basket the sisters had packed for us around to the front of the wagon. Good smells rose from underneath the oilcloth cover. I handed the blanket up to Lily, then started digging in the basket.

There was pone and biscuits. A jar of fig preserves and some meat pies. Jerked beef so tough you had to yank your head to tear off a bite, then chew till your jaws clamped up. Kept me so busy, it took a while before I noticed Em had gotten quiet.

She had her face tucked inside the front of Lily's dress. A muscle at the baby's temple worked. The pink blanket blocked me from seeing any more, but I didn't need to. I knew what was going on under there. I wasn't ignorant, just hadn't stopped before to think about what a two-month-old baby without any teeth might eat. My mouth quit chewing.

"I believe there's some boiled eggs in there, too," Lily said, acting like there wasn't nothing out of the ordinary happening. "And a hoop of cheese. Oughta be wrapped in brown paper. Do you see it?"

"Uh?" I peeled my eyes off the little bit of Emmaline's head that was showing.

"Ain't there a hunk of cheese in there, too?"

I found the cheese, unwrapped it, and got her off a piece. I didn't cut myself, though the knife the sisters had packed was sharp enough to split hairs, and my hands were fumbling. I passed the piece of cheese up to her and tried not to stare. I couldn't help it, though. I finally had to go around back and sit with the goat to finish off my strip of jerky.

Even that didn't help. I kept seeing that little muscle at Em's temple, imagining her mouth sucking at Lily's tit. And that got me to churning inside, made my neck sweat and my clothes feel tight. Brought back her white ankle sticking out from under that Tennessean. I had to walk off from the wagon for a while, out into the brush till my blood stopped pumping so hard. My mouth dried up so's I had to spit out the last bite of jerky, and I gave myself a good cussing.

It was a natural thing for a woman to suckle her baby, and it wasn't as if I hadn't seen it done before. There was a haggy woman named Vallencourt had lived over the Knobs from us back home. And it seemed like any place she went she had a young'un latched onto her like a leech. All us boys had snickered and teased each other about her. Just mooing like a cow could make any of us roll up laughing.

That, somehow though, was different than this. There wasn't nothing laughable about its being Lily up there with her dress peeled open, just a flimsy little blanket shielding her from my view. I think it was her hiding behind the blanket that made it all the worse for me.

A flock of geese honked overhead. I focused on them V-ed up there against the sky. I made myself think about shooting one, plucking him, scraping out his guts, and chopping off his head. Getting him ready for the stewpot. Anything to take my mind off Lily's white foot and the buttons open under that blanket. By the time I'd cooked the goose, I felt able to go back to the wagon.

Em was asleep and Lily had her dress closed up again. I untied the harness lines from the wheel and climbed onto the seat. She didn't ask me any questions about where I'd gone off to, and I didn't offer nothing. I wondered, though, how long it was going to be before I quit thinking so much about her being female.

We stopped again, at a store in Lagarto just before dark. I was letting Lily safekeep the money this time. I knew she could do better with it than me. Em was still sleeping sound when we got to the store, so Lily pulled the meager roll of greenbacks out of a slit she'd cut in the hem of her skirt, and handed the money to me.

We needed a few things—a wagon sheet for one; a map so's I could route our way, for another. The storekeeper had both those things, and he had a gray wool hat, whanged around the edges with buck lacing. The hat had been used but still had a lot of good wear left. My forehead and the tops of my ears had already sunburned. I paid the man the two dollars he was asking for the hat.

I thought it'd be nice to buy a pint of the whiskey he had on a shelf behind his counter, to help me sleep at night, stave off bad dreams that might come. But my bill already tallied to four dollars and sixty cents, and I wanted a gun. I didn't plan on making a four-hundred-mile trip without protection. Not just from highwaymen, either. There were bears and panthers and such roaming the lands we'd be covering. I didn't want to have to depend on just the little pocket pistol Lily had packed in her trunk.

The storekeeper must've noticed me counting my pennies. He took down an old percussion cap, double-barrel shotgun with a broken hammerlock.

"She still fires," he said. "Just gotta hold her down with your thumb whilst you aim." He showed me. There wasn't no need in pressing the trigger. It wouldn't do nothing if you did. He let his thumb go and the hammer snapped down on its own. "Takes some getting used to," he added, handing over the gun for me to heft. Both barrels were orange with rust.

I eyed down the sight. "How much?"

"Five dollars."

Without a word of argument, I gave him back the gun. "I'll just take these other things." I motioned at the canvas wagon sheet and the map lying on his counter. The hat I already wore on my head. It felt made for me, though I did get a bare twinge of longing for my snake band.

"Four-fifty for the gun," he said.

"Two dollars." I was ciphering in my head, which I wasn't much good at doing. The way I reckoned it, paying two dollars for the gun ought to leave us right at ten dollars. Not much for a four-hundred-mile trip. I wasn't at all sure we'd make it.

His gaze moved past my head, and I figured he was looking out his window at Lily sitting in our pitiful wagon with the broke-down mule, holding little, sleeping Em on her lap. He said, "Will you be needing some powder and caps with that?" It was the first hint I'd had that traveling with a woman and a helpless child could do a fellow some good.

"Hat fits you nice," she said, when I came out to pack the store goods in the back of the wagon. I climbed up on the seat, took the lines, and drove Sassy down to a motte of trees forty rods from the store, where we stopped for the first night.

My strength hadn't yet returned to me fully, and during the night, the fever crept back. Not as strong as before. I didn't slip off into a nether world or nothing, but fitful dreams did keep me awake. Dreams and the hard ground. The storekeeper's rooster, crowing right at dawn, woke me for good.

Lily already had a fire glowing, and coffee brewing. Em laid on a quilt spread down on the ground to make a pallet, and she rested content, watching her ma make gravy out of nothing, a little lard, flour, and chopped-up boiled eggs.

"You ain't well yet," Lily said, glancing at me as I sat up. She poured me a cup of the coffee, spooned in some goat's milk. "I heard you shivering all night."

I took the cup and wrapped my hands around it. The morning damp was on the air. She sliced a cold biscuit in half, laid it on the tin plate, and ladled the egg gravy over the top. She handed me that too, and a fork.

"You can rest in the wagon," she said. "We've got level road through here. I'll drive the mule."

I forked in a bite and shook my head, but not because I didn't like her suggestion. What I was thinking of was how good the food tasted, and how I couldn't seem to fill up. Like I had a yawning pit open in my belly.

She frowned at me. "I can drive a mule," she said.

"I've done it plenty. Near about all my life. I can do it good as you can."

"Fine. Drive the mule if you want to." I poked my empty plate at her. "Is there more of this?"

She blinked and opened her mouth like to jower at me some more, till she realized I was letting her have her way about it. I wasn't much interested in nothing besides the food.

She split another biscuit, scooped on more gravy, and handed me back my plate. "It's good you're eating," she said, and her voice had gone mothering again.

We got the wagon loaded and I did rest a while in the back, least till the swaying and the smell of pissy baby rags soured my guts. Besides, it didn't seem we were going at a brisk enough clip. I knew that godforsaken mule would pace down if you let her, and I could tell Lily had let her. I glanced in the cradle at Em, and wished I could sleep so peaceful.

After I crawled up to the high-seat and took the lines, we made better time. Lily puckered up about it for a few miles, but the silence overcame her finally, and she got to talking. Told me that while I'd been holed up in the Banquete jail, she'd wrote a letter to her folks back at McDade asking after her sister and two brothers, and telling them of the arrival of Emmaline. She'd wondered, too, though she didn't say so plain out in the letter, if she could expect decent treatment if she went home.

"I didn't know if you were coming back," she said,

explaining, but I felt like slime again at how I'd walked off and left her sick and in the hands of Mexicans. We were both lucky they'd turned out to be good folks. "Anyhow," she went on, "Papa's married to Miz Kennedy now, and it was her that wrote back. She said he hadn't softened his mind towards me any. Said he made no remark at all when she told him he'd become a grandpa."

I knew of the woman she was talking about, a soured-up old busybody widow woman who'd never borne any children of her own. I didn't know what to say. As I could recall, it was the first time Lily had brought up her family problems to me. Until then, all I knew had come from Shot about how she'd chosen him over her security, and how he couldn't stand thinking he'd caused her to make such a racking decision.

"But I don't care if Papa likes it or not," she said, more to herself now than to me. "I'm gonna keep on writing to Dellie and to Nathan. I've got a right to know how they're getting on. I practically raised them by myself. And Dane'll read my letters to them, I know he will. Even though he might hate me by now, too. He'll read them my letters."

It was her brothers and sister she meant, and I watched her that night by the fire, with paper and a pen from her trunk. We posted the letters in Oakville, though I never asked what words she wrote in them, or things she chose to tell them about where she was or what she

was doing. I was curious, though, and there wasn't any
call for me to be. It wasn't my business, yet it made me
wonder what was going on in her mind, and realize that
she'd been missing parts of her past life as much as I'd
been longing for mine.

We stopped at Belle Branch so Lily could wash
Emmy's clothes in the river there. She took a battling
board out of the wagon, and a gourd of soft lye soap,
and she beat the dirt from the smelly clothes. She tried
twice to get me to let her at my blue shirt, but the clothes
on my back were all I owned. I was reluctant to part with
them. Even for a little while.

I went off into the woods with the shotgun and came
back an hour later with two squirrels for our supper. But
I had missed a big coon and a ringtail learning that the
gun pulled to the left.

At New Hope, I studied our map good and long.
We weren't but twenty-two miles from San Antonio. I
didn't much want to go through there but I couldn't see
any easy way around it. Nights, so far, we'd been able
to spend out in the air, but it was well into November,
and I worried we might run into winter before we got
all the way to Weatherford. That was the only town my
map showed in Parker County, so that was where I was
headed. But I couldn't figure a way to get us there in a
hurry, without tearing smack-dab through the middle of
San Antonio.

"I just don't see why you'd even think about going there." Lily sat with one of her nuns' quilts wrapped about her shoulders.

I stirred in the fire with a stick. "Could stop and collect the wages I never got from Poe Terry." I chuckled.

"That doesn't seem funny to me."

"I wasn't trying to make you laugh."

She blew out some air, then shook her head, gazing off into the night. Her eyes were circled dark in the firelight. She'd already put Em to bed, and was looking ready for bed herself. After four days, the wagon had gotten tiresome for both of them. For me, too. And we weren't but a quarter of the way there yet. Coyotes yowled not too far away, but I didn't think she was listening to them.

"Can't we find some other route?" She sounded disgusted with me. "I've got a bad feeling about going through San Antone."

I chunked my stick in the fire and handed the map around to let her see for herself. She took it, spread it down flat on the ground beside her, holding up one corner so's the firelight fell good enough to read by. Her head bent, studying.

"There's Floresville." She raised her face at me, hopeful. "We could loop around that way."

"And add two maybe three days to the trip."

"So?" She stood up. "So what if it does?"

She swished herself off to the wagon before I could

answer the question. She left my map laying on the ground, too, and it liked to've blew right into the fire and burnt up. I saved it, though, and while I folded it, I watched her climb in the back of the wagon with Em.

I wondered was it for herself or for me that she worried? Was she afraid somebody would know just by looking at me that I had killed a man in that town three months before, or was she scared we'd run into another Tennessean? I hadn't ever had any woman concerned over my welfare before, so I figured it couldn't be that bothering her. I reckon she must've had bad memories haunting her, and knowing that made my own memories come back. They caused a tremble to run up my spine.

"All right," I said, loud enough she should hear me if she was listening. "We'll head through Floresville, and pick our trail back up north of San Antone."

No sounds came from her. Nothing. No movement within the wagon at all. I knew she couldn't be asleep already. She hadn't had time. I waited for her to answer. She never did. But I reckon she heard me.

14

It took us three days longer going by way of Floresville. Mostly because north of there the road petered down to ruts. And the land got so rocky, several times I had to climb down and clear us a path before we could wend our way onward.

Once we got past New Braunfels, the road disappeared altogether. I thought we were sure enough lost till a teamster happened by and showed us the pass through the hills. He traded us coffee and tobacco, soothing syrup for Em's colic, and a box of California oranges, all for our one nanny goat. The nanny had come to be a bother to milk, holding us up of a morning. And what she gave was so rich it churned to clabber cheese in the back of the jostling wagon before we could drink it all up. The teamster fellow made down his bedroll to camp with us that night, but Em's bawling ran him off before he got too comfortable.

Those oranges were the sweetest I ever laid my mouth around. I ate four of them that night while I sat up keeping watch. The area we were in was uncivilized, and I'd already heard a wolf howl and the growl of a cat mingled in with the croaking toads and hoot owls. It looked to me like Indian country, though the government swore they'd routed out all the savages hid up in these hills. But I could feature them in the shadows, all night long, lining the high ridges in the moonlight above us. I sat awake till daybreak, smoking up the tobacco, and eating those sweet oranges.

At Spring Branch, we picked up the road out of San Antonio again. It was on the stage line to Blanco, so we had a good crossing over the Guadalupe River gorge, but we had to pay the ferryman out of our dwindling store of cash.

From there, the going got slow and rough. The hills rose higher and higher, and pretty soon were mountains. Our wagon didn't have a brake, so I had to keep pulling Lily and Em out to walk the downgrades, while I tied on logs or rocks or anything else I could find to keep the wagon from overrunning the mule. We didn't make but about ten miles a day.

The work, getting in and out of the wagon, heaving the heavy rocks and logs, and holding back on Sassy, liked to have whipped me. Every muscle in my body screamed. For some reason, I couldn't seem to get back my strength. I didn't remember ever feeling so puny before.

At Blanco, we stopped at a blacksmith. The owner, a gruff-talking German man, sold me an old drag-shoe for chocking the back wheels of the wagon as we went downhill. Cost us six bits, but he considered it enough spent that he let us sleep in his wagonyard, and use his wellhouse for washing. In a lean-to were some cots that didn't appear lousy, and there was an actual cookstove so Lily could make a proper meal. With a bath and a shave, and a good night's sleep indoors, I felt like a new man.

We left Blanco, climbing out of the long valley the town laid in. Despite the bumpy ride, little Em fell right to sleep in Lily's lap. The soothing syrup had started to ease her colic. Even Sassy didn't balk at the climb, and once we crested the rise, the drag-shoe worked like a charm going down.

It seemed a good way to be starting out the day, with everybody in a good humor. I even felt it some myself, though heaven only knew why. Heading north to become a farmer hadn't ever been my idea of paradise. Yet it had become the one thing driving me—getting up there, getting settled into some kind of steady life, putting down some roots.

I thought about Jack, wherever he was, and Az—

I knew where he was—and the memory of them both took a softer edge. Shot came to mind, and I felt relief to finally be doing what I'd told him I'd do when I left him in that Bastrop jail. Silently, and across the miles from me to him, I thanked him for giving me Lily and Em to keep me out of trouble.

Next thing I knew I had started in singing. A song bubbled right up and out of me, the words coming from deep in the back of my memory. And I didn't feel at all bashful about letting it rip at the top of my voice:

> *From this valley they say you are going;*
> *I will miss your blue eyes and sweet smiles,*
> *For you'll take with you all of the sunshine*
> *That has brightened my days for a while . . .*

Lily wanted to sing along too, but she didn't know the words. She made me teach her that song, and "Aura Lea" and "Yellow Rose of Texas," and she took pleasure in learning. Even kept it up that evening around our campfire, till I was too weary to, and too dry in the throat.

She said, "Marion never told me you were a singer." And her bringing him up made me wonder if he would mind me teaching her songs about a mulatto whore or the maid with the golden hair. I decided then I'd better stick with "The Red River Valley" and "Dixie's Land" from here on. I had to keep it in mind that I had me two innocents on my hands.

We ran into our first norther outside Lampasas. The weather came in wet, swirling wind and rain in all directions, and held us up for three days in that town. While we were laid over there, the malaria swamped back on me, wouldn't let me loose, it didn't seem, from its grip. For two full days I floated in and out, my mind muddy, dreaming sometimes, most times not.

A doctor came. He made me drink a foul-tasting, gritty draught that gave me a skull-crushing headache, and made me so thirsty my tongue stuck to the back of my teeth. Lily used up the last bit of our money paying off the doctor. And before I could get back on my feet enough so's to find a little work someplace to tide us over till we got to Parker County, she went and sold off some of the handmades she'd got at the convent to a storekeeper in town. She bought me a coat, too, and a shirt, some pants, and a pair of wool socks. And she wouldn't listen to me grouse about how I couldn't keep on taking her money from her.

"You had to have a coat," she said, plain out. "It doesn't make sense us heading on north without you having one, does it?" And there wasn't much way for me to argue with such clear thinking as that.

As we passed through the main streets, with her driving the mule, I saw in the store window one of the nuns' quilts and the frilly tea napkins from the Rosales women. It made me feel small, and weak, seeing those things inside that window. Yet I felt something else

too, as I turned the coat collar against the wind, and
shoved my fists down inside the warm flannel pockets. I
couldn't recall anybody ever buying me nothing before,
and especially not sacrificing something of their own to
do it with. It was puzzling to me, and I cut my eyes at
her once or twice, wondering just who it was looking
after who.

The nights were cooler up in the north of Texas.
Though the norther had blown on through and left the
days fair, we got lucky Emmaline didn't take sick, too,
with us sleeping out under the stars.

After a day or so of me seeing visions and near to
swooning, the doctor's draught finally took hold. I felt
well enough to take over the driving lines. Even went
out after some game meat. We spent Thanksgiving din-
ing on a coon stew beside a crystal-clear creek outside
Granbury. By late the next evening, we were rolling into
Weatherford.

The lay of the land reminded me of down around
home. The hills were a little higher, and the soil loamier,
but it seemed to me I'd been in this place, and since
I knew I never had been, I figured it was just the resemblance to home making things feel so familiar. We
passed over creekbeds, running draws, and washouts;
went through pecan bottoms and post oak levels. Night-
fall came, and a curtain of fog dropped down in the
valleys.

It was a week-ending night, so the town was full

of folks, men mostly, since saloons or dancehalls took up nearly every corner. The wheelwright let us park in his wagonyard, which seemed to be a regular hotel for families in town doing their trading. Young'uns ran around playing wolf and crack the whip, climbing trees and laughing loud.

There was a common house with a bathing room, and while Lily washed Em and rinsed out their clothes, and did whatever else all the other women were doing in there, I strode out to join the men around the blazing fire they had built.

There was some shifting of their circle when I stepped in. Their faces were all lit yellow from the flames. Sparks popped skywards, hovered above the fire a second, then turned to ash and drifted back down around us. I brushed some of it off the shoulder of the coat Lily had bought me. I smiled around at the men in the circle, told them my name.

"Wouldn't any of you happen to know of a Jones has a lawyer for a brother down in Bastrop County, do you?" I said. "A Jones has some farmland he's needing a man to work?"

A mumbling went up around the circle, heads shaking. One standing next to me and wearing worn coveralls scratched underneath his hat. "Jones down at Lazy Bend?"

"I dunno." I felt hopeful. "Maybe so."

Another spoke out, "There's some Joneses up at Poolville."

"He said farmland, Amos," the one in the coveralls said. "Gotta be down in the big valley."

"I believe Silas Jones done hired a man," somebody else said.

"Could be Doc Jones over at Poe Prairie," another said.

"*Farm*land, Matthew." The one wearing coveralls, and with the itchy head, turned to me. "There's lots of Joneses around." He was nearly apologizing.

"I guess I didn't expect it to be so populated up here." I felt like a fool, not even thinking to get a first name from Wash before I came all this way.

"The rail line's to blame for it. Got folks pouring in on account of it. Can hop on here and ride her plumb to California now."

He gazed off like he was dreaming of California. He was a homely fellow, about thirty-five years' worth of hard work lined on his face. His smile, when he flashed it, was bright, though. He gave a little shiver. It was plenty chilly, even with the fire warming our front-sides. He reached into his shabby coat and brought out a silver flask.

"Interest you in a nip?" He nudged the flask my way and I took it. Tasted like some kind of brandy. I wiped my mouth and handed it back.

"Obliged," I said.

"You come from down around Bastrop yourself?" he said. I nodded. "Well, don't expect it to be no better up here. Times is hard everywhere."

"It can't be worse."

"You lose your home down there?"

I thought about his question, and my answer, when I nodded, was as true as death. "You could say that."

The music from one of the dancehalls close by came over the crackle of the fire and the kids' play and breathless running. The other fellows had started back to talking amongst theirselves. The one standing next to me tucked away his flask.

"This Jones you're looking for—he a lawyer, too?"

I shrugged and shook my head, feeling more and more foolish by the second.

He nodded. "I'd look for Silas Jones down at Lazy Bend. Only Jones I know has land and is a lawyer, too. Lawyering tends to run in families. Sorter like green eyes and red hair." He gave me a wide grin. "He keeps a house just this side of Brock's gin on Grindstone Creek. Head southwest. There's a fair good road runs through there. Can't miss it."

"Brock's gin," I repeated.

"And if you don't have any luck, just keep on the creek road till you get to Soda Springs. Ask anybody around there how to get to Pete Strickland's place. That's me. We don't live fancy, but you can help yourself to whatever you find in the smokehouse."

"Much obliged," I said, and we shook hands.

The next morning, we found Silas Jones right where Pete Strickland said he would be, living in a house of ship-lap siding and cypress roofing shingles, with a wide gallery around the upper story. He was up there on a high-back chair set on cartwheels, like he was a cripple and needed somebody to push him around. Yet, when I stopped Sassy at his yard gate, he rose from the wheeled-chair and came to the gallery railing to watch me alight. He was tall and straight, hoary-headed, and from where he was standing, he could've reached out and grabbed a handful of pecans off the tree limb stretched before him. He leaned on a duck-head cane, and looked down at me.

I hollered out my name and asked was he the brother of Wash Jones of Bastrop County. I had cleaned up, wore the new clothes Lily had got for me in Lampasas. She stayed in the wagon, her pretty pink poke bonnet tied under her chin, Em on her lap, wrapped inside a blanket. I thought to somebody who didn't know different, we probably looked like a trustworthy little family.

Silas Jones said that he was indeed the brother of Washington Jones of Bastrop township. That was how he talked, lawyerly, using words like township and calling old Wash Washington, which I hadn't even known was his rightful name. I glanced back at Lily, felt myself smiling. We'd found the right place, were finally here. She smiled, too, like she read my mind.

"Your brother sent me," I called up. "He said you were looking for a good man to work your land for you." I started to step inside the gate so's I wouldn't have to shout as loud, but a load of dogs came barking around the corner of the house. They snarled at me through the fence palings. There were five of them, none over a foot and a half high. Yapping little things.

"Stamp your foot at them," Silas Jones yelled. "They're harmless pests."

I did like he said and it sent them a-scatter. They came back, though, their barking louder than ever. I heard Silas Jones shout, "Shut those infernal animals up!" like there was somebody else listening. I didn't see nobody, and thought for a minute he maybe meant me. I glanced again at Lily, to see if she had any ideas what was going on. She was staring at the dogs and didn't notice me looking.

I should've just gone on inside the fence and to hell with the barking. I'd been raised around dogs bigger and meaner than these five, but I was trying to do the polite thing here, act like the good man I'd just declared myself to be.

It caught me by surprise when the gun fired. I nearly jumped out of my skin, then flattened myself behind the pecan tree's wide trunk. It was instinct made me do it, and for a split second, I wished I'd brought the old broke double-barrel out of the wagon. When I peered again, Silas Jones held a smoking pistol in his feeble hand. I didn't know where he'd aimed his bullet, but all five of the dogs had run off yelping. There wasn't any blood or fur bits on the ground anywhere. I heard Em whimpering.

"Now then," Jones said, handing the pistol to the black houseboy standing at his side. "We can hear ourselves think. Take this along, Puddin." Silas Jones raised his chin my way. He wore an old-fashioned imperial, a little gray tuft of whiskers just under his bottom lip. "Washington has already sent me a man. And I'm afraid he is working out perfectly well."

My heart sank. My shoulders sagged. This couldn't be right. I took two great gulps of air. "*Wash* sent you somebody?"

"He did. A hard-working chap. Stevens by name."

"Stevens?" I was having a hard time hearing. The gunshot had my ears ringing. I ran my little finger in there, plumb to the eardrum, to clear things out. "Did you say Stevens? Not R. J. Stevens?"

"Yes, that's right."

"Bob Stevens is here?"

"Do you know him?"

"Like a brother," I said. A burst of joy built in me, made up some for the loss I felt over having come so far for nothing. If Bob was here, at least we wouldn't be alone. I'd have somebody to help me decide the right thing to do next. "Where's he at?" I called up at Mr. Jones.

"He lives right there on the land. You take this road until you come to a cemetery. The house is just beyond."

I sprang for the wagon. Lily handed me the lines. "Robert Stevens is here?" she said. She didn't sound near as glad as I felt.

"I'm sorry, Mister Beatty," Silas Jones called after me.

I barely heard him, but I thought to touch my hat before I slapped the lines on the mule. The dogs had started barking again. They chased us all the way down the fence, and kept up their racket even after we were out of sight.

15

ob Stevens had been Jack's best friend clean back to when they were both in shirttails. He had stood up for Jack when Jack married Estelle. That fact hadn't set too well with Az or me at first. We'd figured it should've been one or the other of us, or even Shot, witnessing Jack's marriage, seeing as how we were his blood brothers. But Bob Stevens had always been able to put on the dog real good, spruce up and pass himself off as a respectable gentleman, and that was what Jack had been needing for his wedding, since Estelle Odom had come from good-educated, well-bred stock, and since Jack had been trying to impress her people. He made the three of us, me and Azberry, and Shot too, stay at home while he flitted off to Rockdale and married hisself into the Odom family.

Bob was about my height, but thinner so he seemed over six feet. He had one of those sunk-in faces that made his cheekbones stand out clear, and long, almost delicate hands. He had always worried over keeping his nails clean, his dark hair combed, and his face shaved smooth as a baby's butt. To see Bob Stevens for the first time, you would have thought he was a businessman, a musician maybe on account of those long hands, a cattleman even, but never, ever a farmer. I couldn't push Sassy fast enough to get us there.

The last time I'd seen him, he was leaving the Bastrop jail with Charlie Goodman. That was just after Wash Jones had brought them clear in court, though I don't reckon much of anybody believed from the outset either of them fired the gun that killed Willie Griffin. Neither one of them was even out on the street still when Willie went down. They both high-tailed it right after the shooting started.

For a while I'd held a lot of bitterness about that, the way they'd left me alone in the street, with Mr. Milton and Tom Bishop trying their damndest to kill me the same way they had my brothers, filling me up with lead; just like I'd held a grudge against Shot for a time, for not going into town with us at all that day. But bygones were bygones, and there wasn't nothing good to come from dwelling on a thing. I whacked the lines down on Sassy's back and nagged her to a harder trot.

The road had been dropping down steady, not so much as you'd notice with your eyes, but could more

feel with each groan of the wagon. We were in the Brazos
River valley, and all around was growing land, mostly
oats coming up. Some wheat. Around the houses were
kitchen gardens, fenced in on account of hogs roaming
free, some of which we like to have run into rooting in
the middle of the road. Sassy raised her head in alarm,
but the blinkers on her kept her from running off with the
wagon. The hogs disappeared into the woods alongside
the road.

We came to the graveyard Silas Jones had mentioned, and just past there, set back up on a bluff, stood
the house. It was made of split logs, a double pen with
a gallery running between the two sides. It was old,
but neat with hollyhocks underneath the windows, and
winter grapes tangling up a fan trellis. A wooden fence
surrounded the yard. Inside the fence, a half-dozen red
pullets pecked at the ground.

"Reckon this is it?" I said out loud, but more to myself than anything. Somehow it didn't seem like the kind
of place where Bob would live. Too homified for one
thing. And I couldn't think of Bob as the sort to raise
chickens. Not unless he'd changed one whole hell of a
lot. I held back on the mule while I looked. I didn't see
a soul about.

"There." Lily nudged my arm and pointed the opposite way from where I'd been looking, out over the level
going down to the river.

It was Bob, sure enough, way out there chopping at
a big stump. I could tell by his form, the straight back

and neck, that it was him. He had a horse and chain with him. I watched him set down the ax and whip the horse to pull out the tree stump. It was a big, hairy workhorse, a Percheron or a Belgian.

I whistled through my teeth, as loud as I could, waved my hat high, whistled again. I got Em's attention. Her blue eyes opened wide under her little bonnet, even in the sunlight. I clucked her under the chin. When I looked up, Bob was running our way, his arm thrown up over his hat to keep from losing it. He left the horse out there, chained to the stump.

I stood up. Lily took the lines from me.

"Light down from there, you old sonofabitch!" he hollered at me. He had on jeans-cloth britches, brogans, the slouch hat. He looked like a farmer, fit and happy, grinning ear to ear.

I jumped down from the wagon, jarred my bad leg. I was all the time forgetting about it till it was too late. I limped towards him, my hand stuck out. But he grabbed me in a bear hug and pounded on my back, laughing. We were both laughing.

"I thought I was seeing things," he said, out of breath from running and from bouncing me around. "How the hell are you?"

"You stole my job," I answered. "Wash Jones told me his brother needed a good man to work his place, and here I am. I didn't know I'd find you."

"He told me the same thing."

It stung me some hearing that, to realize Wash Jones

hadn't meant nothing sacred when he used the word *good* to me, but I didn't let on. Bob was shaking my hand now, still banging me on the shoulder. I was so glad to see him, I felt almost awkward about it.

"How long you been here?" I said.

"Since summer. Got five acres in oats." He pointed to the dark green field beyond where his work horse was chained to the stump. "Gonna put down twenty in corn and twenty-five in cotton come spring."

I looked out over the land. "Fifty acres? How you gonna tend to that much? Just one man?"

"Green guts and bitter gall." He grinned and spit a fine brown stream on the ground. I hadn't known he was chewing. Leave it to Bob to dip snuff tobacco, and do it as delicate as a woman. He dabbed the back of his hand to the corner of his mouth. "Got a hundred and sixteen acres here. On halves. I was thinking to try and buy it from him, if I make out all right and he's willing to sell. He owns land all over this valley."

"You?" I shook my head. "A farmer?"

"Well, what was you gonna do when you got here? Mine for gold?"

I laughed, but it still didn't seem natural, for either one of us. But Bob was going to need plenty of help. That much I knew for sure.

Em let out a fussy cry, and he looked up like he just noticed the two in the wagon. "You remember Lily?" I said. He took his hat off for her, but then gave me a peculiar frown. "Shot asked me to take care of her and his—while he's doing his . . . You knew he got two years?"

"I heard," Bob said. "From old Wash. After I wired him looking for you."

"Why were you looking for me? Were you gonna ask me to go in partners with you here?" I glanced around, felt a pang of disappointment. It would've been perfect. For Lily and Em. For us. I shook that thought away as quick as it came. "Let's turn my mule out and I'll help you with that stump," I said. I reached up to take Em from Lily's lap. She gathered my shirt in her little fist. "Drive up to the house," I told Lily and she popped the lines down, pleased, it seemed, to be doing something useful.

On foot, Bob and I followed the wagon. Em was warm against my neck. Bob made a remark about her hair, which stuck out all over her head like orange broomstraw. He mentioned that she took after Shot, but otherwise he was unduly quiet as we strolled towards his house. I didn't much notice it, though. Not right then.

At the top of the hill, I could see into his horse lot. His gray, the one he'd had for a few years, was in there, Luther by name, after the man he'd bought the horse from. Two chestnut mares came towards the fence, and just behind them came Dash. Jack's stallion. There was no mistaking it. He was a horse looked like no other—almost pure black, save for his chin whiskers and a ridge down both haunches. No blaze, no star, no socks. No other color at all save for those brown points. He was an awful handsome horse, and tall. Almost seventeen hands. I'd have known him anywhere.

"That's Dash," I said, turning to Bob.

His cheeks colored red, even under his sun-dark skin. "I've been holding onto him for you."

"How'd you get him?"

"Well, I was gonna tell you—"

A door slammed, and then a voice cried out, "Lily!" By the time I looked, Estelle was already down to the wagon.

The sight of her didn't make sense to me for a second. As I watched her and Lily embrace, I thought how I'd never known they were such friends. And then she— both of them, arm in arm—headed towards me. Emmaline saw her ma and squirmed in my arms.

"I was gonna tell you—" Bob said again and stopped at the same place. He couldn't seem to get any further with his words.

I looked at him. A muscle at his eyelid ticked. "Tell me what?" I said.

"There she is." Estelle was coming for Em. "Oh, isn't she just so precious." She pulled the baby from my arms, and reached on tiptoe to brush my cheek with a kiss. "Haywood." She cupped my chin quick, and let go. "Look at you. Thin as a rail."

Estelle had dark hair, sea-green eyes, cheeks like peach blush. She was a fine-made woman. Jack would've never had less. Her dress was of pale blue, a bit of white lace at the collar. Not mourning colors. Her apron was stitched with pale pink flowers, and tied up over a belly that was more than a little bit pregnant.

I glanced at Lily, and she frowned at me. Then I looked back, for an instant, at Estelle's smiling face, before I turned to Bob. "You sonofabitch," I said, and I gave my back to all three of them.

"Wait! Haywood!" Estelle called after me. I kept on walking away, headed straight for the fence where Dash stood with his head poked over the top rail. I heard Bob say for her to take Lily and the baby into the house.

Dash nudged his way past the mares, as if he knew me by sight. He'd always been a smart cuss. Lots of brain between those wide-set eyes. When I reached him, he stuck his nose in my armpit, got my smell, then lipped at my hat. I ran my hand down his neck, and he let me hang onto him for a second before he turned away from me, more interested in the grass around the base of the fence post than in remembering me.

I watched him graze and flick his tail, and I could practically see Jack coming out here, his saddle on his shoulder, cinching it up, getting aboard. And I could see them loping off across the hill, taking the fence easy. Jack with his black hat, light hair hanging out the back, and wearing the fringe vest he liked to shine in for the ladies. Sitting tall on his tall horse . . .

"I tried to wire you," Bob said from behind me.

"Wash sent back word that you were out and gone already. I wanted to tell you."

"Tell me what? That you've been sticking your tail in my brother's wife?"

He rushed at me and caught me off my guard. Dash rared back, wheeling away from the fence where Bob pinned me, chest down. My hat fell over sideways onto my shoulder. The wind-string held it there, but also choked my neck. My fingers clawed at it.

"Listen here, goddamn you," Bob hissed in my ear. "She's my wife now, and I won't have you talking rude about her."

I rammed my left elbow back into his ribs. He grunted and let me loose. I whirled and belted him a right to his jaw. But that only made him madder. He came back at me, punched me square on the spot where my brow and cheekbone meet. The force of it knocked me into the fence again. He'd got stronger since the last time I'd rastled him.

"Stop it! Stop it! Both of you!" Estelle barged between us. "Robert!" She pressed him backwards, then turned on me. "Shame on you, Haywood!"

"This is between Bob and me," I said, keeping my eyes on him.

"Do you think Jack would want the two of you acting this way?" she said.

"What the hell do you care what Jack would want?" I didn't want her even speaking his name.

She stepped back like I'd struck at her, too. "How

dare you say such a vile thing to me. You know how much I cared for Jack."

"It sure don't show. It looks to me like you forgot him pretty goddamned quick."

"Hold on there." Bob made a move forward. Estelle held her hand against his chest and he stopped coming. I could see right away who wore the pants around here.

She said, "I know in my heart Jack would've wanted me to go on with life."

"If you think that, then you didn't know nothing about him." I looked past her, past her quivering bottom lip. "Lily," I said. "Get in the wagon."

"Oh no. She's staying here," Estelle said. "Can't you see you've worn her out dragging her and the baby all over tarnation."

"Lily?" I narrowed my eyes. I could feel the left one swelling up. "Let's go."

"No! She's going to stay here." She turned towards Lily. "I insist that you stay. We have an extra room."

Lily stepped around Estelle, careful, patting Em on the back, bouncing her quiet. "Thank you, Estelle, that's kind." She reached out to grip ahold of Estelle's hand for a second, then came on towards me. "Can we talk alone for a minute?"

My jaw clenched up. "So you're turning against me now."

"I just want to talk to you a minute."

I pulled my eyes off her, looked at Bob, caught him rubbing his jaw where I'd socked him. He dropped his hand right quick, straightened to the full height God gave him.

"I'm taking Dash," I said to him.

"I told you I intended you to have him."

"Where's his saddle?"

Estelle gave a little cry and whirled for the house. She ran off carrying her skirts high. Bob's gaze followed her. "In the barn," he mumbled and started after her. He caught up to her at the fence gate, and opened it for her to go through.

I looked at Lily. "You're not coming with me?" My voice sounded accusing.

"Where're you going?"

"Away from here."

Her eyes turned down. Against her shoulder, little Em was babbling, soft and tender. "Estelle's right, Haywood. I *am* tired of traveling. Emmy's tired of it. We gotta settle down someplace. And since Estelle's here—" She glanced back towards the house. They'd disappeared inside. "It'll be nice to be with another woman. And she's gonna need somebody."

"Fine." I spit out the word, then started up the path to the barn. I heard her footsteps behind me, but I kept on walking. I took her right to the barn door without saying anything. When I turned, she jumped. "Shot's gonna feel the same way I do about this. You know that, don't you? He ain't gonna want you staying with these people."

"He might *not* feel the same. He might think Estelle's too young a woman to of stayed a widow long. And too pretty. Maybe he'll think it's lucky Robert Stevens took her in marriage rather than some stranger."

"He won't think like that. I know my brother. Shot'll see Bob as a traitor just like I do. If you wanna stay here with these people then I can't stop you, but don't try to change my mind about them."

I ducked inside the barn, had to let my eyes adjust, it was so dim. My left one was closing up fast, but I caught a glimpse of Jack's saddle thrown over a rail. The leather was worn smooth and stained dark on the seat and down the skirt. My own blood had made that stain. Blood from the wounds Milton and Bishop had given me. And it was Lily who'd saved me, when she came past the ditch where I hid. She was riding Jack's horse. I ran my hand over the stained leather and looked back at her, wondering if she remembered it was this saddle we'd been on that day, together.

"Where will you go?" she said.

"I don't know yet. I'm about out of ideas."

"Then wait till morning, why don't you? Give it some thought before you leave." She gave me a little smile. "Do it for Emmy. So's she won't worry over you. She's gotten fond of her . . . Uncle Woody."

I smiled some then, too, and reached out to curl my finger in Em's soft locks. It felt like something was pinching up inside me. I didn't want to leave without them. I never knew you could miss somebody before you'd even gone.

"I don't reckon I can blame you for rathering to stay here. For Em's sake. But I can't dishonor Jack thataway."

"Will you at least let me know where you are? As soon as you get there? Don't wait around and forget."

"All right, I won't. But why?"

"Well, because . . ." She looked unsure, like she didn't know the answer herself. "We're family. Don't you think we ought to keep up with each other?"

I shrugged, then nodded.

She put her hand on my arm, and before I knew what she was doing, before I could jerk back, she brought her cheek next to mine. "Godspeed," she whispered. I lost my breath to have her so near, and then she moved off, went out of the barn. Left me standing there, strangling.

If it was all right for Estelle to give me a hug, or a kiss even—if that was all right, never mind that she had betrayed Jack's memory, her hugging me had always been all right before—then why wasn't it the same for Lily? She was my sister-in-law too, and rightfully entitled, if she wanted, to hug me or press our cheeks together. But I knew, as my hand came up to touch my face where hers had just been, as I moved to the barn door to watch her carry Em to the house, as I noticed the smooth, swinging way her back-end swayed when she walked, that I had better not let it happen again.

16

ash had always been a bit of an outlaw, pitching and bucking whenever he was first mounted. Jack called it spirit. I took it for pure orneriness, but I held on fast to him, knowing that just as sudden as he threw his fit, it would be over and then he'd stand as sweet as a baby's heart. He didn't disappoint me on either count. But when he calmed, I noticed a founder in his gait he hadn't had before. Bob had been letting him go barefoot, and his toes were overgrown. So our first stop was the blacksmith I'd seen back at Brock. We didn't get any further.

I told myself later that either luck or fate one was working for me that day, but the truth was I didn't much want to leave that country. It felt like the place I ought to be. And if, after all, I was going to keep my word to Shot and look out for his family, I would have to stay close by them.

The blacksmith was closed down. The man who had run it, a Joseph Kelley by name, had just recently died of a cancer in his stomach. All his tools, the forge, anvil, everything right down to his leathern apron and sleeves, was still there in the shop. But the building owner was, by chance or fate, Silas Jones. This was told to me by Riley Davis, who ran the store next door and also paid rent to Silas Jones.

Since it was getting on to early evening, my first thought was to visit Mr. Jones again, see if he'd let me use the shop long enough to bend a new set of shoes for Dash. I also hoped for permission to throw down my bedroll in the shop's backlot for the night.

Old man Silas had another idea. He thought if I could shoe my own horse, why, I'd surely be able to run a blacksmith shop, too. I knew better, but I jumped on the chance, anyhow, seeing as how the work would keep me within six miles of Lily and baby Emmaline. And I couldn't think of nowhere else to go just then.

Silas advanced me two months' rent, and opened me up a line of credit at his store next door. That was what he called it—his store—even though Riley Davis bought and paid for all the goods stocked on the shelves out of his own profits. But that was the way Silas Jones's mind ran. He called the whole settlement of Brock his town, and though he did own a goodly portion of it, I reckon Henry Brock, who the town was named for, and who had the cotton gin and gristmill on Grindstone Creek, might've disagreed with Silas's claim.

The signboard above the shop—my shop—said BLACKSMITH. But what I really was, was a farrier, the shoeing of horses being the only kind of smithing I knew much of anything about. Even there I had plenty to learn. Lucky for me, the dead smith Kelley had been an orderly sort of fellow. Several dozen already bent horseshoes hung by nails on the soot-black walls, and underneath, written in chalk, was the name of the man whose animal each set fit. Made it easy for me, and time saving, since most of the effort came from fitting the iron to the animal's foot.

My living quarters were in a shed attached at the back of the building, full of mud daubers' nests and spiders' webs. There was a cot back there with a rope mattress Kelley had used when he was ailing, or had drank so much laudanum his reason left him. The cot was spread with a dark comfort made from old coveralls and wool trousers left whole, so's at first glance in the night, you might think a man was laid out there like a corpse.

Right behind the shed, with wood from Brock's sawmill, I built a box stall for Dash. On the wall between my lodgings and his, I cut a hole and covered it with a board that I could slip back to look in on him without leaving my room. Now that I had me a good horse again, I couldn't rest easy with him. I fixed me a shelf for the old shotgun right above the cot.

Liam Brannon, Henry Brock's partner at the gin and mill, wanted Dash for seed stock in a horse ranching venture he had going. I said, "I'll let him stud your mares for a price, but he ain't for sale." Riley Davis, the storekeeper next door, had a weakness for the match races held every Saturday at the track a mile outside Weatherford. He offered me a hundred dollars for Dash, and I said again, "He ain't for sale." Finally, I hung a sign outside the front doors that read, NO HORSES FER SALE, in clear letters for anybody that maybe saw Dash grazing in the backlot. Even if I had been willing to sell him, which I surly wasn't, he'd have brought me a good two hundred dollars at the least.

Word went out that there was a newcomer at the Brock blacksmith, and pretty soon folks from all over the valley came to see me—some with animals to shoe, others with just a desire to see what sort of fellow I might be. I got invited to church, to a barn dance, and to a cockfight, all in the same day. I didn't go to any of them.

One man, a Coop Mullholland, came to test my mettle with a pair of oxen that needed shoes. I should've just turned him down, since I didn't own any stocks to hold them still while I worked. But instead, like an idiot eager to prove myself, I took the bait, spent all one afternoon rastling the bellowing beasts while Mullholland looked merrily on from Davis's store.

Finally, at my wit's end to get one surly ox necked to a blackjack oak, I bonked the animal over the head, right at the base of his horns, with a two-pound cross-peen hammer. That brought Mullholland out of Davis's store right quick, cussing me. But at least, from then on, he helped. So did Riley Davis, and three other of his customers. Together we got the job done, squeezing the oxen between two iron wagon wheels. After that I vowed, out loud so Coop Mullholland would hear it plain, that I was out of the ox-shoeing business.

Pete Strickland from Soda Springs paid me a visit one cold, rainy morning a week before Christmas. He brought his flask of brandy and a Galveston newspaper which we sat and read together. The news was mostly all about the coming inauguration of Grover Cleveland as president. Being the first Democrat to take office in twenty years, everybody had high hopes that he could end the trade depression going on in Texas, and bring the price of cotton and cattle back up to the level it had been in the '70s.

Pete said he was sorry I'd lost my wife and baby, so I figured there must already be tongues wagging in the neighborhood. I said, "They belonged to my brother. I was just watching after them while he's away. They got another place to stay now." I tried not to sound downhearted about it.

"Oh," he said, and let it go at that, but before he left, he invited me to his place for Christmas dinner. It was a day I'd been dreading, the one-year anniversary of Jack and Az getting killed. I said I'd think it over, and after he was gone, I nailed his newspaper on the wall behind my bed, to help block out some cold-seeping cracks up there.

Bob found me, or more likely heard where I was. He brought in a link of chain that had broke apart on him. Then he stood outside smoking a cigar in the cold, while I welded the link back together. The break was at the end of the length, and the chain could've easily been used with that one link pulled off. All Bob had come for really was to show me he knew I was here.

"How much do I owe you?" he said when I gave him back his mended chain.

"No charge."

"How much?"

"I said, no charge."

The furrow between his brows deepened, and we stood there staring at each other's eyes, like it was a game we were playing, to see who'd look away first. Bob lost.

"Why've you gotta be so goddamn pig-headed?" he said.

"Did you come here to fight me again? There ain't no women around to stop us this time."

He looked back at the doors. They were both open enough so's our breath made smoke when we talked, despite the welding heat from the forge. "No," he said.

"I came to tell you Lily wants to see you."

"What for?"

"Hell if I know. To see if you're faring all right."

"She's a good driver. She can come here if that's all she wants."

"Dammit, Haywood." He blew out a big steam of air. "I tried to find you to tell you about Estelle and me. You and Shot both. I wanted y'all to know beforehand, but I had her saying yes to me, and so I went ahead and I married her. I didn't think you'd take it so hard."

I turned back to the forge, took the tongs and dipped them into the slake trough to cool. With the poker, I banked up the coals, damped them with my water can. Bob stood right over me, getting into my line of sight, casting a shadow across my work. He didn't appear to be fixing to leave.

"Jack himself knew I fancied her," he said. "He used to pester me about it. You gotta remember that, how he gloated over finding her first. It can't be such a big surprise to you, if you'll just think back on it a bit."

I rubbed my hands off on the apron tied about my waist. Joseph Kelley'd been a big, strapping fellow, and I could nearly wind his apron around me twice. "What's the matter, Bob? Conscience got ahold of you? You know Jack'd kill you if he was alive."

He nodded at me; smiled, except it came out looking more like a grimace. "That's just the point, Haywood. He ain't alive no more."

"No. He ain't." I dashed the poker into the trough, too. "No thanks to you."

"What d'you mean by that?" He shifted an inch closer to me. "Tell me what you mean by that?"

I glanced at him, could see the blood just under his skin. "You know what I mean."

A silence hung between us, so thick you could've painted it red. He didn't move. I didn't. For a good half a minute or more.

"What did you expect me to do?" he said, talking slow now. "I went into McDade unarmed just like Jack did. Was I supposed to stop Tom Bishop in my shirt-sleeves when he had a pistol?"

"Maybe so. Anything besides scampering for your horse. Lighting out like you had a wildcat nipping at your ass."

He stared hard at me, nostrils flaring, hands shoved deep in his coat pockets. It wouldn't have surprised me at all if he had pulled out a pistol himself just then and blown my brains out. Most men don't take kind to getting called a coward.

"That's been festering in you all this time, hadn't it?" he said.

"I reckon so."

He wet his lips and looked like a ghost had stung him, took out all his vim. His mouth turned down three notches, eyes clouded over. "Jack and Az was both already down when I left. Mister Milton come outside with his shotgun, and commenced to shooting at me. I got afraid, Haywood. It ain't something I'm proud of."

A choke closed off my throat. I couldn't swallow; didn't try to speak. I nodded once, took up the poker again, and bent back over the forge, banking the coals, giving the fire room to breathe. I could feel him behind me, his eyes boring through me like spikes.

He stood there a moment or two longer, watching me or watching something, his own haints maybe. Then he picked up his chain and went for the doors. We didn't say goodbye.

After I heard his horse move off, I sat down on the wood bench next to the wall. I felt like all the wind had gone out of me, and just plain mean in my spirit. Of course, he'd been afraid. Hell, I was afraid. So would anybody be with a shotgun firing at them point-blank. And it wasn't really even Bob's running I was mad at, yet I'd caused him to leave here with his tail tucked under, slumped low as a snake's belly.

Memories came pouring down on me, of Bob about fourteen, skinny, freckled, and naked as a bean, swinging out on the rope above our swimming hole; of us racing our dogs across that same creek, mine against a boy's who'd bullied me all summer, and Bob over there on the other bank with a piece of fatback to help my dog win. And I thought of him and Jack, sitting with their fishing poles, fat, wiggly maggots for bait, talking about the mysteries of a female. I learned all I ever knew, or thought I did, from the two of them. And now, here I was, one of them dead, the other my enemy. It just didn't seem right some way, but I couldn't see how to fix it. Bob shouldn't of married Estelle so quick, not with Jack's bones hardly cold in the ground.

The next day Lily came, driving Sassy. She didn't have Em with her and I was let down by that. She sashayed right in, caught me in the middle of making some fence stakes for old Silas. He had me doing all kinds of extra work for him in exchange for my rent.

She was a sight, done up in a dress I'd never seen, coffee-colored with a high, stiff collar. She was already getting new duds, hand-me-downs from Estelle no doubt. Seemed her shape had changed some way, and then I realized she had on a corset. I tried not to smile at her too much, but she acted glad to see me, too.

First thing she did was peek into my living quarters. "Could use some cleaning up," she said, then, "Are you keeping warm?"

"As a biscuit." I nodded at the forge. It was nearly always burning.

"Well . . ." She put her hands on her hips and gazed around. I couldn't get over how small-waisted she seemed in that dress with those stays. Her hair was all piled up and curlicued like a city gal. Pearl eardrops hanging down. "This looks like a profitable business for you." She was even starting to sound like Estelle, using a ten-dollar word like *profitable*. I caught a scent of lilac water, even over the smoldering iron smell of the shop.

"Could be," I said, "if I knew more. Folks keep bringing me work I can't do."

"It's the best way to learn, I reckon. By diving in on something and see what you come up with."

I laughed. Just having her standing right in front of me was making me feel giddy. But an uplifting kind of giddiness. I hadn't known how much I missed her, or how easy with myself I felt in her company.

"That's probably so. The man who had the place before, he left a book back there. The pages is all blacked up, but I read a little bit each night before I hit the bed."

"So you're a scholar now." Her eyebrow tweaked up. She was flirting with me, I could swear it. Was she flirting?

"Just needing to learn," I mumbled.

"Come to dinner Christmas," she said, blurting it out all of a sudden. I let go of a breath I didn't know I'd been holding. This was more like her, coming right out with what was on her mind. She wasn't any better than me at small-talking. "It just seems like time to get things settled between you and . . . I probably shouldn't say, but Bob's so long-faced he can't hardly work. And Estelle, she—"

"I got other plans."

She blinked at me, surprised, doubtful. "What other plans?"

"Pete Strickland. Remember him from the wagon-yard in Weatherford? He invited me to his house for Christmas."

She looked disappointed. It tickled me a little bit, seeing that shade of regret cross her face. "Have you written to Marion? I know he'd love to hear from you."

And there he was. Right between us. His name from her lips jolted me, reminded me, in case I'd forgot, of who she was. I shook my head, partly to answer her question, and partly to get the pollywogs out of my skull. "You write to him for me. I ain't much for letters."

"I already have. He should've gotten a dozen from me by now. But I haven't gotten not one back from him yet. I've been wondering if I should get worried."

"He'll write. We'd have heard from Wash Jones if something was the matter."

She reflected on that a second, and then the smile came back to her. "Will you come *after* Christmas then? Emmy'll be so pleased."

I had to chuckle. I could see she wasn't going to let me off with a no. "All right. We'll see," I said.

I walked her out to the wagon, helped her up. Sassy looked as tired as ever. I watched them roll off down the Lazy Bend road, towards Bob's place.

That night, I dreamed of her. She was nursing Em and I lifted the blanket away to see, ran my finger down her neck and smooth skin to where Em's mouth was latched on. Lily stared at me with her big, watery eyes, and I reached for the hem of her skirt next. She was barefoot, barelegged. I rubbed my hands around her white ankle. . . .

I woke myself up in a sweat, the bed underneath me wet and sticky. I cussed as I got up to clean myself off. What the hell was happening to me? My mind was bent and jangled, turning me into a filthy person.

A whore was what I needed. A nice rowdy whore to take away all my starch. It had been too long, that was all. So long I was starting to dream dreams I shouldn't be. I vowed right then that I'd ask somebody, the first fellow I met who seemed like he'd know, where I could find me a good clean cathouse to visit.

I slid back the board into Dash's stall and talked to him awhile, tried to make myself sleepy again. He stayed on the slouch in his corner and didn't even prick his ears at me, but it helped. I yawned, crawled back onto the cot. Pretty soon, I dozed off. And I'm damned if I didn't take that dream right back up where I'd left it.

17

ete Strickland's place wasn't much different than Bob's. A house set up on a bluff overlooking bottomland broadcast in oats. The house was a sight bigger, newer, made of plank instead of log. Pete had more outbuildings, and children were screaming everywhere.

The day had turned off cloudless, as Christmas in Texas was apt to do. Warm. Before I ever got there I'd had to pull off my coat and wad it behind me on the saddle.

Pete came out to greet me, saying how proud they were to have me. His wife, Alice, a short, pudgy woman, came right behind him. She took my coat and handed me a cup of spiced cider, which would've gone down better on a colder day. They called one of their older boys to come and take Dash down to the corral.

They had a girl staying with them, a girl named Ruth who cooked and tended to the kids, and made eyes at me. I wasn't sure if she was kin or just a foundling they'd taken in. She looked about seventeen or so, and it came clear enough that Pete and Alice would invite a courtship if I had the desire.

Trouble was, Ruth didn't move me in any way. She was all right to look at, doe-eyed, a brown-head, not too skinny. But what did you say to a girl such as her? I just never had learned that art like Jack had, or like Shot.

After a huge supper of roast turkey stuffed with sausage dressing, brown bread, yams, stewed currants, and black-haw pie, Pete and me went out to the front gallery to smoke. We sipped his brandy and talked about cattle, what we knew and didn't know. Pete, like me, had a hankering to be a rancher, had, in fact, ten English steers in his back pastures fattening up. He planned to sell them come spring, though. "Costs too much to winter them over these days," he said. "I'll be lucky to break even."

I drank too much of Pete's brandy, or else had filled up too much on their food. I found my eyes closing while he talked. I heard him tell Alice to fix me a bed in the hayloft. I roused myself, saying, "No, I have to get on home." Yet, even saying it out loud, I couldn't think of the shed with the cot and the mud daubers' castles in the crannies as home.

"Nonsense," Alice said, and she took off for the barn with an armload of bed things.

After dark, all the kids sat on the floor in the front
room and sang Christmas hymns. There were eleven
kids, ranging all ages, and I marveled that such a small
woman as Alice could've borne so many young'uns. They
didn't have a Christmas tree, but strung laurel and cedar
boughs hung in swoops over the doorways and window
sashes. They passed around more of the spiced cider,
and lit candles. Ruth stayed to a corner, smiling shy at
me now and then.

Pete said a Christmas prayer, and it was the first
one I could recall ever sitting through that wasn't said
over a table full of food. He thanked the Lord for their
meager pleasures, and for each and every one in his
family by name, and for Ruth, and for me. I had never
had anybody pray for me before. I didn't know what to
say when he finished. I mumbled an "Amen" right with
everybody else, and it felt strange rolling off my tongue.

All in all, though, it was the right kind of day for
me. Kept my mind from Jack and Az and last Christmas.
After everybody else turned in, Pete and me had one last
nip of brandy out on the gallery. He wanted to be sure,
he said, that I slept well, and sound, out in his hayloft.

The barn was a good one, made solid with a rock
foundation and weather-hardened oak above. Pete held
a lantern while I climbed the loft ladder. Each rung had
a groove worn down in the center from all the years the
boots on Pete's feet had made this same climb.

"If you need anything, you holler, hear?" he said,

and he hooked the lantern to a pulley to hoist up to me.

The floor of the loft was softer than my rope bed at the shop, and warm snuggled down in all that hay, even with the hatch open for the moonlight to come in. I realized right off, though, that I should of drank more brandy. As soon as I'd doused the lantern, I heard every mouse skittering, every hen roosting up in the rafters.

I laid there and thought of Lily and Em, wondered what they'd done today. Then I allowed myself to think of Bob and Estelle, and of their baby coming. And again, I felt sorry for casting blame on him like I'd done, damned near accusing him of killing Jack and Az with his own bare hands. He'd run off because he was scared, and big enough to admit it. He'd been shot that day, too, in the arm, so he knew the heat of bullet just like I did. I wondered if it pained him still, the way my leg sometimes did me, reminding me, keeping the sorrow of my losses fresh within me.

The shifting and creaking in the barn changed, got louder. I held my breath and listened, recognized the sound of somebody climbing the loft ladder. I raised my head, waiting, watching in the shaft of moonlight.

"Evening," Ruth said, her voice dark and husky. I realized I'd barely heard her speak all day. "Are you asleep?"

"No."

She knelt on my pallet. I saw she had on her night-dress. "Me neither."

She laughed a little. I thought she should be quieter. I put my finger to her mouth. "What are you doing here?"

Her tongue flicked out and touched my wrist. At the same time, her hand gripped on tight to my thigh. In just my longhandles, she might as well have been touching bare skin. I pulled her up to me, and we didn't say anything else.

She wasn't shy in the dark. No virgin either, rocking on top of me like a squaw. I had to keep my hand over her mouth to stop her from raising a racket to bring Pete from the house. I didn't think he'd much appreciate me taking more than a meal and a smoke and a nip of brandy. It was about the queerest thing that had ever happened to me. Almost like Ruth was another wicked dream I made up to slake my lustful thirst.

"When're you coming back again?" she said afterward, when she was pushing herself from me.

"I ain't sure." I needed sleep, rest. I felt weak in the belly from all Pete's brandy I'd drank.

"Missus Strickland cooks up a whole pig on New Year's. And they've got sweet potatoes buried out back by the garden. Come then, why don't you?"

I didn't say I would or wouldn't. The moon had gone too high to filter much light into the barn. I could just barely make her out enough to watch as she pulled her nightdress back over her head.

The sweat on me made me cold, yet I laid there a

long time after she'd gone, before I worked up the energy to yank my handles back on.

I didn't rush right over to Bob's the next day like I told Lily I might. After my romp in the hayloft with Ruth, it would've seemed peculiar to me seeing Lily and Em so soon. Not that I felt unseemly. I'd have done it again and right away if I thought I could sneak it by Pete and his family one more time. I just didn't feel like seeing folks I knew so well as I knew Lily and Em, and even Bob and Estelle for that matter. Ruth was the first female I'd ever had and not paid for, and it gave me pause for thought, was all. Like I ought to feel something deeper than just the desire to bed her again as soon as possible. It worried me some that there wasn't anything else. As if I had such a tiny heart it couldn't feel no love for anybody.

Which was why it struck me odd for Estelle to say what she did, when I first rode up two days later. She saw me coming, and ran down through the dooryard and through the fence gate, to meet me turning onto their land. She said, "Come with nothing but love and peace in your heart, Haywood, or turn right around and go back."

I kept on walking Dash up the hill. "I've come to see Emmaline. My niece."

I had a dolly for her in my saddlebag that I'd picked up at Riley Davis's store. It was the only one he'd had in stock, made of straw mostly, with a drawn-on face, and plug-ugly, but I hadn't wanted to come empty-handed so soon after Christmas.

"Well, you picked a bad time," Estelle said, keeping pace with me. "She's sleeping."

I was working up to it to ask next was Lily here, when I saw her walk round the side of the house. She had her hair loose and tied back with a head scarf. On second look I saw it was the same bandanna I'd given to her to wear on the trek from San Antonio to San Patricio. It made me feel kind of fluttery inside, seeing her wear something of mine. And then I silently scolded my insides for feeling anything at all.

She carried a laundry basket wedged between her hip and arm. With her free hand, she shaded her eyes from the sun, then waved at me. She was smiling, or maybe squinting at the brightness of the morning. I liked her better dressed like that, just plain, not all tarted up the way she'd been at the shop the other day.

I lit down off Dash and started leading him by his tether rope. "You can turn him loose inside the fence," Estelle said, nodding towards the horse lot. She sounded resigned to me being there. "Just bring the cow out first. He never got along with her."

On the other side of the fence, along with Sassy, Bob's gray, and the chestnut trotters I'd seen before, stood a wary-eyed milch cow of some kind of Dutch descent. She ran from me, her udder flipping from side to side, as I tried to herd her into the barnyard. But I finally caught her calf, pulled it along by the ear, and that got her to come along, too.

When I turned Dash into the fence, he charged right at Sassy, backing her off into a corner. Evidently, he didn't much like mules either. But she stayed to her corner and pretty soon he forgot about her, preferring instead to try to mount one of the chestnuts. It was then Lily came up. It made me blush to see her, what with Dash right there in front of us, acting so brash with the unwilling mare.

"You came," she said. "I didn't think you really would."

I threw the saddle over the fence and dug the doll out of the pocket. "Here's something for Em. Estelle said she's sleeping."

"But you can stay till she wakes, can't you?" She took the dolly from me, rubbed its straw hair with one finger. "I got a letter from Marion I want you to read. They've farmed him out is why he hadn't written in so long. He wasn't getting my letters."

"Farmed him out?"

"Leased him like a slave. To a rich planter at Rosenberg who doesn't hold to letter writing and such. He's been chopping sugar cane like a colored hand."

I didn't know what to say. It didn't sound so bad

to me. At least he was outdoors with the sky and the ground around him, instead of hemmed up in a prison cell.

She took me up to the house where we sat on the back gallery. She read me Shot's letter, skipping over the sentimental stuff, except for one part that slipped out and caused her face to color quick, about how he laid awake nights picturing her face. And how it still came as clear to him as a crystal star.

Now why couldn't I dream up words like that, I wondered, sitting there, watching her cheeks redden. It would've never come to me to think of stars and a face together in one notion, but I could see it pleased her to have him write those silly thoughts. If that was the way this sweethearting game was played, I knew I'd never learn the rules.

My coming had interrupted their chores—Estelle's mending, and Lily had wash to hang out. Em kept on sleeping, so I wandered out to look the place over, a thing I hadn't taken the time for when I was last here.

The house was old but solid, and with a rain trough at the roof line that ran into a claybanked cistern just off the back gallery. They had a bucket hanging on a rope for dipping out the water they needed. There was a root cellar, a falling-down corn crib, and out behind the privy, a wagon shed with a nice-size two-horse buggy inside, which explained the chestnut trotters that Dash was so fond of.

I was on my way to the barn for a good snoop, when I noticed Bob out in the field across the road. I'd seen him on my way in, and felt pretty dead certain he knew I was here, too, but he hadn't come up and I'd been putting off going down to him.

He was out there still clearing his field, working out cedar stumps now. He'd already harrowed about half the ground, but there was still one stumpy section left to do, and he was out there at it. I had never known him to be such a hard worker. Was it the love of a woman, and the child growing inside her belly, could change a man so?

I went down across the main road, and into the lower field. He was struggling over one big stump with rubbery roots that didn't want to pull free. He was already stripped down to his undershirt, and just as I came up, he stopped to wipe sweat out from under his hat brim. He looked at me, his face squenched up from tired, and the heat, and the beaming sunshine.

"Hard to believe it's nearing January," I said, venturing forward, unsure how he'd receive me. He nodded, kept squinting. Distrustful of me, I reckon. I motioned at the stump. "Pa used to burn them out. Bore a hole in the center, pour in some coal oil. After a couple of weeks, them roots'll let loose."

He watched me a second more. "Neighbor down the way said dynamite."

I chuckled. "Might work."

"I'm about ready to try anything."

"Can't say as I blame you."

He picked up the harness chains around his work-horse, to get back at it.

"Could you use a hand?" I said.

He looked me over again, lingering this time, pondering me. "Grab that grubbing bar."

I jumped over to it, levered it deeper under the stump, and when he drove the horse, I heaved with all my weight on it. A few more times like that, and we got the stump out. He drug it over to the edge of the field, lined it up with all the other stumps he'd pulled. He had him a pretty fair fence forming over there of stump roots.

I stayed all afternoon working with him. I knew I should've been back at my shop, but it seemed right to me, helping Bob. The labor, the heat and sweat of it, and the progress we made, two instead of one, thawed the ice between us. Come evening, back muscles sore and cramping, I walked with him to the house, where we washed up out of the cistern.

They made me stay to supper, a stew I recognized as coming from Lily's hand. Thought I recognized her fingerprints in the cornbread, too. Estelle brought Em in to sit on my lap, but she was cranky, cutting teeth Lily said, and didn't sit still for long. Seemed to me she'd grown a mile in four weeks.

After supper, Estelle read aloud to us from a book called *Treasure Island*. Once, in the middle of the reading, Bob hollered out, "Don't he know it's the man with the wooden leg?" talking about old John Silver, the peg-legged pirate.

Despite he'd gone a term or two to school back home, Bob could barely read a word hisself. I didn't know if Estelle knew that, but maybe she did. She seemed to enjoy reading to him as much as he enjoyed listening, casting her voice down to sound like the mutinous pirates, or up when she was speaking for young Jim Hawkins. Even little Em calmed to the sound of Estelle's voice, and fell asleep on Lily's shoulder in the rocking chair.

The cedar logs in the fireplace hissed out gas, sizzled sap, and glowed yellow flames. The mantel clock of Estelle's, that I recognized from when she was with Jack, ticked lazy yet steady. I didn't much want to go back to my cold shed room behind the shop. It was a sweet, sleepy, slow-warming I felt sitting there inside their house with people I knew, who knew me, all around.

And I wished I could trade places with Em on Lily's lap in that rocker, for about an hour. I felt an hour would do me, would cure me of whatever this new malady was that I had growing inside me. The daydreaming, and nightdreaming, and wondering why it hadn't been me to see the beauty in a thing that had struck me, so long ago, as a stringy-headed stick of a girl with black eyes bugging out of her head.

She was my brother's wife. I never for one instant forgot it. To allow any feelings at all was dangerous. Yet, she had an easy way about her, easy to watch, and relaxing in a way I couldn't help. Like right then, rocking Em, the soles of her shoes rasping quiet against the grit on the floor. Her eyes as intent as Bob's on the tale Estelle was reading. I wanted to gather up handfuls of her hair and bury my face in it, or just run my knuckle back behind the velvet of her earlobe.

I couldn't put into words what I thought about her. I didn't try, just tried not to think about her at all, but that was coming harder and harder all the time. She was my brother's wife, for Christ's sake. And she would've never looked at me thataway, anyhow.

18

I skipped Pete Strickland's on New Year's Day. Didn't even think of it, really. Or of Ruth. She'd done for me all she ever would, so far as I was concerned. Instead, I went to help Bob clear his field, and later, to listen to more of *Treasure Island*. The fact was, I got in the steady habit of riding out the six miles to Lazy Bend every day. I couldn't stand staying at the shop anymore, couldn't stand being alone. It was like an itch inside me. So I'd work till noon or a little after, then hang a sign on the door saying CLOSED, and I'd saddle up Dash and go.

Bob seemed glad for the help. After a few days, we were back to poking fun with each other like in times past. I almost told him about the Tennessean. I wanted to, even yearned to get it off my chest. And I knew if anybody would understand, Bob would. But I remembered how Lily didn't want Shot knowing, so I figured she wouldn't be wanting Bob to, either. And to tell the one thing, I'd have to tell the other. I kept it to myself.

Though she never spoke of it, Estelle didn't appear to be packing a grudge against me anymore either, for acting jackassable that first day like I'd done. I reckon she understood it was just the shock of seeing her with Bob, and that I needed time to get used to the idea of them together, to realize that neither of them meant it as an insult to Jack's memory.

Em liked seeing me come. She'd get to kicking and gurgling as soon as she recognized me. She liked for me to carry her on my shoulders, her chubby, little legs necked onto me. She pat her hands on my head, tasted my hair, slobbered in it. I couldn't have liked her any better if she'd been my own.

And Lily—well, I couldn't tell what she thought of me coming around so much. She seemed to accept it just as if I was a piece of furniture, or a cold snap that wouldn't break. Only once did she make any mention of it to me at all. It was the middle of January, one morning when a light-powdered first snow laid upon the ground.

I had come early to help Bob get the barn weatherproofed for the animals, to bring down plenty of hay from the loft, to help him chop firewood and stack it inside the dog run. He said, "It's colder than toad farts," just before we went inside, stomping jackfrost off our boots, to warm ourselves by the stove.

Lily caught me at the door, nudged me into the kitchen larder with the sacks of flour and meal and coffee beans. "I hope you ain't doing all this work to earn me and Emmy's keep," she said, whispering so's the others wouldn't hear.

Being in such tight quarters with her made me squirm. It took near everything in me not to lay my hands on her. I said, "I ain't."

"Because I'm earning my own way," she went on. "I do the cooking and the laundry. Estelle doesn't know a piddling thing about housework and I'm helping her. So I don't want you thinking you gotta do for me."

I shook my head. "No," I said, nearly choking on the smile I was struggling to hide. "I don't."

She leaned forward, raising her nose at me. "Who've you got doing your laundry?"

I arched away from her, unnerved by her inching up closer to me. Sometimes I could swear she knew what her nearness did to me. I said, "Nobody."

"I didn't think so. You're starting to get gamy. Bring your things with you next time, and I'll do them when I do all ours." She slipped out around me and stepped back into the kitchen.

My next trip, I did like she said and brought my dirty clothes with me. It gave me a good deal of pleasure that day, thinking about my britches and shirt and underwear stirring around in the vat of boiling water, alongside her dresses and her scanties—the corset covers and camisoles, and the bell-shaped drawers I saw hanging on the line later.

I reckon I'd gone plumb goofy by then. I blamed it on the cold weather, being from further south and unused to such things as snow and the ice curtains that draped the rooftops. I figured my brain could chafe the same as my hands and face did every morning riding that six miles. Or maybe I still had the malaria weltering inside me. Whatever caused it, I was having trouble keeping Lily down to a small quickness under my skin.

Silas Jones put a stop to my trips out to Lazy Bend when he sent his colored boy, Puddin, to pin a dun to my door, saying it was time to pony up February's rent. Ten dollars I owed, and once I paid him, it left me near to broke. There was still Riley Davis to pay for the charges I'd run up. Lonesome or not, I had to get back to my own work.

Pretty soon, plowing commenced, and all the farmers in the valley needed their animals shod, their shares reforged and sharpened, or a new point welded on. I kept busy, learned a few things, too, from some of the old-timers who were in the habit of taking over the shop and doing their own work to save theirselves money. Joseph Kelley had been an agreeable sort of fellow, and evidently hadn't hungered for no great wealth. Folks expected me to do things the same way as he had, and I didn't gripe.

I made a trip to Weatherford after scrap iron and coal. Coming back, once I crossed Patrick Creek ridge, as far as I could see, dust clung like mist over the fields the farmers were turning. I vowed right then that I'd have me a piece of this land someday, even if it took every dime I could save to get it. For some reason I didn't yet understand, this valley beckoned my soul.

Estelle surprised me by showing up at my shop the last day of February, with a pair of scissors she needed me to put a new edge on. Right off, it seemed like an unusual request since I knew Bob had a grinding wheel out in his barn. But I took the scissors and worked on them a while. They were sewing shears, not the highest quality, and with a loose screw hitching the blades.

"I've been using them a lot. Making things for the baby." She laid her hand on her belly as she spoke. I had already noticed she didn't mind mentioning her condition, not like some women who no matter how far out their paunches poked, didn't want a word said about their coming child.

While the grinder was whirring, she wandered to the back of the shop, peered into my room the same way as Lily had. She opened the door out to the horse lot, and shut it fast when it looked like Dash would nose his way straight in to join us. He could always hear the voices, and stayed just outside the door like an eavesdropper. Weren't many horses with more smarts than old Dash. Sometimes I expected him to come right out and start talking.

When I got down to putting the finish on her scissors with the emery, she came back near to me.

"Are you going to the dance tonight?" she said, lazy, as if she was just jawboning the time away. Something in her tone, though, made me think there was more.

I looked up from the shears. "What dance?"

Her mouth set up in a firm line then. "I didn't think you knew." The way she livelied up and held her eyes so straight on me, it was clear this was the real reason she'd paid me a visit. "They've been having one every Saturday night for the past three weeks. The Fairadays over in Sandy Hollow."

"Don't know them."

"They've opened a store there. Well, it doesn't matter. The whole valley's invited. You can go with us."

"Go? Tonight?"

"Yes, and don't you think of saying no, Haywood. You know how Robert loves a get-together, and I can't refuse him. But Lily shouldn't go unescorted. I know she's been aching to, but it would be improper, her being a married woman. But I thought if you were to go—oh, say yes, Haywood. She needs to have some fun."

My thoughts quickened. "She sent you to ask me?"

"Good heavens, no. I waited until she was elbow-deep in pie pastry before I said I was going up town. I plan to tell her *you* mentioned it to *me*."

I handed over the sharpened scissors and felt myself get flush. "Well, don't that seem improper to you, too? Me asking a married woman to a dance?"

She frowned at me, two little dimples dipping in right above her eyebrows. I thought she looked a mite suspicious. She spoke slowly. "You're her brother-in-law. I should think that would make you a thoroughly proper escort."

I straightened; felt like I'd just had my knuckles rapped. "I ain't got nothing to wear to no dance."

She smiled, and the suspicion was gone. "I swear, Haywood, you sound just like an old spinster."

She turned and left the shop, so sudden, I almost raced after her. I hadn't said I'd go yet, and she was giving up too quick. I wanted to go, and I aimed to. If anybody could use a little fun, it was me, hard as this shop had been working me. I sure wouldn't mind seeing Lily either, or escorting her. I'd just expected Estelle would beg me a little longer, so's I wouldn't appear too over-eager.

I took two faltering steps towards the open door, to catch her before she got off too far. But then she was back, as sudden as she'd gone. Instead of the sharpened sewing shears, she had a pile of clothes folded neat in her hands.

"I've wanted to give these to you. . . ." She shook out a pair of pants, and I recognized what it was she was holding. Jack's wool wedding suit and his stiff-bosomed, front-button white shirt. "We can make them fit you just fine, Haywood. If you'd take them . . ."

For some reason, I had thought Jack had got buried in that suit, yet here it was, shook out in front of me. I took the shirt, held it up. He hadn't been so big, nor broad, as I remembered.

"Here's his sleeve garters." She held them looped over two of her fingers. "All these things have been packed away in my trunk, getting musty. Somebody might as well get some wear out of them. Before the moths find them."

I pulled everything from her. "What else of his have you got that you're giving away?"

Like she felt cold, she crossed her empty arms over her breast. "Giving to *you*, Haywood. There's a difference. It's been hard for me to know what to do where you're concerned. I know how you admired him, and I just thought you might like to have—" She patted at her skirt, and her petticoats crackled. Her eyes, wet and gleaming, stayed on Jack's clothes. "I remember the day I saw him in that suit. He was all a girl holds hope for in her heart." She gave me a troubled look. "You do believe that I loved him."

"I know what he felt for you."

"If I could change things, I would. If I could bring him back—Robert's been a comfort to me. He doesn't ask for anything in return." Her voice caught.

I looked down at the loose bundle in my arms, the black silk, four-in-hand necktie still stained with Jack's sweat, the satin sleeve garters limp in my hands. It struck me that this was the real reason she'd come alone here today, not for me to sharpen her scissors, nor to give me Jack's suit of clothes or even to invite me to the dance, but to ask me to understand her marrying Bob so quick. It was something, evidently, that had been eating at her to get said.

Her face was fearful, hopeful, both those things at once. I took a deep breath, said, "Fellas get up this fancy for the dances around here?"

She laughed, clamped her hand to her mouth, near giddy. A tear tracked down her cheek, and quick, she daubed it away—so quick, I thought for a second, I hadn't seen it fall.

"We may have to brush out those trousers," she said, lively again; relieved. "You go put them on, and let's see if they need hemming. I brought my sewing box, in case. I'll trim your hair while I'm here."

"I don't need a haircut."

"Yes, you do too, Haywood. You have the prettiest blue color to your eyes, but you never let the girls see them. You've always got your hat pulled down low, or that hank of hair hanging in your face."

My cheeks burned. "Estelle—"

"It's the truth. A strong, sturdy man like you, I should think some girl would latch herself right to you."

"I ain't after no girl."

"Well, why not?"

"I just ain't. Now, go on and get your sewing box."

She gave me a broad smile, but she shut up her carping. She'd got what she wanted from me. Not exactly my blessing, but near enough.

I put the trousers on and let her pin them up. I stood about two inches shorter than Jack, so it wasn't no quick job. While she was sewing, I took care of a customer that came in needing a rod bent for his wheel jack. Then, I hung up the CLOSED sign and let her cut my hair.

That evening, bathed and shaved and all primped up in Jack's suit, I took a gander at myself in the dressing glass behind my room door. The glass needed resilvering, and so made my face wavery and weak-chinned. But it was me in there. The same old me, only clean and with my hair freshly shorn.

I squinted closer, looked straight into my eyes. They were blue. Always had been. Like Azberry's. Like my ma's, I reckon. Hadn't done either one of them any good. Hadn't done me any neither. Eyes were just eyes. For seeing, nothing else. Leave it to a woman to find something romancing about them.

Still, as I went out back to slap the saddle on Dash, I couldn't help torturing over what it was made a thing fetching to one person and not to another. Why did it all have to be such a mystery? Why were women such strange creatures? And how come it to take so little—a bit of lace, a scent of lilac—to muddy up a man's mind?

19

The dances were advertisement for Mr. Fairaday's new feed and seed and general merchandise store. He hoped that by buttering up all the farmers in the valley with drink and music and jollifying, he'd get their business this planting season.

Signs hanging around said he carried all grades of cotton seed, and corn, bagged or bulk, or on the ear for fattening hogs. For the ladies, he had garden seed, flowers, and vegetables. FRUIT TREES FROM LOUISIANA! POULTRY FEED! THE NEWEST FERTILIZERS AVAILABLE ANYWHERE! The signs fairly shouted at anybody who could read. But there was one sign, not near as big as the others, that I knew proclaimed his doom. It said CASH ONLY.

Months later, folks would be calling Mr. Fairaday's

the "cash-only" store and trading there just when they had no other choice. But that night, inside the Sandy Hollow Hall, nobody appeared to even notice that little sign. All were merry and feasting on the free food, dancing, and draining the beer barrels, one by one.

There was a string band playing, and a song caller. Took me a minute to recognize old Pete Strickland up there, hollering the figures: "Toes to the center! Backs to the wall! Chaw your tobacker, and promenade all!"

And sure enough, a second later, I saw Ruth dancing in the circle with a fellow wearing a dandy brown tweed Prince Albert with a black velvet collar and cuffs. He had a bright red-and-white-striped ribbon tied at his neck. I turned my back on them to keep from being spotted, even though I knew I couldn't dodge her all night.

The babies were laid out on pallets underneath a line of tables shoved against the wall. A pipe-smoking old woman had taken charge of them. While Lily and Estelle got Em nestled in, me and Bob went to fill our beer pails at the keg outside the open front doors. After just that short while inside the hall, the cool felt good to us both.

Bob didn't seem like he'd noticed I was wearing Jack's suit. I had skipped the tie and the vest, and now that I'd seen how hot it was inside, I was glad of it. But Bob had gone for the whole hog with a blue satin vest and cravat to match, hair combed back slick, reeking of rose water.

He spewed his little stream of snuff tobacco out on

the ground, then downed half his pail in one long, gulping swallow. From then till the end of the night, he kept a gratified smile on his face. I knew right off that it would have to be me to see that little Em and the ladies got home safe.

But I wouldn't have wanted to get lit anyhow. Not that night. Not with Lily right there watching me, dancing with me even, her hair loose and flowing down her back, shining like a sorrel pony's. A lacy shawl was tied about her shoulders. She wore another one of Estelle's castoffs of pink and lace, taken in at the waist and up at the hem, for even when Estelle wasn't swollen up pregnant, Lily was half her size.

We weren't either of us sure of the dance steps, and she laughed every time we made a mistake, having the fun Estelle said she'd been needing. Her eyes glowed and twinkled, set my heart to pounding so hard I expected to see it come flying out of my chest and bounce on the floor at my feet.

We played the rounds, changed partners, laced our hands together on the promenade. Even working as hard as I knew she did out at Bob and Estelle's, her skin felt silky smooth to me. I grinned so much my cheeks ached.

Directly, as was bound to happen, Ruth came swinging my way. It wasn't but just for a second the first time, as old Pete's calling kept us going round the circle. But in a while, the two of us got caught in a do-si-do. She blushed and dipped her head, said, "I'm monstrous glad to see you."

I didn't say nothing. Didn't have time to, but there wasn't nothing for me to say anyway. I'd long since realized the mistake in what I'd done that Christmas night succumbing to the ways of the flesh practically under Pete's nose, while he'd been trying only to be my friend. I didn't know who the fellow in the bright tie and Prince Albert was, but I wished him well. Except that now Ruth knew I was here, and she started in with that same damned eye-batting she'd done in the Strickland's kitchen Christmas Day.

Lily pretended for a while not to notice, but I was addled, and pretty soon, I backed out of the circle. She came with me. We went over to where Estelle stood, watching out the door, waving a paper fan in front of her face.

"Did y'all get tired already?" she said, smiling, but then her gaze returned to outside. I saw where she was looking. Bob was tight as a tick, tottering out there among a bunch of other drunks.

"I think Woody got girl-friended," Lily said, with a giggle.

"No, I didn't."

"Where? Who is she?" Estelle got suddenly interested. Ruth picked that second to favor me with a smile, and another bat of her eyes. I looked away, feeling my neck get hot.

"See?" Lily said.

"Who is she, Haywood?" Estelle asked.

"Nobody, I told you. She ain't nobody." I walked past them, out into the night air.

Bob had my beer pail with him, and he filled it for me when he saw me coming, held it out to me. It brimmed with foam, and I was reaching for it, when somebody shoved me from behind, upset my balance.

I went sprawling forward, and would've knocked into one of the beer kegs, save for the quick action of three of the fellows standing there. They tipped the barrel up on its rim and rolled it to the side, allowing me to fall flat-smack on the ground.

It wasn't muddy down there exactly, but spilled beer, and the weeping bunghole on the barrel, had things damp. My hands slipped as I was pushing myself up to see what had hit me. The fellow in the Prince Albert took a swing at me before I got to my feet good. I managed to duck him.

I heard Bob say, "Hold on there, friend." He tried to muscle in between me and the other fellow, but he was too drunk to do much good. He got pushed aside as Prince Albert charged past, aiming for me again.

This time, I didn't dodge quick enough. His fist landed square on my nose, blinded me with my own tears and the singing pain. I took two more blows to my body before I came around enough to fight back.

He had some kind of mistaken idea about me, and I wanted to tell him so, but he was mad as a hatter, and there wasn't time for talk. I got in five quick, solid gut punches, and could feel the sand going out of him, when somebody tripped me. I stumbled sideways, and then it wasn't just the fellow in the Prince Albert, but three of his cronies fighting me, too.

I heard men hollering. Women screamed. With four on one, it was me getting the worst of it. And then the next thing I heard was the pop of a gun. Once, then twice more real fast. Like firecrackers going off.

The fight stopped.

I drug myself up from the ground, and saw Bob standing there with a Colt's .45 Model P aimed at the fellow in the rumpled Prince Albert coat. A toadstool of smoke rose from the pistol's muzzle and joined the cloud of it already hovering overhead. I glanced around to see who'd got shot. Didn't see anybody. I hadn't even thought about Bob's carrying a gun, though I reckon I should have. I wondered where he'd kept it hid.

He said, "Now then. That's just fine," to Prince Albert, and to me, "Get around behind me, Haywood." He wore a bloodless smile, and I hoped there wasn't anybody in the crowd dumb enough to doubt he'd use that six-shooter, especially pissed on beer like he was.

I moved around behind him, said, "Why don't you put away the gun, Bob. This is just a misunderstanding."

And then Prince Albert, even with Bob's pistol stuck in his face, opened up, calling me every vile name he could lay his tongue to. I was just about ready to resume the fight, when my nose decided to gush. Blood poured down the front of Jack's shirt, and speckled the ground.

"What's going on here, Noah?" Pete Strickland said, marching up through the ring of people around us.

Estelle stepped in. "Robert," was all she said, but I heard the disappointment in her voice.

Lily came beside me at the same moment, pushing a frilly lace handkerchief at my face. It wasn't near big enough to catch all the blood that was coming out of me, but she made me give it a try.

"What happened?" she said, pulling me out of the crowd. I had my hand and the handkerchief to my nose, and her hand was in there too, pressing. Didn't make it easy to talk. I just shook my head in answer.

Several of the men were trying to get the crowd to break up. Pete's voice said, "Either get back inside or go home." People started milling back towards the hall. Pete came over to where me and Lily were. "I hope this ruckus wasn't over Ruth," he said. "Noah Steelman's got designs on marrying her, and unless you're thinking the same way, I wish you'd step out of it."

"I didn't think I was stepping into it, Pete," I said, and I sounded like a pug dog barking, all nasal and high-pitched.

Somebody I didn't know, a man in a white coat, was talking to Bob, talking right up close to his face, but I didn't see the pistol anymore. Estelle was hanging onto his arm.

"We don't like folks bringing firearms to our dances,"

Pete said. "I know you all're newcomers, but . . ."

"We're leaving, Pete," I said, holding Lily's handkerchief to my nose, and taking her elbow with my other hand. "Go get Em," I told her.

"Well, dern it, I wasn't meaning you had to go," he said, but he didn't sound convincing enough.

Bob appeared to've sobered up some. I still made him let me drive the chestnuts. As it was, they were such even pacers I believe they could've got us home without a driver.

The women sat in the rear passing Em back and forth between them. Otherwise, they were mostly quiet, except for the crooning women like to do, for some reason, when they get around babies. Wasn't necessary. Em wasn't kicking up any fuss. She was a good little traveler, mostly slept. Same as Bob did up front next to me. By the time we got to Lazy Bend, he was practically slouched over in my lap.

Estelle saw him off to bed, and Lily took Em in, leaving me to unhitch the horses and rub them down. Before I finished, Estelle came out. My nose had quit bleeding by then, but I think she felt the need to fret over it some. She brought a wet cloth for me to clean my face with, and one of Bob's old raglan-sleeve shirts with a frayed collar and the pocket ripped off.

"Put this on, and leave that white one here," she said. "It's going to take some work to get out those blood stains."

I did like she said. The blood had soaked through to my undershirt too, but I ignored it, and slipped Bob's shirt over my head.

She said, "Don't plan on going back to Brock tonight. It's late. You can sleep here."

"I've gotta open up the shop in the morning. I reckon I'll make it there all right."

I expected her to argue with me about it, but she stood quiet, like she was pondering on something, while I hooked the four front buttons on the raglan shirt.

"Do you know that girl well?" she said, finally, and I knew she meant Ruth.

"She ain't nothing to me. I just hope old Noah whoever believes that by now." I laughed. It didn't sound all that mirthful. "A fellow holding a grudge can make life miserable."

"You think he'll cause trouble?"

"Nah. Not after Bob showing his pistol." I smiled. She didn't. I pushed my shirttail inside my pants. "Ruth lives over at Soda Springs. A long ways from here. I reckon that Noah fellow's over that way someplace, too."

"That's her name? Ruth?"

I nodded.

She watched me turn the mares out the other end of the barn. They plodded, tired, still blowing some from the long drive home. I made to follow them out to the lot, grabbed Dash's catch-rope off the nail beside the back doors.

"It's Lily, isn't it?" she said, stopping me. I turned towards her. She had her face aimed right at me. Something in her features caused my heart to race.

"What is?"

"The reason you aren't interested in this Ruth. Or in any other girl."

I started to laugh; couldn't. I nearly choked on my own spit. "That's crazy."

She shook her head. "It's all over you. I watched you while you danced with her tonight. I couldn't settle it in my mind at first, but then it came to me. You light up when she's around you."

"Good godamighty, Estelle." I tried to sound like I thought she was joking, but my face burned, and suddenly, the bridge of my nose hurt like blue blazes. "She's Shot's wife."

"Yes. She is."

"And you think I—you think . . ." My neck felt sweaty. I gripped the rope in my hand tighter. I couldn't stand the smug look I saw on her face. "I ain't talking about this," I said.

I went through the doors out into the lot with the horses. Estelle came right behind me. She brought the barn lantern with her. The circle it cast swung along at my heels.

"Deny it to me all you want to, but admit it to yourself, at least." She was shrill and out of breath, trying to keep stride with me.

"I said I ain't talking no more."

Dash, with his good night eyes, saw me coming with the rope. He swerved off into a far corner of the pen.

"You don't have to. You've told me enough already."

I turned. "I haven't told you one damn thing." I didn't pretty up my words. I wanted to shock her so's she'd go on and leave me be.

She stopped dead, and held the lantern high enough it made me squint. "You're in love with her."

"You're crazy."

"No, I'm not. Not about this. I can tell it by how you're acting right now." Her face looked feverish with the lantern fire flickering in her eyes. "And all this time, while you've been condemning me and Robert, holding it against us because we found each other—"

"I ain't holding it against you no more," I mumbled.

"All this time while you judged us—"

"I said I ain't holding it against you." I brought my voice louder in case she didn't hear me clear the first time.

She lowered the lantern out of my face. Her eyes stayed on me. "But you did. You said things to make me feel low and horrible. Even today when I gave you Jack's suit, you got angry—"

"Only because you surprised me. I just didn't expect you to have it still."

"What did you think I'd done with everything? Thrown it all out the first chance I had? Burnt it?" She stomped her foot down. "I loved him, too. You aren't the only one who misses him."

"I never said I was."

"But you thought it. In that sanctimonious way of yours."

"What? Are you calling me something?"

"A hypocrite. You're a hypocrite, Haywood."

I stood there and tried to feel insulted, though I didn't have one clue what none of those words meant. She'd already turned her back on me, headed for the barn, taking the lantern with her. I followed after her.

"All right. I'll give you that," I said. "But one thing, Estelle. Estelle." She was walking fast now. "Things we said here, it don't have to go no further, all right? It's between us. Just you and me. All right?"

She stopped at the barn door, then smiled, though it looked more fearsome than happy. "You don't have to worry. Lily's my friend. I won't tell her you're smitten with her. She has enough on her mind like it is, with Marion serving his time, and with trying to raise Emmaline on her own."

After she left, I spun around, kicked at a dark clod on the ground I took to be horseshit. The raw smell of it came to me. Dash, over in his corner, bobbed his head my way, daring me to come chase him. The other horses were off up the rise, nipping at some clumps of tickle grass just outside the fence. I raised my face to the moon and the sky, then glanced as Estelle's figure moved across the clearing towards the house.

A light glowed in the window where Lily's room was. Her silhouette passed behind the curtain. She had Em in her arms, walking her to sleep. I'd seen her do it a hundred times, in just that same, quiet-going way. I felt pulled by the sight, like a magnet had hold of me, drawing me towards the fence to watch.

The night closed in around me till there wasn't nothing else, just me leaned against that fence with Lily up in the house pacing in front of her window, while the only brother I had left in the world chopped sugar cane at the other end of the Brazos River. I hoped like hell Estelle kept her mouth shut.

For a while I couldn't move from that fence, like my boots had sprung roots into the ground, staking me down. I just stared, my mind as dry and empty as a desert. It was Dash, nosing me between the shoulder-blades, that finally nudged me out of that trance. I turned and slipped the rope over his head.

20

The weather faired up. Trees budded, then leafed out. Grasses began to grow, and pretty soon, flowers. All colors of flowers, like somebody or thing from on High had spilled paint all over the valley.

Farmers were like ants, busy planting if they'd held out for a late freeze; or, if they were the gambling sort like Bob, watching the young shoots of corn and cotton split the earth. Rains came. Not too much wind blew. The ground stayed moist, and the corn, especially, grew by leaps. It wasn't long before the women were stuffing scarecrows to keep the birds out of the fields.

I went out to Lazy Bend to help a lot, my work at the forge having slowed with the onslaught of planting.

Slowed so much, in fact, that I worried I couldn't make my rent, until a bank draft came from Wash Jones. He'd leased out the farmland back at McDade, took out what Shot and I owed him for his services at both our trials, and still, it left me with sixty dollars. I felt rich, and also generous. Silas cashed the draft for me, and I took half of it to Lily. It was only fair. After all, the land belonged as much to Shot as to me. Wash said in the letter he sent that it might take some time to find a permanent buyer, seeing as how money was scarce.

After the night of the dance, me and Estelle didn't talk again about what feelings I might or might not have for Lily. We were friendly enough with each other, but things weren't ever the same. There was a new distance between us. Between me and Lily, too, since I felt Estelle watching us all the time. And it got so she called Lily away to do the least trifling thing if it looked at all like we might have one second alone together.

I didn't much miss feeling close to Estelle, but it was harder with Lily. Em was growing fast, doing things like rolling over on her own, then sitting up by herself, getting her first new tooth, and learning to creep that Lily wanted to tell me about. And there were letters from Shot to read, and once, a letter from her brother with a picture her little sister had drawn of a cow. And I couldn't share one minute of Lily's joy, on account of Estelle nosing in, though I wanted to hear it all. In a brotherly, uncle way. I thought if I willed it so, I could change my heart off of anything more.

For since Estelle had brought everything out in the open, I couldn't seem to stop thinking about Shot. Every day we ever spent together flickered through my mind, which took up a lot of my time, since being the closest in age, him and me had shared everything from our bed to the clothes we wore, to beatings from Pa because we wouldn't snitch one on the other. And Pa could lay the beatings out if he took a mind to, and was drunk enough.

Once Pa had got after Shot with his fists and a razor strop over something I'd done. And Shot would of probably had some broke bones when Pa got through with him if Jack hadn't stepped in, bashing Pa over the head with his own crock whiskey jar, knocking him out cold till the next morning. Pa woke with a headache but sober, and I don't think he ever remembered how come Shot's lip was busted, or his ear cabbaged out to twice its size.

But even though I felt resentment towards Estelle, downright mad at her sometimes for bringing back boyhood memories I could of done without, and for making me feel guilty about Shot and uneasy with Lily; even though I wished I could've reacted different that night in the barn, and not gone storming off like a kid in a temper fit, giving my fool self away as I did; and even though I wished Estelle hadn't been so damned nosy in the first place, asking things wasn't none of her business to know. Even though I felt all that, and had come to regard her with more and more dread each time I saw her, I never wished her ill.

It was the middle of April. Oats were all ripe, and the price so low, Bob had turned the animals out to clean off the five acres. The evening before, we chopped cotton. Even Lily was out in the middles. A boy from down the road, a neighbor name of Wilson's boy of about twelve or so, had been helping us. And it was him, that Wilson boy, who came busting into my blacksmith shop, red-faced and winded, like he'd run afoot the six miles.

He said, "Missus Stevens is bedfast and laboring hard. They said tell you to come quick. And bring a doctor. Her baby's trying to land heels first."

I didn't know of a doctor. Hadn't had need of one. But Riley Davis said one lived up on the Millsap road, eight miles away. I pushed Dash to a fast lope, but once I tracked the doctor down and took him all the way back to Lazy Bend, the damage was already done.

The baby came out a girl. Clarissa Marie. Estelle stayed together long enough to give her baby a name. But her insides were too tore up to linger much longer. And even with Bob sitting at her bedside, holding her hand and telling her not to go, she went. In the wink of an eye, it seemed to me. One minute here, a cheerless smile upon her pale lips; the next, gone. I didn't even have time to know what I felt.

The doctor placed the coins over her eyes. The newborn babe started to cry, as if it felt its ma, beside it on the bed, grow cold. Bob lit out like he had a fire under him, slamming through the door and disappearing before I could chase him.

"Let him go," the doctor said, stopping me, patting my shoulder, his head hung low. "It's difficult for the men, but he'll come around. Give him his time alone."

It was bad advice. I should've gone on and followed my instinct, for we didn't see Bob again for quite a little while.

I paid the doctor his fee and sent him on, though it seemed to me it should have been him owing us, for all the good he'd done. The neighbor, Mrs. Wilson, stayed to help Lily clean up and get the corpse laid out. Before they finished with that chore, six other women showed up to lend a hand. It was as if word of Estelle's passing had leaked out on the wind.

Some of the men came, too, and since Bob wasn't there, I sort of took over in his stead. We got a coffin built, using boards off the old falling-down corncrib for lumber, as Bob had no other anywhere that I could find. Took nails from there, too. When the box was finished, we carried it into the house where the women lined it with some pearly blue satinet somebody had thought to bring.

Three of us men lifted the corpse careful, and laid her away in the coffin. She was heavy as a slab of concrete by then. The preacher, come down from the Methodist church in Brock, warned me not to wait too long to put her in the ground. "The body'll start to putrefy," he said, shaking his head like it might make the difference on her getting into heaven.

It was after sundown before the folks trickled out, one or two at the time. The women left the kitchen brimming with food—loaves of light bread, corn flitters, sausages, fried chicken, beafsteak pudding, and custard pie. There was barberry jelly, potato cakes, stewed carrots, and rice custard. Fresh fruit, milk and cheese. And at the end of the cupboard, a brown store-bought bottle of Runnymede Rye stood, inviting me.

I peeled the wire and wax off the top, prized the cork out with my thumbs, and started to drink straight from the bottle, but thought better of it. I got down a tin cup, stirred in some honey to quiet the bitter.

Lily was in her chair facing the window, still and silent, her neck bent, watching the newborn at her breast. Em laid in the cradle across by the stove, sleeping gentle and sweet.

I sat down on the bench at the table, cup in hand, and drank, watching the back of Lily's neck. Her hair was twined up in a tired knot. She'd been so quiet—quiet and strange—ever since Bob slammed out the door. A breeze blew in the window, moved the whispers of hair around her neck. She had a mole there, just under the hairline. The baby made little grunting noises, like a roothog.

"Reckon I oughta go hunt down Bob," I said, my voice sounding loud and out of place in the stillness.

She moved the baby up to her shoulder, patting its back. It was asleep, little screwed-up face and acorn head, limp. "Maybe he'll come on back on his own." She rocked. The chair thumped the wood floor.

I stared past her at the darkness out the window. We stayed like that, saying nothing, me staring out the window at the night, and her rocking the chair back and forth.

"Reckon we oughta write her family a letter for him? In case he ain't able," I said, after a while.

"You know how to reach them?"

"Leon Odom is her pa's name. Down at Rockdale. Shouldn't be all that hard. He runs a cotton gin there. I met him before."

She got up, holding the baby like a sack of flour against her shoulder. The front of her dress was fastened. She looked towards Em, then at me. Her eyes were lined under and swollen.

"This poor child," she said. "Ain't even got a bed of her own." Two tears, one after another, dripped down her face and hung, jiggling, on either side of her chin. "Robert kept saying he was gonna build one, but he never did get to it. And now there ain't no place to lay her down. I can't keep on just holding her. I got things to do. I got Emmy to tend, and my back aches. I can't just go on holding her, day in and out."

She looked near to the hysterics, and I couldn't spare her to them. I needed her too much, what with Bob gone, and things left up to me.

I stood up, stepped around the table, and took the baby from her. It squeaked and wiggled a little bit, but then sank right into me, wore out and full of Lily's milk. A pity stirred inside me, yet something else, too; something akin to wonderment at the newness of her, her perfect little fists and nose and chin.

"There now," I said, almost whispering. I raised my head at Lily. "We'll figure something out. You don't need to cry about it. Everything's gonna be all right."

She stood silent a moment, then she came against me, her arms circling my back. It gave me a start at first, having her so close. Made me think about the last time she'd come to me for comfort like this. A year ago back at Bastrop. Standing in the Widow Dillard's boardinghouse kitchen. Me holding her at arm's length.

This time I didn't do that. I drew her in to me with my free hand, the one not holding tight to the baby. I could feel Lily's heart, her trembling shoulders, every curve of her. She pressed her face against me. Her hair smelled like fresh-cut grass.

"It ain't the end of the world," I said, not knowing what to do for her, feeling my own heart thud. Another part of me started to rise, and it was just the baby in my arms that kept me sane, saved me from doing something I shouldn't have.

I moved Lily away from me, brushed the tears off her face. Her eyes shone, and I thought she looked as pretty as I'd ever seen her. Soft spirals of hair fell about her neck and jaw, her cheeks the color of new cream.

"I'm sorry," she murmured.

"Can't we make a bed out of that basket there?" I pointed to the wall over the jelly safe. The basket she used to haul wet clothes from the washtub to the line hung there. She raised her face at where I pointed, but it was me that took the basket down from its nail.

"There ain't no call for me to be acting so selfish." She tucked a baby quilt Estelle had pieced inside the basket. "Least I ain't as alone as she is. Her papa never even gave her one glance."

I laid the baby, face down, in the basket. "You ain't alone," I said.

She looked at me. "I know I got Emmy, and there ain't any reason for me to feel so hopeless. But sometimes, I swear, I can't even say what good it's done me leaving home. Traipsing off up here where I don't belong." Her eyes clouded again, and she waved her hand at me, like to say she couldn't go on without bawling some more. "It's just silliness." She gulped for a laugh, blinked, and dabbed at her face with the back of her wrist. "Reckon we oughta try eating some of this food. There's plenty of it."

"You wanna go someplace else?" I said, watching

her pick at the cracklings on a piece of fried chicken. "I'm willing to go someplace else if you want to. We could try the piney woods. We ain't been there yet."

"You like it here. That's what you told Robert. He said you were gonna save your money till you had enough to buy you a piece of land around here someplace."

"I was daydreaming."

"You know you could do it." She took the piece of chicken and sat down on the bench, facing away from the table. "How come you're so good to me? When I ain't been nothing but trouble for you?"

"What trouble?" I sat down too, straddling the bench a foot away from her, resting my elbow on the table.

"You already forgot about San Antone?" She looked off, then forced her eyes back, steady on me.

"It don't nag at me anymore."

She tore off a bite of chicken and, after a second, ate it, licking her fingers. "It doesn't even seem like something real that happened. Does it seem like that to you?"

I watched her chew, her fingers lit right in front of her mouth, hanging in the air, delicate as a butterfly, her eyes round on me. I looked away from her. I had to. There wasn't a day went by I didn't see in my mind her white foot hanging off that bed in Markin's inn. It made me ashamed, and sick at myself, but I couldn't help it.

"Maybe we *should* write that letter to Estelle's people.

I reckon they oughta know they got a new grandbaby." I stood up from the table. I felt weaker than if I'd been all day at the plow, or hoeing cotton middlings.

"And then what? Are you gonna leave? Go back up town tonight?"

I stayed where I was standing. "I figured I would."

"What if Robert comes home?"

"That's what we want, ain't it?"

"I'd rather you were here if he does. I can make you a pallet in this room. Or you can take their bed if you like."

I frowned. "Are you afraid of Bob?"

"I'd just rather you were here."

I helped her cover all the food on the cupboard and move both the babies into her room across the gallery. She found some blankets in a chest in Bob and Estelle's room and brought them to me in the kitchen. Didn't either of us check in on the corpse in the front room.

The candle she left me was of tallow, and so soft the heat of my hand nearly melted it. I stobbed it into a can lid that had caught drippings before and set it on the floor by my bed. By the flickering flame, I drank another cup of rye before I settled down to try and sleep.

It took a long while to drift off. I did my best not to think about Lily just a few feet away across the middle gallery, and us alone here at this farm. One time in the night, I heard the new baby wail, and then Em joined in. I wanted to go over and help, but I feared I'd walk in on

Lily nursing one of them, and maybe lose my head this time. What could I do, anyhow? Sing. I thought about us singing on the trip up here, and it helped coax me off again.

I dreamed of Shot, and of something that had happened once. We were kids, seven and eight, out in the woods, hunting below the Knobs. We heard a screaming. A horrible, high-pitched, banshee-sounding scream. Not human. We followed the sound to a clump of juniper.

Shot spotted the snake first. A big rattler, eight buttons on his tail, his jaw unhinged and clamped around a squalling baby rabbit, sucking it in whole and alive. We killed the snake, broke its spine with a rock and the club end of a shotgun. Shot pulled the baby rabbit from the snake's jaws, but it was too late. The quivering body had already been crushed, and we saw its suffering, felt it in the palm of our hands. Both of us stood there, with a rabbit small enough to fit in a boy's hand, and we cried tears.

It was the wailing of the new baby, I reckon, coming across the gallery and through the walls, that made me have that dream. In the morning, I couldn't think of another reason for it.

21

We held off on the funeral, waiting for Bob to show himself. He didn't, so I went looking for him. First, I rode across the river, as far south as Granbury, where I mailed a letter to the Odoms. The second day I headed west, all the way to Palo Pinto. I searched Weatherford twice, asking in all the saloons and billiard halls. Nobody had seen a soul answering to my description. By the fourth day, we had to nail the lid on the casket in the parlor.

I went to Brock to call on Silas Jones, to get permission to plant Estelle in the little graveyard out at Lazy Bend, since it was on his land. Then I checked on my shop. I hadn't even had time to lock it when I left, going after the doctor that morning, but nothing had been disturbed. Somebody had left me a dollar and a note saying they'd needed an iron rod and had gone ahead and taken it.

The fire in the forge was long out, and it took me a good while to get it burning hot enough to bend strap metal around the anvil horn. It would've taken every dime me and Lily both had to buy a stone marker for Estelle's grave. So I welded two straps together in the shape of a cross, added some curls along the base and at the top, like I'd seen on the German graves down in Bastrop. Mine didn't turn out as fancy, but I made a round plate for the center and, with a wedge and hammer, etched these words:

> *Estelle Odom Beatty Stevens*
> *Died April 12, 1885*

Since I didn't remember ever knowing her birth date, I just put:

> *Age 21 years*

And under all that, I carved these words Lily had wrote out for me on a scrap of paper:

> *To Live In The Hearts*
> *We Leave Behind*
> *Is Not To Die*

It was the same thing as was written on Lily's ma's tombstone back at McDade.

The job took me the whole rest of that day, and into the dark, working by lamplight.

We buried her on Friday, April 17th, without Bob. A daylight moon hung above us, flat on the bottom, thin and wispy, like a scratch on the blue sky. Neighbors came, some I knew, but most I didn't. The only song they sang I recognized was "In the Sweet By and By." Lily knew them all. The neighbors and the hymns.

The preacher said, "Be with us here, oh Lord, and accept this soul into paradise," and that was nearly all I heard of the speaking he gave. None of it meant too much to me.

My back and shoulders ached from digging the hole. Even though some of the neighbor men had pitched in, it took all morning. We'd hit quicksand about four feet down, and had to start over in a different spot.

I stood there in Jack's suit, sweating, watching the eardrops Lily wore glint the sun onto the crushed love-grass beneath our feet. She stood stock-still, eyes shut tight, holding baby Clarissa. I had Em, and she was twisting, and blowing spit bubbles through her lips. I had to bite my cheeks from the inside, for it wouldn't do to laugh at her right then, not with everybody else so solemn and weepy.

Later, I heard some of the ladies say how generous Estelle had been about giving, and how she could turn her quilt corners to a tee. One said, "She made the smallest stitches and had the smallest feet of anybody I ever saw." And I thought that was one hell of a sorry way to be remembered. Sort of took the shine off the words I'd lettered out on the iron grave marker.

I started thinking Bob had run into some kind of trouble, got himself killed or, even worse, was stinking in some jailhouse somewhere. It would've been like him to find some innocent somebody to take out his miseries on. I could understand it. I'd been known to do the same sort of thing in the past, although I felt that was a different fellow than the one I was now.

A lot had happened in a year, yet not much of anything, too. I turned twenty-one, but I was still just me, still living day to day, hadn't got rich yet, always busted, always figuring on tomorrow to bring some great change inside me. Yet things *were* different in a way, gradual different, slow enough so's you didn't see it right off unless you stopped to think and ponder on it. But I *had* changed.

For one thing, I wasn't depending on anybody to make my way for me anymore, to tell me how and why I was doing things the way I was. Even if I wasn't sure myself sometimes, even if it was a sort of treading water kind of life, it was mine. I'd chose it. Well, it had been chose for me at first, but I'd kept on with it. And I'd come to take a kind of pride in myself, that I could work all morning at my shop, then ride out to Lazy Bend to

tend Bob's fields till dark, though I'd about decided to let
half the cotton crop go if he didn't show up pretty soon.
Twenty acres of corn and twenty-five in cotton was just
too much for one man to handle part time.

Lily tried to help me, but she had her hands full
nursing two babies, cooking, cleaning, and keeping a
garden. I woke up every morning at dawn, my eyes
popping open on their own with the first sign of light,
and she'd usually already fed the babies and milked the
cow by then. She'd have coffee going, and corn mush or
maybe fried meat if I'd had a chance to kill some game
the day before. All that was missing was a good morning
hug and a smooch from her, and me rising from a warm
bed we shared, that kept her from seeming like my own
wife, with our babies, living in our house. Though I'd
have been too ashamed to admit it, I felt a relief, with
Estelle gone, that I was the only one, now, who knew
my secret.

I slept in Bob's room, and I kept on waiting for
him to come back and ruin my daydream. Then I didn't
know what would happen. Lily wouldn't stay here alone
with Bob, I knew, even if he needed her to take care of
little Clarissa. Some other arrangement would have to be
made, and I didn't want to stop the dream long enough
to figure out what. In the meantime, I went on how we
were, treading water as I said, glorying in the little bit
of happiness that had stumbled on me. Even if I was

so tired each night I barely had the strength to get my clothes off before I fell into bed.

In June, with the corn ripening in the fields and the cotton putting on bloom, the Odoms came. Puddin, Silas Jones's boy, showed them the way out to the farm. They came in a black canvas-topped buggy with a little portico cut in back for a peephole, behind a span of black trotters with the Weatherford livery brand on their necks. It was Mrs. Odom I recognized, prissing out of the buggy in her wide-brimmed hatty hat with a long swooping feather and fancy doodads flashing all over the brim. Everything she wore, the feather, her gloves, everything, was as black as Puddin.

They didn't come up to the house, where we'd just sat down to dinner, but headed straight out into the graveyard. Mr. Odom held tight to his dreary-dressed wife's arm as she high-stepped through the switchgrass and johnny jump-ups. None of the neighbors around, nor me, had had time to take a scythe to the weeds in the graveyard lately.

Lily said, "That's just plain rude, them ignoring us," and I hadn't seen her come up behind me on the gallery. She carried Em on her hip. Clarissa was already down for a nap. It's what she did mostly—sleep.

Em had a biscuit she was chewing to pieces, with most of it clinging to her face rather than in her belly. She burped, then leaned way back from her ma and dropped the gummy biscuit on the gallery. It landed in the dust down there, and she grinned at me with her two big, new front teeth showing.

"Go see what they want," Lily said.

"I reckon they come to look at Estelle's grave."

I went on down the three steps and across the yard path. Em started hollering. She didn't like for anybody to go off without her in tow, but I didn't turn back. I'd forgot my hat, though, and the sun was a bright orange fire overhead. Forgot my shirt, too, and just had on my underwear shirt. So many washings had turned the color of it to pink. I straightened my galluses up on my shoulders and tried to scrape off with my fingernail a stain of milk gravy I'd dropped on my belly.

Mr. Odom saw me first, and left Mrs. Odom beside the iron marker. He came with his hand stuck out, grinning polite. "Leon Odom," he said to me, as to a stranger. "I was told Robert Stevens lived here."

I shook his hand. "I'm Haywood, Mister Odom. I reckon you don't remember me. Jack's brother."

"Why yes. Yes. You wrote us the letter. I want to thank you for that."

I nodded, and wondered why he kept on shaking my hand so long. Finally, he stopped. He was dressed in a fine suit, silk hat.

I said, "Bob ain't here right now. He's—well, he's—"

I looked off down the road. I didn't know where to say he'd gone, but it didn't matter. I saw right off Odom wasn't really interested in Bob's whereabouts, anyhow.

"We came to see our granddaughter. Clarissa Marie," he said, getting wet-eyed, or else glittering eager; I couldn't tell which. I remembered him as being a kindly old gent.

"She's at the house."

His mouth drew up, and he waved at his wife. "The child," he cried out to her, pointing for the house.

She looked away from the grave plot and stood still a moment, like she expected him to come take her through the weeds. But he didn't even pause for her. He started for the house where Lily and Em still waited on the gallery.

I looked towards the fancy rig out on the road and motioned for Puddin to drive the team on up into the yard. He did. Mrs. Odom yelled out something I didn't hear, and I turned in time to see her marching her way out of the graveyard. She didn't look happy.

Mr. Odom beat me to the house. He was in such a hurry it struck me that maybe he had the mistaken idea Em was his little grandbaby. She'd got suspicious of folks she didn't know, and I thought was going to wail when he wiggled a finger in her direction.

"This is Lily," I said, and then to her, "The Odoms have come to see Clarissa."

Lily looked wary, heels dug in. She said, "Well, she's sleeping right now. I'd have to wake her."

"Please do." Mr. Odom took off his hat. He was nearly bald-headed. I saw clear now that it was a merry twinkle he had in his eye.

Mrs. Odom came huffing up the yard path, her silly hat tilted cockeyed on her head. She fumbled with it. "My lands, Leon, you could have come and helped me out of that mire over there. I was getting eaten up by redbugs."

"There ain't no mire over there," Lily said, surprising me with her sassy tone of voice. She was usually polite with people. "Haywood worked all one afternoon digging ditches to drain that graveyard."

I frowned at her, trying to understand why she had her chin raised and her shoulders held so stiff. It was unlike her to take such a quick dislike of somebody.

The old lady said to me, "You're Haywood? I didn't remember you as being married."

I was about to correct her mistake, but Lily said, "Coming two years this fall," and I gaped at her, out in the open enough, anybody could've seen my surprise, had they been looking. But it was Lily's proud smile they watched. She had that kind of smile. It could take away anybody's attention.

She reached to loop her arm through mine. I didn't mind it. Hell, it was like part of my dream. I smoothed her hand flat into the crook of my elbow, and took a great joy in her softness. I even forgot, for a second, what it was we were all doing standing out on the gallery.

"Lily was just about to show us to Clarissa Marie," Mr. Odom said.

Lily let me go, then put Em into my arms. "She's sleeping sound. But if you're quiet, you can peep in on her."

"You could sit down to dinner with us till she wakes," I said, and knew right away from the flinty look Lily gave me I'd done wrong. I guess I'd got too caught up in pretending we were married-folk.

Mrs. Odom stopped right in front of me. Em shied from the woman, clinging tight to my neck. Despite she was all gussied up with that hat and clouds of perfume, Mrs. Odom sure enough looked like somebody had beat her all the hell with an ugly stick. I didn't much blame Em for backing away.

"Thank you, but we wouldn't dream of eating your food. We'll just take Clarissa Marie and be off again. Out of your way."

"Take her?" Lily stopped up short.

Mrs. Odom turned. "Why yes. That *is* why we came."

"Take her where?"

"Why, back to Rockdale with us, of course. We thought we'd have to coerce Robert, but we understand he's disappeared."

"Where'd you hear that?" I said.

Mr. Odom spoke up then, glancing out at where Puddin held the buggy team. "Mister Jones told us he'd been missing for some time now."

"It comes as no surprise to me he would walk away from his own daughter," Mrs. Odom said. "Estelle never did show good judgment in the men she chose."

That got me mad. The hair on my neck stood up. It was Jack she was talking about now.

Mr. Odom must have seen my face change. He said quick, "Oh now, Lucy. Estelle didn't show good judgment about anything as far as you're concerned." Turning to me, his lip sweating and his hands shaking, so's I realized he was scared of me for some reason, he said, "I'm sure Robert is having a difficult time with this. Missus Odom and I are grieving as well. You know, Estelle was our only daughter. As for the child, Robert will always be welcome to come visit us." He reached into his breast pocket and shook out a kerchief to mop off his brow. "And the two of you are welcome, of course."

"You can't take her," Lily said, getting that wild, mama-coon glint in her eyes.

"I beg your pardon." Mrs. Odom's back stiffened.

"You can't. Her papa ain't here and we can't let you take her without him agreeing to it. That's just the way it is." Lily glanced up at me. She jerked on the strap of my galluses. "Do something, Woody."

"S'cuse us a minute," I said, and steered her off a little ways, to the other end of the gallery. I kept my voice low. "What can I do? I can't stop them. They got every right to take her. And even if Bob *was* here, do you think he'd wanna try and raise her on his own? You think he could?"

"*My* papa did it. Your own papa did."

"Bob ain't your papa. And thank God, he ain't mine, either. Look around you, girl. Bob ain't here anywhere. And she is their grandbaby. We're gonna have to give her to them, Lily."

"Well, I ain't gonna have no part of it. You hear me? No part of it." She gave me a look that turned my heart to ice. She yanked Em out of my arms, then she stormed right past the Odoms and down the three steps, headed for the barn and the horse pasture.

I thought she might be leaving, going for good, and my first notion was to race after her, find some way to calm her down. The Odoms stood there waiting for me to show them to the baby sleeping in Lily's room. So I took them through the middle gallery to the door at the back of the house, pushed it open. They went in, oohing and aahing at the fat baby asleep in the box cradle I'd nailed together, sanded down, and painted at my shop one Sunday morning. I stepped around to the back by the cistern, gazed over towards the barn, and then the wagon shed. I didn't see Lily anywhere.

"Oh, she's a jewel. Just a jewel," Mrs. Odom came out cooing, with the drowsy baby in her arms. Clarissa had turned out a pretty thing, with her ma's black curls and peachy cheeks. "Where are her clothes? And her bottles?"

"She ain't got no bottles. Lily's been . . ." I glanced around again, out towards the tree motte at the top of the bluff. "Lily's been feeding her."

"You mean, *wet*-nursing?" Mrs. Odom sounded horrified. Clarissa started crying. She'd always had a soft cry, more like a little kitten than a human baby.

"Is there something wrong in that?" I snapped, my temper overcoming me. "I should think you oughta be grateful for it. She's alive. And she's healthy. And she's been loved like she belonged to us."

Clarissa's howls got louder, and angrier. Mrs. Odom pulled up her starchy shoulders. "But the fact of the matter is, she doesn't belong to you." She put Clarissa against her chest, crooned, "There, there," and turned her back on me. The baby didn't stop her wailing.

Mr. Odom lifted the trunk with the baby's things inside. Most of the clothes Estelle had made, but some were Em's hand-me-downs. Odom was so weak, putting the trunk down every two steps to get a new grip, that I gave in and helped him haul it to the buggy. They didn't need the cradle. They were taking the train back to Rockdale, where Clarissa had brand new furniture waiting for her, and her own room.

No matter how Mrs. Odom bounced her, the baby wouldn't stop her screaming. Her belly was empty, I knew, but I didn't want to say anything to delay them going. It was better if they left fast. Got it over with. And Riley Davis carried bottles with rubber baby nipples; I'd seen them in his store. They could stop there for one. Even after the buggy was way off down the road, I could hear Clarissa cry. She hadn't ever seemed so loud to me before.

Lily wasn't in the barn or the wagon shed. All the horses were in the pasture. Dash looked up at me, his ears pert. Then he turned his head another way, in the direction of the old falling-down corncrib. I went towards it, and heard Em before I got there, gurgling and jabbering. She was pulled up on one of the rotten sideboards, and was stepping careful on her fat feet, along its length, holding on.

"Doo-dee," she said when she saw me, and fell flat on her bottom. She crawled for me, and she was devilish quick with it.

I scooped her up and went around to the other side of the corncrib. Lily was sitting there in the dirt, her head between her hands, like she was closing up her ears. I reckoned then she'd heard Clarissa bawling, too.

"This ain't a good place to be letting Em play," I said. "There's rusted-up nails and splinters all around here. Could be black widow spiders in there . . ."

She glared at me, got to her feet. She didn't bother to dust off her skirt. "She ain't yours," she said, and snatched Em from me so sudden it made Em's chin go to quivering. "So don't be telling me how to do with her." She started off towards the house.

Watching them go, I felt a heat come up my back. I almost ran after her and begged her not to be mad at me, to please forgive me for letting Clarissa go. But I found my pride in the nick of time.

The ax I'd been using to hack down the corncrib whenever I needed wood was buried in the stump where I'd left it. I heaved it out and rammed it into the side of the rickety building. Half the boards caved in. A choking dust rose up. I pushed the short rear wall in with my foot, and stood there breathing hard, looking for something else to smash down.

Over at the fence, Dash stood watching me. I looked at him, and said, "To hell with all this." His ears flickered like he understood how hard I'd been working, and that it didn't any of it mean one thing to anybody.

While I had him in reach, I grabbed his halter and led him to the barn to saddle up. I threw some grain in the bin for the other animals, but that was the last thing I was going to do.

I stepped into the stirrup and hiked myself over his back. And I rode away from there without saying good-bye. Not that it mattered. I doubt I was even missed.

Riley Davis said the Odoms had stopped into his store. He said, "Fact is, you just missed them." He leaned around me to look out his front windows. "That stallion of yours could catch them pretty easily." But I wasn't interested in catching them. I just wanted to know if they'd bought a bottle for baby Clarissa. He said they had, and I said good, and asked to buy a bottle for myself, only I picked rye instead of one with a baby nipple.

I went over to my room in back of the shop, left the CLOSED sign on the front doors, and set about getting myself good and drunk. It wasn't any fun. All it did was put me in a mind to feel sorrier for myself than I did already. I considered riding into Weatherford, seeing if

I couldn't find me a whorehouse to spend a night in. Maybe a ripe woman could bring me out of my blight, but I couldn't seem to get up the energy. In the end, I fell asleep right there on my rope bed, with my boots still on my feet. Didn't even dream.

The next morning, Liam Brannon woke me up, banging on the two outside doors to the shop. He had a couple of his working ponies with him that needed to be reshod. Since I didn't have the forge burning, he left them in the back lot for me to get to when I could.

I chocked the doors back with the bricks I kept for that use. The sun was already bright and hurt my eyes. I lifted my head and let the breeze cool my face. The sky was empty, cloudless. Remembering Lily's last words to me yesterday, and the hateful look on her face, I felt just as empty inside.

It took a little while, banking the coals and pumping the bellows, to bring the fire in the forge back to life. I led the first pony into the shop. He was skittish with me at first. His skin quivered and snaked. I talked to him till he got settled down.

The thought came to me that I could talk to a damned horse better than I could a woman. Understood them better, too. I didn't know what Lily had wanted me to do yesterday to stop the Odoms from taking Clarissa Marie. Pull a gun on them? Fight Mr. Odom with my bare fists? But I knew I shouldn't have reprimanded her about letting Em play around the corncrib. I'd been so relieved to see them both there, still there with me, I hadn't known how to act. That was always my trouble. I had to hide what I really felt.

By the time I finished with the second gelding, folks were gathering at Riley's store across the street. It was mail day, and the wives and sisters and some of the farmers had come in to wait on the postal rider to come down from the mail station in Weatherford.

I wasn't expecting any mail, but I let the second pony out into the horse lot with his mate, and since I couldn't decide whether I should go out to the farm or not, I strolled on over to hang around the store front with everybody else. I was standing there listening to Daniel Porter tell about how he'd gotten nine dollars and fifty cents a head for his three Durham bull calves at the stock auction in Millsap yesterday, when I felt a tap on my shoulder.

I jerked around. The fellow doing the tapping jumped back about three feet from me. He was just a kid really. Fifteen, maybe sixteen. Slight and lanky. He wore a short-brimmed hat with a peaky crown, and a pair of wire spectacles that glinted the sunlight and hid his eyes. His britches were made of ducking; striped galluses. He looked so familiar to me I scratched my head, trying to recollect his name or where I'd seen him before.

He said, "Ain't you Haywood Beatty?" And he had a gloomy, unsteady sound to his voice. He kept the three feet of distance between us.

"That depends on who wants to know?"

"I'm trying to find my sister," he said, and I was about to ask his sister's name when it dawned on me it was Lily. She was his sister, and I remembered now seeing him a time or two rattling around McDade in an old farm wagon. I still couldn't recall his name, but he was sure enough a DeLony. He had the same thin lips and nose, same point to his chin, and hair the same color as hers. He even had the same cowlick spiking out on the right side of his forehead.

He didn't look all that fond of speaking to me. I stroked my face. I needed a shave. Probably smelled bad, too. I looked towards the Lazy Bend road, thinking about how I'd feel seeing her after what she'd said to me. Her words were still smarting.

I said, "You got a horse?" He nodded towards a brown, cow-hocked, swaybacked cob tied over by my shop doors. I recognized it, too. "You didn't come all the way up here on that thing?"

He started for his horse, and didn't answer me, didn't even appear to hear what I'd said, though I know he couldn't have missed it. I watched him for a second. Then I went to saddle up Dash.

As soon as we turned in off the road, I saw Lily, bent over in her garden, yanking weeds. Em sat in the shade of the elm tree, in the play-box I'd made for her. Her babbling carried on the air to us, even above the clop of our horses' feet striking the ground.

Lily's brother rode beside me, blank-faced and silent. He hadn't said three words the whole six miles. I couldn't read nothing on him, why he was here, if he was eager to see his sister, or if he had plans on taking her back home. His glass spectacles were like sunspots over his eyes. Looking at him made me uneasy, so I didn't.

Lily heard us coming and rose to her feet, shielding her eyes with her forearm. She stayed frozen like that for a while, studying, not on me, for she'd have known me and Dash in an instant, but on the stern fellow beside me. I could tell it when she finally recognized him. There came a slight lifting of her shoulders, a sort of lurch to her footsteps as she moved between the garden rows to the wire gate.

Her face was shaded by the slat bonnet she wore, but I didn't think she was smiling. She came around the end of the fence. Her feet were bare. She stepped one foot on top of the other and hugged onto the corner post. Neither one of them spoke, not even after we stopped the horses. They just stared at each other. It seemed a peculiar greeting to give to your kin.

Em pulled up in the play-box, called out, "Doo-dee," at me, and rattled the side boards.

I lit down from Dash. "Got somebody here to see you," I said to Lily. "Found him up town outside Riley's."

She looked ragged, like she'd been up all night, pining for baby Clarissa. She never glanced my way, but came three paces closer as her brother swung down off his brown. "Dane?" she said, cocking her head, dusting garden dirt from her hands.

He looped his horse to the fence. "Papa don't know I'm here," he said with that gloomy voice of his.

I kept hold of Dash and waited to hear what else they said. I felt out of place, like an eavesdropper.

"Is something wrong? Is somebody sick?" Worry came clear in her tone.

He shook his head. "Nothing's wrong." He reached to pull his grip off the saddle. "I've had enough of that stingy old wife of Papa's. Had enough of him, too. You done right to leave. If you'll let me bunk here a spell, I'll make myself useful. You know I ain't lazy." He glanced my way, his eyeglasses nearly blinding me. I wondered how long was a spell?

"Course you ain't," she said. She reached to give the old brown a rub. "You've never been lazy. Come on inside."

Over in her box, Emmaline started to fuss. Dane glanced at her. "She don't look like you," he said.

"No, she don't." Lily went to lift her out of the box. Then she motioned for her brother to follow her to the house. All of them went up the steps and disappeared inside, leaving me to myself and my longing. If she'd have just looked at me once, I could've let her see I was sorry for speaking sharp to her about the corncrib.

I pondered on the cotton field across the road. I hadn't finished busting out the middles. There was still half the field left to do, yet. But she hadn't spoke one word to make me think I was welcome. Maybe I ought to just leave the rest go. Let it grow up in jimson weed. Let the bugs eat it up. Corn was tasseling out.

I glanced towards the corral, wondering if she'd fed the animals. They were all lined up at the fence rail, watching me, and Dash was pulling that way, thinking he ought to be over there bullying the others. I could turn Dane's plug out there, take his saddle off and scrub the horse down good, but what the hell if it wouldn't bring me up any higher in Lily's eyes.

As if she'd heard my brain thinking, she stepped again out on the gallery. She'd taken off her bonnet but still had Em on her hip. I raised my face at them and she patted Em's little back, looked out at the trees. "I'm gonna put Dane in your room—I mean, in Bob and Estelle's room."

I nodded, peered off down the Brock road. I reckon I looked pretty glum. I felt it.

"He could be a big help to you," she said. "He's been farming since he could walk."

I didn't say anything, but a stab of hope flashed through me. She still wanted me here, just not sleeping here.

She came down the three steps, closer. Her face had gone soft, eyes sad but dry. "I'm sorry for what I said to you yesterday. About Emmy not being yours. It was pure hateful of me."

"I'm sorry, too." Em reached for me with both of her arms.

"You got nothing to be sorry for. It was the right thing to do, letting them take Clarissa. I guess I just let myself get too attached to her."

"You couldn't help it. Maybe we can go visit her as soon as we get the crops laid by."

Em reached for me again, grunted this time. I took her, and Lily didn't seem to mind. She even smiled. Em pressed her face against my neck and smiled back at her ma, made baby noises, like she thought she was talking.

"She doesn't know she ain't yours," Lily said. "I mean, she might as well be—"

"She ain't, though. I didn't have no part in making her."

"I know." She had come close to whispering. "I'm sorry."

And it sounded peculiar, her saying both those things, and in that order, like she was meaning something she wasn't, that she was sorry I hadn't taken part in making Em. I knew that wasn't how she meant it, but I was sorry for it. Damned sorry. Also, pretty sorry for other thoughts roaming through my head just then.

Wind billowed her hair out from her shoulders, and I decided she ought not to be wearing it loose so's to tempt a man. And I looked down at her bare feet, pink toes, trim ankles. And without another word, I gave Em back to her, led Dash over to the corral and turned him in, giving his ass-end a pop to get him moving out of the way. I caught up Shorty, the big, slow-footed Percheron, and led him to the tool shed for the plow. When I glanced back up at the house, the gallery was empty.

23

After Dane came, things changed. I moved back to my room at the rear of the shop, and there weren't any more alone times with just Lily and me and little Em. My daydream faded, disappeared down to a memory shining bright in my mind. It was just work then, in the fields getting Bob's crops laid by, and at the shop of an evening, the heat of the forge becoming more and more unbearable as summer wore on.

Dane was a help to me, a good farmer like Lily had said, but he didn't like me much. I wasn't sure exactly why, but he stayed sullen and didn't seem to trust me, not even to feed the damned nag he called Joe. Fact is, I got the feeling it was me he'd come to save his sister from.

She acted glad to have him, and to get from him

news of her other brother and little sister, who evidently got along better with their new stepmother than Dane did. At first, they did a lot of talking, but never in front of me. Dane would clam up whenever I came around. I heard him once, before he knew I was there, say, "Papa only married Miz Kennedy to get ahold of her land, and now that he's got it, he doesn't wanna be bothered with nothing else." I knew a little bit about their pa, mostly from things Shot had told me. Josh DeLony was a hard man most folks learned to steer around.

A week or two after Dane came, him and Lily and Em started coming in to the Methodist church at Brock on Sundays. I'd see them sometimes from the shop, or pass them on the road, us going opposite ways. Em would call out "Doo-dee" at me and grit her little grin.

Finally, one Sunday in July, I let Lily persuade me to go along with them. I sat there in the pews wearing Jack's suit. I felt like everybody was staring at me. I'd kept the crease in the trousers by spreading them flat underneath my mattress. But the coat had a steeple jutting up in back, just under the collar, from the wall nail it had hung on since Estelle's funeral.

I got a headache trying to listen to what the preacher said. With Lily beside me, the paper fan in her hand blowing her scent my way with each swipe, I couldn't concentrate. He read from the Bible but it sounded more like Latin or Greek to me, than English, what with all the *whither thou goest* and *whoso hearkenth unto me*. Leastwise, I never had heard anybody talk like that. Not even a lawyer like Silas Jones. When Em decided to fret loud enough the whole congregation shifted, I scooped her up and took her outside, grateful for an excuse to leave.

Almost as soon as we stepped through the doors, she stopped her racket. She was just too much like me—didn't care for church or the preacher's speechifying, or for being cooped up inside on such a bright morning. I let her walk, with me holding onto one hand, in the little patch of grass by the front steps. She was getting steadier, about ready to go it on her own. She tired real quick of the grass patch and wanted to venture off further. I wasn't much in the habit of telling her no.

We visited the chestnuts tied to the wagon rails along with all the other folks' teams. The off mare, Razzie by name, was rounding out at the flank with Dash's get in her belly. Em squealed and spanked at Razzie's nose, laughing when the mare snorted. Em had a hankering for horses, too—like me. I swear, we were peas in a pod, Em and me.

We crossed the road, stopping at Riley's store for some of the arrowroot crackers he sold in a barrel. Em loved them and knew by sight what they were. She leaned nearly out of my arms to grab one with her stubby little fat hands.

"How-do, Miss Sunshine," Riley said, reaching out to tweak her cheek. She was too busy with the cracker to care that he was talking to her. I asked him to draw me a beer. It was hot enough to drink a whole pitcher full.

Pulling on the tap, he said, "I saw you head inside over there, and I says to myself, that can't be Beatty taking up with churchfolk." He set the beer on the counter in front of me. "I'm pleased to see you didn't take the message too much to heart. Some of them women have been in here spouting temperance at me, wanting me to get rid of the beer keg and whiskey shelf. I tole them wasn't even the Lord Jesus Christ a teetotaler."

"He wasn't?"

"Hell no. He drank wine like a fish."

The beer had foamed up a good head, and that took Em's interest. She poked her fingers into it, and jostled them around, making more foam.

"I know one thing," I said, "it's too damned hot for all these clothes." I loosened the tie at my neck and raised the beer glass to drink. Em's serious little eyes watched every move I made.

"Seen Stevens was back," Riley said. "Reckon he'll stay this time?"

I set the glass down on the counter and Em leaned over to dabble her fingers in it some more. "Seen him where?"

"This morning. While you were over there getting religion." He glanced at the clock tocking on the wall. "Came by here maybe an hour ago. Headed out to Lazy Bend. Had him a different horse, but it was Bob all right. I had a suspicion you might not know he was back."

"You were right."

I leaned against the counter and turned to look

through the open doors. Church was letting out. The preacher had come onto the front steps to shake hands. Lily and Dane stood off to the side, searching around for me and Em. I drained the beer and hiked her back onto my hip.

"Thanks, Riley."

"Tell Stevens he still owes twelve dollars on account to me," Riley called as I left the store.

Right away Lily remarked on Em's smelling like beer and then on me smelling that way, too. I told her, "Jesus wasn't a teetotaler either." Dane just lifted his nose the way he always did, like I wasn't worth bothering about, so I didn't let him drive. Didn't even offer to, and I knew how much he liked it. I was in a hurry to see if Bob would still be at the farm when we got there.

I spotted the horse he was riding, a dapple gray, tied to the horse ring outside the graveyard. Bob had always been partial to a gray horse. He was up by Estelle's plot, kneeling there, his hat off his head. His hair had grown out long, and was so greasy it shown like a polecat's pelt in the sun. I slowed the chestnuts.

"Is that Robert?" Lily said from the back.

"Riley Davis told me he was here," I answered.

"How come you didn't say anything?"

"I wasn't sure it was true." I tossed the lines at Dane and hove myself down from the wagon, careful not to stun my bad leg. "Y'all go on up to the house. I'll be there in a minute."

"Maybe you ought to leave him be for now."

I waved off her words and started up the hill.

Bob had seen us and stood. He came at me walking, met me halfway up the bluff, and hugged both his arms around me hard. He stunk of soured whiskey and cigar smoke, and of the road and his horse's sweat. His eyes were syrupy, like he'd been awake so long the brown parts had bled into the whites.

He let go of my shoulders. "I ain't staying long," he said, still holding his hat by the crease. "I just come to tell you whatever you get for the crops is yours. You done all the work anyhow. And I already told Mister Jones I ain't staying around." He fished a folded paper out of his vest and held it to me between his first and middle fingers. "Here's this. I had him make it out to you."

I took the paper. It was a bank draft, drawn on Citizens National in Weatherford for $45.25, and signed by Silas Jones.

"It's the way we agreed," Bob said. "He pays me by the quarter against the harvest. So you're his tenant now."

"Already was." I tucked the check into my breast pocket. "He'll just get it back from me as rent on the shop."

"Yep. Pretty soon men like him'll be owning the whole country. Already do." He grinned. "You and me ain't the lucky kind."

"Where you been, Bob?"

He gave a little chuckle, but mostly it sounded like

nerves. "Here and there. New Mexico for a time. Too damned dry to suit me there. And I got in a little scrape, so . . ." He let out another rasping laugh. "Had to light out."

"What kind of scrape?"

"Fella tried to rob me at poker." His smile grew weaker. He hadn't shaved in a week or more, and had a jaw full of whiskers shading his cheeks.

"Somebody ended up shot," I said, knowing I'd got it right even before he nodded.

"The robber."

"He die?"

He nodded again. "Took him a couple of days to. It was self-defense, but of course the law don't see it that way."

"Wouldn't."

"Never do." He looked over towards the house. Dane was helping Lily and Em out of the wagon. "I went down around McDade for a little while. Found out Charlie'd moved over to Lockhart. He's got married. Got him a little place. Got a little bride."

I glanced up the hill at the metal cross I'd made, poking up out of the ground amidst all the other markers of stone. "Estelle's folks came and took Clarissa Marie," I said, knowing he wouldn't ask. He'd wonder, but wouldn't ask. "She's in Rockdale with them now."

He looked down at his boots. He had a faraway glaze on his face for a minute, then he came up smiling again.

"Guess who turned up at Charlie's while I was there? Bird Hasley. Ain't changed a bit. Still mean as piss. Been living over at Louisiana. Trading horses. He tried to talk me into going back there with him. Going partners in business. Might do it yet. Put some more miles between me and New Mexico."

"Mister Odom said you was welcome to visit anytime," I said.

That brought a frown to his face. His jaw muscle clenched. He palmed his hat back on his head, so his eyes were in the shadow of the brim. "You can have Shorty. I reckon if you're staying here to farm, you'll need him more'n me. The buggy mares I'll sell to you. A hundred dollars for the pair, whenever you get rich."

"That might be a long wait."

"I'll call it an investment."

We looked at each other for a while without talking. There didn't seem to be anything else needed saying. The pain plain on his face moved a pity inside me, but it wasn't nothing I could do to help him. He'd have to find his own way through it same as I had to do with Jack and Azberry.

And it was right then, staring at Bob's dark face and sad eyes, I came to realize I'd finally laid my brothers to rest. I wasn't sure when I'd done it, but that part of me was at peace now.

He put his hand on my shoulder, gripped me. I gripped him back. "Take care of yourself," he said.

"You, too." It felt like the end of something, and I got wet-eyed.

We walked down to where his new horse was tied, and he pulled up into the saddle. He struck an easy lope going down the road, the shoes on the gray flickering like mirrors with every step. Before they hit the first bend, Bob turned back, waved his hat at me.

"Where's he going?" Lily had come up the road behind me. Dane stayed back on the footpath in front of the house. But all of us were watching Bob leave.

"He don't know," I said. "Someplace there ain't no memories."

"Not coming back, then?"

"I reckon not."

She stood next to me, calming her skirts in the wind that had come up. "Did he say what I'm to do with Estelle's things? Her clothes and her whatnots?"

"Keep them," I said. "Wear them if they fit you. Or give them to the needy."

She pressed her lips together and looked up at me. I could tell by her eyes she believed I was quoting words Bob had said. "Ain't too many around here much needier than we are."

I dipped my fingers into my breast pocket and came out with the bank check. "He gave me this." I handed it to her. She read it. "I'll sign it over to you, so's you can buy whatever you're lacking. It's considered the same as cash money."

She studied the check and then me, my eyes and

face. I wished I could tell what her mind was thinking. "I didn't mean to seem resentful," she said.

"But it's true. You've done without long enough. Maybe things is gonna get better now. He gave the harvest to me. Said Silas Jones agreed to it."

"I'm happy for you if it's what you want." She gazed off in the direction Bob had gone, and slipped the check into her skirt pocket. "Nice he waited till the crops were laid by to show his face around here. Come any sooner and he might've had to work."

"Ain't the work he was afraid of," I said. I looked back towards the house. Dane had sat down on the gallery steps to whittle on a piece of wood. Every Sunday he sat there and whittled. He glanced up at us now and then, keeping watch with those glass owl eyes of his.

I started up the hill to the graveyard again. Lily came along with me. We hadn't had any rain in a few weeks, and the sun had beat down most the weeds. Still, she held her hem up enough I could see her trim ankle sheathed inside her white stockings. I tried not to notice.

Both of us headed straight for Estelle's grave, curious to see what Bob had saw when he knelt there. On the clean mounded earth, there laid a handful of orange zinnias, the same as the ones growing beside the house. Lily glanced that way to see where he'd picked them. I spotted his wedding ring, looped on one of the curlicues I'd forged onto the cross. Inside was an inscription embedded in the silver. It said, "Never doubt I love."

I turned the ring over in my hand, poked my fingertip inside it. Losing a wife changed a man, I reckoned. I'd seen the change on Bob's face, the lines and bitterness. The same way Pa had looked. The same old age in the eyes. Folks that knew Pa before had said he was different when our ma was alive and I believed it. I figured he must've been different, because wasn't any woman would've had him the way I knew him.

"I reckon he was a sad man." I said it out loud, then gave a half-laugh when Lily looked curious at me. "My pa, I'm meaning. I was thinking of him just now. I reckon he was sad was why he fell into the bottle." I hung the ring on the curlicue where Bob had left it. "He was a hard man to feel sorry for. Never liked nothing. Or nobody. Just wanted to be left alone with his jug and his dogs."

"I remember all those dogs y'all used to have."

I looked at her. "That was the first day I ever seen you. That day Shot brought you out there to our place."

A wash of red spread up her neck. I wondered what caused it. "I remember," she said.

"You sure did rile them dogs up that day. Rousted me out of bed."

"You shouldn't of been sleeping anyhow, in the middle of the day." She laughed, and it came to me as gentle as music. The wind took her bonnet ribbons and flung them across her face. I reached to move them aside, but she curved away from my hand. "Don't," she breathed, then plucked aside the ribbons herself.

The smile came back quick to her, but I'd seen the dark glitter in her eyes. She knew. She probably knew everything, my daydreams, my wicked dreams at night. All this time, she'd let me believe it was my own secret to keep inside me. But she knew. That *don't*, and that quick smile and that glitter, had given her away.

"Now, don't you dawdle too long up here," she said, gay and stepping light back down the hill, pretending nothing out of the ordinary had just passed between us. "I'm fixing to make us some dinner. You have to eat before you head back up town."

"All right," I said, going along with her game. But underneath my hat, my ears were burning.

I stayed standing there, and there wasn't one reason for me to. It wasn't my wife buried in the ground, wasn't my habit to visit Estelle's grave for long, either. I watched Lily all the way down the hill, and I stayed back because I knew she hadn't wanted me to walk with her.

She got to the road and turned up towards the house, and when she reached the gallery, Dane stood up from his whittling. He let her go by, then looked out at me for a good half-minute before he followed her inside.

At the end of August, the Baptists came to the valley. Missionary Baptists, or "two-seed" Baptists some folks called them. They were revivalists from over Dallas way, come to convert the sinners. It was so hot by then the sky came down to waver together with the earth, forming clouds of steam every evening that promised to rain but never did. All a farmer could do was sit out the heat and hope the dirt held enough moisture left from last spring to bring off the cotton crop. A tent meeting along the banks of the Brazos to get some good out of God was one way to take a man's mind off his worries. And Lily wanted Em converted, finally, from a Catholic.

It was something to do with the dunking that made

the difference. The Methodists in Brock were of the sprinkling persuasion, pretty much like the Catholics down in San Patricio had been, and that method didn't cut no ice with Lily. Em had to get doused. Lily was settled on it, even being a backslidden Baptist herself like she claimed she was.

She spent all one day, sunup to sundown, cooking enough grub to last a week. She had Dane pack the light wagon, and she asked me for directions to Littlefield Bend, where the evangelists had built a brush arbor to shelter their flock.

"I don't guess there's any need in me inviting you to come along with us," she said, and I shook my head. Religion, it seemed to me, was something a fellow ought to put his whole self into, and I had serious doubts as to the strength of my convictions.

"I'll see you in a week," I told her, and after they'd gone, I spent the next two days fighting a bolly worm that was trying to get into the cotton.

I mixed equal parts coal oil and soft soap with water, and hand-dippered the poison onto the soil around each plant. If that didn't work, my next trick would be to soak the plants directly with a soup made of cayenne pepper. I'd been learning some things from the old-timers that hung around Riley's store of an evening. Grinless as Dane was, I could've used his help those two days.

By Thursday, I'd gotten tired of shuffling around the farm alone. Brock was deserted, so there wasn't much need in opening up the shop. I rode into Weatherford and spent some time in the Lone Star Saloon, swilling ten-cent whiskey and bucking the faro bank, till I ran out of money, which didn't take long. I'd only allowed myself six dollars to paint the town red with. And I'd lost the knack for painting anyhow.

I rode back to Brock in the dark, and fell asleep sober in my rope bed in back of the shop. I hadn't even learned the way to Faymon's Pleasure Parlor that I'd heard fellows tell about around the cracker barrel at Riley's. Somehow none of that held much charm for me anymore.

Friday I rode out to the farm to check the cotton. I couldn't yet tell if my worm killer was working. I fed the horses and the milch cow, sprinkled some cornmeal down for the chickens. Then, I went back to the shop to putter around. Made some new horseshoe forms, hung them up on the wall. I opened a tin of sardines and un-wrapped a loaf of light bread—the gun-wadding Riley sold—for my supper. Played a solitary card game till nearly dark, before I made up my mind to get Jack's suit out from under the mattress.

Even so late in the day, it was too hot for the coat and tie, but I brushed the rust out of the trousers and put the vest on over the white shirt with a black fleck that used to be Bob's. I filled up a nosebag of oats and corn for Dash, saddled him, and, after a quick stop by Silas's to ask Puddin to tend the farm till I got back, I set out for Littlefield Bend to find the rest of the sinful. I'd had my fill of alone.

Word of the meeting had spread to three counties, and folks had traveled from as far away as Palo Pinto. Preaching and singing was still going on even after dark when I got there. Lanterns, swirling with bugs, hung from poles. Rough plank benches were set up underneath an arbor of branch willows and cedar boughs, men on the left; women, decked out in their stiff Sunday skirts, to the right. I couldn't find Lily nor Dane anywhere.

I saw a few people I knew. The Stricklands had come. Alice and all her daughters were lined up on the women's side. Ruth wasn't with them. I figured she must've already married that Noah Steelman who had punched me, though news of a wedding usually traveled around the valley. I hadn't heard, but then I doubt I would've been invited.

Sand fleas were bad and had folks fidgeting, or else it was the call of the Spirit giving people the jerks. The preacher's voice was hoarse and crowing, but he managed to holler out above the singing, calling his flock to come forth and face the Savior. Some already had, and were on their knees weeping, praying at the mourners' bench up in front of the crowd. I felt like I'd walked into somebody's private bedroom. I couldn't help but stand and watch.

One by one, they went. Some crying. Some staggering against their escorts. Some marched, head high and proud, bright smiles on their faces. A woman in purple sat at a pump organ, her dress hiked nearly to her knees, stomping the pedals and banging the chords. Voices sang—"Softly and tenderly, Jesus is calling. . . ."

I had never seen anything like it in my life, folks so overwrought, some of them fainted dead away on the ground with the fleas. And every time one went over, the hollering and hallelujahs went up louder and louder. Didn't anybody call for a doctor.

"Come forth with your sins, brother," a sweet-faced old lady said to me, tugging at my sleeve. I nearly had to prize her fingers off my arm, one by one, before she let go. The second she did, I beat a retreat out from under that arbor. Everybody had seemed to've gone mad.

I found a long food table with nobody guarding it. My hunger overcame me, and I went from dish to dish, tasting all the goodies laid out. There was ham and cakes and sweet potatoes and all kinds of biscuits and bread. Somebody had brought a crate of watermelon. I had to wave away flies. Not even the oil torches stuck down in the ground around the table could keep the bugs run off.

"Woody! Over here!"

I turned and saw Lily coming between the rows of tents thrown down. She was wearing the dress of pale pink with the tiny dots and flowers that made her skin glow, even in the darkness.

"I thought it was you," she said, catching up to me. "How long've you been here?"

"Long enough I nearly got saved," I said, and she laughed, which was what I'd been hoping for. "Where's Em? And Dane?"

"Em's asleep." She pointed back the way she'd come. "And Dane's helping Brother Shaw escort the people." I looked towards the arbor, thinking I hadn't spied Dane anywhere. "He's about decided to become a preacher himself," she said. "He told me last night he'd felt the calling. I said he'd better wait to make that judgment. Revival meetings'll sometimes put a notion in a person's head that doesn't stick once things are back to normal."

"I can see how that's true," I said, listening to the organ, and the singing and clapping.

"Anyhow. I'm glad you're here. The baptizing is Sunday. Are you staying till then?"

I hadn't come expecting to be here longer than one night at the most. I hadn't brought a change of clothes even. But looking at her in that pink fogged my mind. And she'd said she was glad I was here. "If you want me to," I mumbled.

"Emmy would like it," she said, and from the way she dipped her head, I felt sure if there'd been more light than that from the half-moon and the pole lanterns across the level, I'd have seen her blush.

More and more, it seemed to me, that one or the

other of us spent all our time around each other blushing, or else pretending we didn't notice the blushing. It was awkward, and almost easier to stay away from her, except I couldn't stand that either.

I slept that night on the ground outside the tent they'd made by throwing the wagon sheet over a rope strung between two pin oaks. Lily stayed under the canvas sheet with Em, bedded down on a pallet of quilts. Dane, when he finally came to the tent, well after the organ and the music and shouting had stopped, threw his coat on the ground near me and slept like the dead, snoring louder than the toadfrogs croaking out in the river.

Who'd have thought—especially if they'd of known me last year or the year before—that I'd ever be found at a camp revival singing hymns. But I still liked to sing. That part of me hadn't changed. And the song leader, a fellow they called Brother Henderson, hollered out the verses line by line, since there wasn't enough songbooks to go around. With him lining the words that way, I could keep up. One thing I didn't like was how the men kept separated from the women. All I could do was look across the aisleway at Lily, and watch her look back at me. She didn't need a songbook, or Brother Henderson lining the words either.

The boss preacher, Brother Shaw, did sermons at

daylight, ten-thirty, one-thirty, and dark, so's it was just about an all-day affair. Folks got tired was part of why they took to swooning and carrying on, testifying, and in one case, speaking in tongues. It was the fevered pitch Brother Shaw kept everybody in that did it. "Bunkum," Riley Davis would say to me later. "Pure and simple bunkum." But at the time, I got just as caught up in the mood as the next person.

First came the sweats. Then the chills waved over me. I felt about the same as if I was in a sick fever bed. Brother Shaw was crying out above the singing voices, about how all it took to purify your soul was a walk to the bench, a pledge to take Jesus into your heart, and all the sins of your life would be thrown over to the Lord. *All* the sins, he said. And him saying that moved a part of me, made me think what it could mean to me to have all my sins forgiven, to become replenished, born again. It was the fresh start I'd been seeking in San Antonio, the new life I'd been after since I left Bastrop County. And I was hot, and tired, and thirsty from all the singing.

Pete Strickland surprised me by coming to stand beside me. He put his arm around my shoulders. I hadn't seen him since the dance, but I could tell by his face that he'd already forgot about whatever I'd done that evening to provoke the fight there. And as it turned out, Noah Steelman had left Ruth in the lurch, headed off to the Panhandle with a cattle outfit.

"Ye who are weary, come home," Brother Shaw hollered out over the singing. "Come lay down your burdens. Put them down."

I thought about Azberry and Jack, and the Tennessean, and my poor, dead ma I'd never known, and pa with his jug of busthead, and Shot withering away in a cane field at the other end of this river, and of Estelle in her grave, and Bob on the run, and Clarissa Marie without any parents to succor her. And it was all of it almost more than I could bear in one thought.

My eyes welled up and my nose ran. Pete stood next to me, smiling, patting my shoulders. A shine of dampness lit his chin and forehead. He took me by my left arm. Somebody else, a man I'd never met, took my right, and they helped me down the aisleway, clogged with other mourners like me, all of us fighting our way back from the edge of perdition.

I never saw Lily. Never looked for her. Never saw Dane, nor looked for him neither. I was tranced by the promise of salvation, fevered with hope that God and Jesus could be the answer for me, shaking worse than I ever had in a fit of malaria. The voices rose all around me like the choir of ascending angels, ". . . calling, oh sinners, come home. . . ."

25

**B**rother O'Healy, Pete, and Coop Mull-
holland, the man who'd brought me his oxen to shoe,
all stayed with me most of the evening, talking about
heaven and hell and the light of a life lived in Jesus. They
ate with me, sat with me under the arbor, even went
with me, the three of them, when I made my second
trembling trip up to the bench to have Brother Shaw lay
his hands on me and say, "Bless you, brother."

All evening there were those who bore witness, who
stood up to tell of lying and cheating their neighbors,
of drinking binges and bouts of card playing, of tongue-
lashing their loved ones and slapping their wives. Wasn't
one person, though, confessed of ever robbing a store
at gunpoint, or of kicking a stage driver in the face to

make him light down. Of spending months in jail for a crime they might have done, of slitting a man's throat and dumping him in a river. Of coveting their brother's wife for their own.

I stood up, and when the crowd got quiet to hear, which they did since I was a stranger to a good many, all I could bring myself to mutter was "I have sinned."

"Are you sure, Haywood?" Lily said to me at the tent that night, late, after most folks had turned in. She was holding Em, rocking her, though she already slept so sound, I could hear her breathe. "Do you feel changed inside?"

"Changed? You mean, have I found the glory? That's what Pete Strickland asked me."

She waited for me to say more. Her eyes glimmered in the high moonlight. "Well? Have you?"

"Don't I seem different to you? Can't you see it? Don't I look lifted up?" I had all the words going. I'd been hearing them said to me all day.

She studied me, then laughed a little bit, shaking her head. "Maybe. Yes. Maybe you do. It's just so sudden."

"All I know is I've been floundering in deep water without a plank to cling to, and I feel steady now. Rock steady. Like the world could lean on me and I wouldn't falter."

She narrowed her eyes at me, tilted her head, like

she'd never heard such blather, but I kept on going. I was full of it, overflowing.

"I've known such tribulations"—it was a word I'd only just learned, and I liked using it—"in my life. Such sorrow and temptation. Sorrow *wrought* from temptation. It's all come clear to me. Today when Brother Shaw reached out his hand to me . . ."

She nodded, quirked a tiny smile.

"I even thought," I said, still caught in the sound of my own voice, my righteousness, "at one time that God might be just a lie folks made up to fool theirselves into thinking death wouldn't be so bad. Wouldn't hurt, or last forever. I thought that even if God was true he wasn't paying attention to a man like me, that I wouldn't have to make no payments to him, so it didn't matter what kind of bad sinning I'd done. I could steal and lie and swear and cheat my brother—I even thought I had a love—an affection for you in my heart, and I didn't feel it was no craven sin, even if you was—even if—"

My mouth stopped. She was staring at me like I'd slapped her, mouth open, eyes round, forehead creased. She'd quit rocking Em, and just held her, still and sleeping against her shoulder.

"I didn't mean—" I let out a laugh, shrugged. "I wasn't—*it* wasn't—"

Her back had squared up. "You know better now."

I took in my breath; nodded. I couldn't keep my eyes

trained on hers, but I didn't want to look away either, for fear she'd see I was a liar.

"That's good, because it ain't possible for me to love two men at once. It ain't in me."

"No." I shook my head, tried to swallow. I made a choking noise I hoped she didn't hear. She stared at me so long and hard I nearly squirmed.

"I'm glad that's all behind you now," she said, and I nodded. That was all I seemed able to do, nod my head, shake my head, anything but speak. I'd already done enough of that.

"It's good you've seen the light. I reckon you can take Emmy in with you for baptizing tomorrow. She won't be so scared being with somebody she knows."

I nodded again and couldn't find my voice to say anything until they were both well inside the rope-hung tent. "I'll keep her tight to me," I mumbled.

I didn't get a lick of sleep, tossing, thinking about how I'd slavered out my love for her, and mixed it all in with the Holy Spirit and salvation. I felt ashamed and foolish and wished I could have back everything I'd said. By the time the next morning dawned, I was already having second thoughts about my conversion, too.

Could I really give myself over to Jesus? Was that even likely for somebody like me? And if I said yes today and failed tomorrow, would I be branded for hell worse than I was already? And would one douse in the river be enough to wash away all the sinning I'd done? Could it wash off of my soul the blood of the Tennessean? In the light of this new day, I didn't see how it was possible.

It was a big step for me, and I thought of how Jack and Azberry, and even Bob and Bird and Charlie Goodman and the others, including Shot, would laugh at me if they knew. And I thought how Lily was probably already laughing at me inside herself, though she didn't act any different at breakfast.

Folks lined up on the river bank, trampled down the rushes, and Brother Shaw took off his frock coat to wade waist-deep into the muddy water. Dane and some of the other helpers rolled up their britches. The women lashed their skirts down around their ankles with hog-tying twine, so their petticoats wouldn't float up in the middle of the baptizing.

Ruth was there, hog-tied like the others, so tight she couldn't take anything but little hopping steps. Dane went to help her in. She squealed at the sudden coolness of the river, and she clung to his neck in a death-lock. "I can't swim," she moaned.

The water wasn't deep enough to drown, and we all could hear Dane explaining that to her, low and soothing. He'd make a good preacher, I thought. And then her voice rose up, telling Brother Shaw that while she was ready to meet her Redeemer, she had a terrifying fear of going in over her head. Brother Shaw explained that without a complete dousing, the baptism wouldn't take, and Ruth cried all the harder, until Dane finally held her nose and went down with her. He came up wet and brought Ruth up, and there wasn't a man on shore, saved or about to be, that didn't notice the sight of her in her white dress, everything God gave her showing clear as the morning through the drenched garment. Alice Strickland rushed over to wrap Ruth in a blanket.

It came our time, me and Emmaline, and by then it was for her more than me I waded in, and for Lily hovering over on the shoreline biting her lip, waiting with a drying towel. Em whimpered a little, feeling my own jitters, I reckon.

I felt Dane tap my elbow. "Give Emmy to me. Brother Shaw ain't gonna let her get baptized."

"What do you mean *ain't*?"

"He just ain't gonna do it. It's against the rules."

"What rules?"

"Baptists don't believe in dunking babies."

"Does Lily know that?" I glanced towards the shore where Lily was pacing all around the others gathered there.

"She ought to. Now, give her to me. You're holding up the line." He tried to take Em from my arms, but I pulled away, and plodded on past him, out to where Brother Shaw stood, the current in the river swirling around him.

"I'm proud to see you've come, brother," the

preacher said as I reached him, "but we'll have to send the child back to her mama."

He had a down-turned smile, and a kindness in his eyes, and I could see plain on his face the one thing he feared the most: losing a sinful soul like mine.

I said, "Can't you just pretend she ain't here?" Em had a tight grip on me. I patted her back to calm her before she started fretting hard.

" 'Fraid not, brother," he said, shaking his head. "I'm sorry. When she's older and can come of her own free will." But he still had that look on his face that made me think there was room for barter.

"It's on account of this little girl I'm even out here." I hitched Em up higher on my shoulder, and she turned her blue eyes the same way mine were facing, straight on Brother Shaw. "It's *her* free will that's made *my* will free, if you can get what I'm trying to say."

His eyes shifted out at the bank where I could hear the crowd growing restless.

I went on, "And it's my fault anyhow, that she's a Catholic, because, see, I'm the one that left her and her ma down there in South Texas with them nuns where they could sprinkle her head with oil. Or whatever it is they use—"

"I cannot baptize this baby," he said, almost gritting his teeth now.

"Then just do me. And if I'm holding onto her—

well, that oughta be enough to wash the Catholic off her till she grows up like you said. We could clean her slate thataway."

"That's what the trouble is, brother. She's only a baby. No baby's a sinner. Her slate's already clean in the eyes of God."

"Being Catholic don't count for a black mark?" I said.

He frowned hard at me, then out at the crowd growing more and more impatient. "Do you accept the Lord Jesus Christ as your Savior?" he said, his voice rising with each word.

"Yes, I do," I answered, almost grinning. Almost.

He raised up one hand and laid the other on my head. Then he shut his eyes, said, "In obedience to the command of our Lord and Savior Jesus Christ and upon your confession of faith in him, I baptize you in the name of the Father, the Son, and the Holy Spirit. Amen." And then he dunked me under the cold river water.

Em kicked like a bullfrog, and pushed at the hand I held over her mouth and nose. When we came up, she choked and coughed and spit, and let out the most hellish bellow I'd ever heard her make. But Lily, up on the river bank, smiled deep. I only had the one pair of pants that went to Jack's suit, but I'd taken off the shirt so's to keep it dry. Lily brought it to me when she took Em inside the towel.

We had a feast waiting, unmatched by anything the ladies had laid out so far. The newly saved got to go through the line first. I filled up my plate. I recognized a molasses pie as one of Lily's and took a slice, but I ended up feeding most of it to Em, to get her happy with me again. It didn't take but a couple of bites for her to warm back up to me. I only heard one snide remark, made out of my line of sight, about Brother Shaw's changing of church doctrine to include the baptism of infants.

Dane had disappeared, and I noticed Ruth was gone, too. They showed up together later, after we were done eating. Dane's cheeks were flushed just a mite too red, and he wouldn't look anybody in the eye for a little while. I thought I saw a clutch of sandburs clinging in Ruth's hair.

Folks were striking their tents, loading up wagons. Some stopped long enough to congratulate the newly converted, and I got my share. A couple of the ladies put a flower behind Em's ear, but she didn't like that and crumpled the blooms in her hand. She'd got fussy and tired, and Lily was trying to get her quiet, when the man came up to me.

"Are you Haywood Beatty?" he said, and I thought he was just another well-wisher. He had yellow hair and a brown beaver hat, and his clothes were a little dusty. I stuck out my hand, which he didn't shake. He said, "My name is Dunkin. G. W. Dunkin. I've come all the way from Lee County looking for you. Isaac Heffington was my half-brother." And before I could think what that meant, he pulled out a six-gun.

I heard Dane holler "Look out!" just as Dunkin started shooting. I dove for Lily, and knocked her and Em to the ground behind the wagon. Most of his bullets splintered wood. When I thought his gun was empty, I jumped and ran for where Dash was staked.

People ran, scattering and yelling, and I thought, for a second, that maybe the crowd had stopped him. But no sooner did I have that notion than I saw him running up behind me, firing again. He'd already reloaded.

"I ain't armed!" I called at him, but he kept on shooting. The horses on the stake line started bucking and straining at their ropes. I lifted myself onto Dash's back and dug my boot heels into him. He bolted out of there.

Dash hadn't got his name by accident. He was swift and daring when he was on the run. I kept my body low over his neck and gave him his head. He knew the way home to his stall. The only thought on my mind was to get to my shop and the old shotgun in my back room.

The name Dunkin didn't mean anything to me, but Isaac Heffington did. It was Bose Heffington he was meaning, the Lee County deputy sheriff that Jeff Fitzpatrick had killed at McDade. The same Bose Heffington whose corpse I'd carried out of town, and who'd caused George Milton's mob to go on their spree, and my brothers to end up dead in the streets. If this Dunkin was here for revenge, and it was pretty clear to me he was, I didn't intend to face him unarmed.

It was nine miles from Littlefield Bend to Brock, and

we were nearly there, still going at a fast lope, when I realized I had blood soaking down my shirt. I was hit and hadn't known it. Didn't feel the bullet, or know when it happened. I felt it now, though, a deep familiar ache just above my left collarbone.

Dash was frothing by the time we rode into Brock. Silas Jones was up on his top gallery and called out to me, "What is the rush? Have you heard Gabriel blow?" And he laughed.

I didn't answer him. Riley Davis stepped up to his door and hollered. I nearly fell off Dash, and turned him quick into his lot, going in with him. I went through the back door into the shop, got the shotgun down from the shelf I kept it on right over my bed. I loaded both barrels. My hands were shaking so hard I spilled open, and wasted, one paper cartridge.

The hole in my shoulder slowed me down. I pulled off my shirt, about cried out taking it over my left side. I twisted the shirt into a knot and stuck it down inside my undershirt, right over the wound to try and stop the blood. It hurt like the dickens.

I heard a horse come up outside, so I took the shotgun and crept into the shop to the big front doors. The wood bolt was still locked down in its slot, but I heard him try the outside handle. Both doors, and the whole wall, rattled.

"Beatty," he said. His voice was clear and close. Only thin wood separated us. "I know you're inside there."

"I didn't kill your brother," I said. "I had him hung 'cross my saddle but I didn't kill him."

For an answer, he fired three times into the left door, making holes near my body. I sprang to the other side. "Stop that, Dunkin! You've got the wrong man!"

Another bullet came through from outside. I backed away. Leveled the gun. I cocked down the hammer on the first barrel and let it fall. A hole opened up in the door the size of a wagon wheel, but six inches to the left of where I aimed. I adjusted the gun. The second barrel hung fire, then blasted another hole to the right. Nothing else happened. Silence. My ears rang from the noise, and smoke choked out through the holes in the doors.

"Dunkin?" I said. "You go on from here, now. I ain't wanting no trouble. You hear me? I ain't who you're looking for."

Footsteps came running up outside. Another set came. "Beatty." It was Riley's voice. I bent to try to see through the splintered doors. "You better come out here," Riley said.

I leaned the gun against the wall and lifted the bolt lock block, doing everything one-handed. The strength was all gone from my left side. Riley heard me lift the bolt and he swung the door open for me. It broke off its top hinge.

Dunkin was lying out there in the dirt, his clothes all shot to bloody hell. His eyes wide open and staring vacant at the cloudless sky.

"You got him with the first blast," Riley said.

26

I was near collapse when Riley took me into his store. One of his customers rode for a doctor. Silas Jones sent Puddin after the sheriff.

"You don't have anything to worry about," Silas said to me. He'd come down to the store, walked right inside with his cane, and twisted off the duck-head to take out the long flask of whiskey hidden in the shaft. There wasn't much more than a mouthful. "We all witnessed what happened here today," he said. "An act of self-defense. Isn't that what you saw, Riley?"

Riley was getting me settled in a rocking chair with arms I could rest against. "Sure did. Beatty didn't have any choice but to shoot him."

I was weak-headed. "The law won't see it that way."

"Yes they will." Silas laid his cane on my knee. "I'm

your lawyer and I say they will see it that way. This won't ever go to court."

I hoped he was right, would've prayed for him to be except I'd just killed another man, and I wasn't at all sure the Lord was still on my side. I reckon my baptism had already wore off. Least, I didn't feel at all saved sitting there in Riley's rocker waiting for the sheriff to show up. Silas took down a bottle of port from Riley's shelves and handed me the whole thing to drink on.

The sheriff came with a deputy and a wagon for hauling off Dunkin's corpse. By then, most of the folks from the camp meeting, including Lily and Em and Dane, had made it to Brock and were filing by to look at Dunkin. He'd been pulled up and laid out on Riley's front gallery. Some of the people came into the back of the store to speak to me. Nobody seemed against me.

I gave the sheriff my statement. He got about twenty others, too. He didn't arrest me. I couldn't believe it when he didn't. Silas Jones said I'd have to stay around close, though, in case the sheriff needed to ask some more questions of me.

The doctor, when he got there, ran everybody out except for Lily. She helped get my undershirt off, so he could take a better look at the hole in my shoulder. I got a look at it, too. It wasn't pretty. It felt to me like the bullet was lodged against a bone. When the doctor pressed around it, I heard something scrape.

"I can chloroform you," he said. "But it'll cost about five dollars. And we'll have to lay you down."

"Just dig it out, doc. I've been through this before." I had drank nearly all of the bottle of port and was feeling numb and brave. That went away as soon as the doctor started mining with his scalpel.

Lily looked pale. She bit her lip and dabbed away the blood that rolled down to puddle at my elbow. "Seem like I oughta be getting used to this," I said to her, trying to make her laugh. She didn't even crack a smile.

It was all I could do to hold my arm still, and my eyes were swimming. It hurt. Like hell it hurt. I thought I might swoon. I grit my teeth together to keep from hollering, and sweat poured out from under my scalp. Finally—it felt like hours later to me—I heard the chunk of lead ting inside the metal tub of bloody water beside the chair.

The doctor bound me up, fixed a sling for my arm, and sent me home in Lily's care. She made Dane help me into the wagon. She had to *make* him; he really didn't like me at all. Em wanted to sit on my lap for the ride, and Lily tried to tell her no, but I wanted her there, was glad she wasn't holding grudges against me for dunking her in the river this morning.

I didn't sleep good that night. The aching had gone deep by then. That was the way with a gunshot wound. At first it didn't hurt too much at all. Felt sort of like somebody poked you with the tip-end of a lit cigar. Or like a hornet popped you hard. It was later when the hurting came. I know I moaned in my sleep. Every time I tried to roll over, I woke myself up.

Near dawn, I opened my eyes to Lily standing over me. She had made my pallet in the kitchen from the feather bed, hauled in there by Dane, from her room. In one hand, she held a sputtering tallow candle. She was in her nightclothes, the darkness touching all around her head.

"Are you all right?" she whispered. "Need me to get you a drink of water?"

When I nodded, she set to work, seemed glad for something to do for me. She put the candle on the table and went outside, came back in a minute with cold water from the cistern. She brought a whole pitcher full, which she set on the floor beside me. She knelt there, too.

"I've been over yonder in my bed thinking how lucky we are you weren't killed," she said, pouring me a glass. "Or maimed serious."

She tried to help me drink, but I wasn't that much of an invalid. I still had one good arm. I took the glass from her. Water dripped down the corner of my chin. She wiped it off with her fingers before I could.

"Is your binding too tight? You need me to loosen it up some?" She tugged easy at the edge of the bandaging. It reached halfway down my chest. "The doctor's got you all trussed up like a Christmas turkey." She made a quiet laugh, felt of my forehead with the back of her hand, and seemed satisfied by what she found. "More water?"

I raised up higher and took the glass from her. She sat on her knees, watching me drink. I kept my left arm in close to me, so's not to strain my shoulder, and I swallowed every drop of the water.

"Woody," she said, taking the empty glass and starting to pour me more. I motioned I'd had enough. She reached back and set the glass on the table beside the candle. "Woody. I've been over there thinking, that man could've shot me or Emmy, too, if you hadn't pushed us out of the way like you did. And I just want you to—I'm just so grateful to you for—"

"It don't matter."

"No, I wanna say this. You've been good to us. You have. I don't know what I would've done without you all these months. You've been like, well, you've just plain been like a papa to Emmy. And to me you've been—" She took a breath and seemed to peer closer at me. "When I watched you riding off with that awful man right on your heels, shooting to kill you . . ." She made one shake of her head and looked down at her hands clasped on her lap. "I thought, at first, he was somebody come to revenge that man in San Antone. That one who—" Her voice got heavy and faded off.

"The one from Tennessee?"

She nodded; kept her head bent.

"How would he of known to come for me?" I said.

"I don't know." She raised her face at me. "He looked a lot like him, though. Didn't he?"

I tried to recall the Tennessean's face, but all that came to me was that he snored and stank, and how hot his blood had felt on my arm. "I can't remember," I said.

"Well." She let a little smile come, and tugged again at my bandage. "It would've been hard on me not to get a chance to tell you how grateful I am. You turned out to be a lot different than I thought you would."

"You did too." I sounded hollow, but I didn't feel that way. I'd never been so full.

I reached out with my right hand, my strong, good, unhindered hand, and cupped her face. My thumb rubbed her cheek and along her jawbone. She was soft as down, and smooth. Her fingers wrapped around my wrist, but she didn't stop me. I just looked at her and she looked back at me. The candlelight flickered in her eyes. Then she closed them.

I didn't care that my shoulder was throbbing. I barely noticed it. My mouth found hers like a magnet. She tasted of clover, or creamed tea. Every hair on my body stood on end, as if lightning was about to explode on me.

She didn't try to push me away, so I wrapped my arm around her back, and I pressed her mouth harder. And when she didn't stop that, I kissed down her jaw to her neck, and she held her head back, face upwards. Her arms stayed at her side, but she was like putty for a few seconds. I was so lost with tasting her skin, feeling her softness, I didn't hear her whispering at first.

"Woody." She sounded breathless. I was. "Don't, Woody." I felt her hand inside the crook of my elbow.

I had heard her by then, but I didn't think she really meant what she was saying. I kept kissing on her neck, lifting her hair away. All I could think of was the sweet smell of her skin and the way she tasted, and how warm she was, and soft, and that she had kissed me back. And my desire had grown so bursting big, more than I'd ever known, I couldn't stop myself, or even try to, or want to. The powerful thing that had been burning inside me for so long kept me from thinking clear. Her hand clamped onto me like a vise, struggling.

"Don't! Stop it!"

She got loose but I reeled her back in, held her to me. I could've swallowed her against me. She kept trying to bust free, and then she pushed at my shoulders, got me right where Dunkin's bullet had gone in. The pain shot through me, brought me round to myself again. I let her go and she scrambled to her feet. I saw the hurt on her face, her cowering eyes.

"Oh God," I said.

She turned and yanked the door open and was gone.

I rolled off the mattress, knocked over the pitcher of water, getting to my feet. I went after her. She had headed off the back gallery, around the cistern, and was rushing across the dooryard, aimless, just getting far away from me.

Dawn was breaking and shed a gray, edgy light on everything. The Wilsons' rooster crowed. I nearly caught her at the yard gate. I grabbed her elbow, but she slung me away, her eyes quick with fear, and I hated that it was me who'd caused her to look that way.

"Don't run," I said. "I wasn't gonna hurt you. Don't run."

She kept going, down past the privy towards the wagon shed, and I followed her. A possum was rooting around in the wood pile. I could see the glow of his eyes. A whippoorwill up in the hackberry called long and mournful.

I thought back on that black night in San Antonio, at Markin's inn, her beneath that foul Tennessean. I'd been near to doing her the same way, at least wishing to. And not just to her but to my own brother, my own flesh and kin. I hadn't ever felt such loathing for anybody as I felt for myself just then.

"Please stop running from me," I called. She'd gotten so far ahead I couldn't even see her anymore. "Lily! Please. I won't touch you, I swear it. Quit running."

I went up the hill, heading for the oak motte, and there she was, leaning against the rear wall of the wagon shed. She had her back to me, her face turned in towards the wall, but I knew she'd heard me coming. She'd of had to be deaf not to hear. I went up to her, as close as I dared to.

"I didn't mean to scare you. I swear I didn't. I thought when you . . . I guess I thought it would be all right."

She didn't turn around. Her shoulders raised, like

to block my words off her. She was silent. I couldn't even hear her breathe.

"Lily, please turn around. I can't stand to see you hating me."

"Go away," she said.

"No, I can't. Lily—" I stepped in front of her so's she'd have to look at me, and I got on my knees. I'd never been on my knees to anybody before, but I could've crawled to her if it would help, wallowed in mud like a hog for her. She turned her face closer into the wall. "I don't know what happened to me in there. I don't know."

"Get up," she said.

"I didn't mean to harm you. I'd give my life for you if I had to."

"Get up."

"I reckon I love you. I don't know why. I tried not to. But I can't help it."

"Stand up, Woody." She bent to tug at my arm, pulling me to my feet. Dirt, gummed with dew, crumbled off my knees.

I took ahold of her hand and didn't let go. "I ain't ever had such feelings. I love—"

"Don't say it again."

"If it's the truth?"

"It ain't the truth. You're just all mixed up. And we're both tired."

"No. That ain't it." I turned my hand over, twined hold of her fingers, but she snatched away from me.

"Stop it, Haywood. Just stop it. I know you're lonely. I'm lonely, too. But this ain't the way." Her eyes filled up. "I feel a tenderness for you. I do, but—"

"What's a tenderness?"

"It's what I feel." She pressed her hands to her chest. A couple of tears fell out of her eyes. "I have a soft place for you in me, but—"

I couldn't stand that I'd made her cry. I put my hand to her face. She pushed it back at me.

"No! Don't you hear me? It can't ever be more than that. I'm married to Marion. I love him. He's my husband."

"I ain't forgot."

"And he's your brother."

"I ain't forgot that either." I cradled my arm. It was throbbing.

"Then *why* are you doing this?"

I leaned against the shed wall and looked out at the sky, turning to day. Up in the trees, the birds had come awake. I turned my face towards them. There wasn't any answer I could give; not one thing I could say to change what I'd just done, to her or to Shot. To myself.

Hadn't she kissed me back? Or had I imagined it? And all these months hadn't she been smiling too bright at me, and blushing around me, and sometimes flirting, leading me on? Or did I imagine all that, too? She'd told the Odoms we were married, said that to them when she didn't have to. A tenderness? A soft place. What did that mean?

I felt her near to me, but I didn't look her way. And then the quiet pad of her feet came to my ears as she went off around the end of the shed. And I knew, leaning there alone, that things wouldn't ever be the same again, inside of me.

27

The world is full of people gritting on with life. I became like that. You get up of a morning, do what you have to do to stay alive. You take pleasure where you can find it: in a sunrise that burns the earth red; in a sky lathered thick with clouds about to rain; in rich black dirt yielding up its bounty. Anything more that comes your way is gravy. And dreams are for sleeping.

Emmaline turned one-year with the cornstalks drying in the field. My shoulder mended in time for the harvest, though my neck stayed forever stiff. It was just another part of me to ache with a change in weather. We filled the hayloft to brimming with corn, and had plenty left over to sell to Henry Brock and Liam Brannon. We got fourteen bales of cotton off twenty-five acres, which wasn't as good as some in the valley did, but I was satisfied with it.

I didn't get rich but I had enough to clear my standing at Riley Davis's, and I paid Dane forty dollars for all the work he'd done. He disappeared with it for three days, and came back grouchy and tired, like an old tomcat that had been on the prowl. He said he'd been out to Soda Springs, and I near about laughed. I knew who lived at Soda Springs. Pete Strickland. And Ruth. I remembered when my sap was running high like that, just after my first taste of female flesh.

For some reason, after the trouble with G. W. Dunkin, Silas Jones took a liking to me. He agreed in writing to sell me the farm, working out a payoff over the next six years. That was after a grand jury failed to hand down an indictment on me for killing Dunkin. Old Silas was right about the case never coming to trial, but it got me a reputation around that I wasn't much fond of. I bought a pistol and wore it inside my coat.

I had to shut down the blacksmith. Never had time for it anymore and couldn't pay the rent. I moved a bed out to the farm, into the room that had been the front parlor. It hadn't hardly been used since Estelle was laid out in there, and I figured since the place was to be mine now, I could damn well do as I pleased.

Lily didn't pitch a fuss about me being there, but we ignored each other the first week or so. After that, we went back to acting pretty much like we had all along.

She stayed busy, and I did. If ever the old yearning rose up in me, I smothered it with work.

I stayed gone over Christmas, and into the new year, chopping cedar posts up in the hills north and west of Weatherford, and on over into Palo Pinto County. Ranchers in the Panhandle were stringing barbwire all over everywhere, and the price of eight-foot posts went to two dollars apiece that winter. I made nearly as much in two months as I had the whole rest of the year, or would for the next two, on account of a drouth that came and settled in. But I didn't know about that yet. If I had, it might've made a difference on me signing my name to buy that hundred and sixteen acres.

At the end of January, I headed back to the farm, ready to get back to the plow and to breaking out the lower pasture down near the river. I planned to grow more corn this year. The land was suited to it.

Just above the little graveyard, on the Lazy Bend road, I crossed paths with Dane. He was sitting his old horse, coming at a slow pace. The wind was cold and working up to a good blow.

I called out to him, and he raised his face. He wasn't wearing his spectacles, and I didn't know how blind he might be without them. I said, "It's Haywood."

"I see you," he said, and pulled up on his reins, but I didn't notice any big change in his plug's speed.

"Where you headed?" I said. "It's looking like a norther's due in."

"He's here," he said.

"He, who?"

He gave a glum nod in the direction of the house. "Your brother."

My spine stiffened; ears perked up. I almost asked him which brother. My mind was doing cartwheels. "Since when?"

"Came about a week ago. Lily ain't been fit to shake a stick at."

His nag stretched his neck out and tried to nip Dash on the butt-end. I had to circle around to keep check, and I glanced towards the house. A fountain of smoke streamed up from the chimney and scattered with the wind.

"They staying?" I said.

"Don't know." He shrugged. "You got any tobacco on you?"

I lifted the ring tab from my pocket and swung the bag of cigarette makings at him. I felt I was moving in a daze. Shot? Here? Already? I hadn't even remembered he was due out this month.

Dane shook his head at the smoking tobacco I offered. "I meant chaw. I'll just go up to Riley's after some."

"Will you be home for supper?" I said.

"Why're you asking?"

"In case Lily does."

Dane snorted. "She won't."

He kicked his nag in the shank and headed off again at a turtle's pace. There wasn't nothing left but for me to go on to the house. I didn't know how it was going to feel, seeing Shot after so long.

I turned Dash into the corral and he started right in to bullying the buggy mares like he hadn't ever been gone from them. He'd already got both of them swole-up with his foals—one due in March, the other next May. I stashed the saddle in the barn and, coming out the front way, nearly bumped right into him—my brother— going in.

He looked the same, but different around his eyes. Not exactly a hardness, or the hollowness you'd expect with an ex-convict, but it was close kin to that. Sort of used up. And there was a deep scar cutting his cheekbone that hadn't been there before, high and on the right, in an inch-long crescent moon shape. He was still skinny. Seemed taller. Still a devil with that red head of his. His eyes lit up at me and he grabbed my hand for a shake, clapped my upper arm. He felt as strong as a tree. And he moved almost just like Jack.

"You damned old peckerwood," he said, and it wasn't much like him to speak a cuss word. "I've been waiting on you to get here."

I hooked my arm around his neck, put a stranglehold on him, and knuckled his head. He hollered out laughing, and ducked out of my grasp. He'd gotten quick. Quicker. And hard as steel. I wouldn't of wanted to tangle with him. He feinted a left, then butted his right elbow into my gut, but he didn't put his weight with it. I was struck by how truly good it felt to see him. I knotted him up in a hug. The norther blew in hard around us.

Fickle female that she was, Em had taken right to Shot. She sat in his lap most of the evening, seeming to forget all about me, while he talked of his plans. He wanted to go out to West Texas, where he would file on a quarter section of land just as soon as he turned twenty-one next month. He was going into sheep.

"Sheep?" I said, wrinkling up my nose.

"That's right. Wool sheep. Met a fella that already has some land out there, and we're gonna partner up."

Em said, "Seep." She was at that age to repeat everything she heard. She banged her hand on her pa's arm and jabbered a whole lot more words nobody could understand. I swear, she was the spitting image of him, and just as happy as a jaylark.

"They're opening that land up for sheep grazing," he said, "and there's water from the Concho River. Ground water, too, if you wanna dig for it. I know I won't ever get Lily to leave Texas." He leaned backwards in the chair and threw a big smile Lily's way. She glowed and fumbled with the supper dishes she was washing, and I saw right then he'd always been between us. "I don't got the patience for farming, Woody. I've had my bellyful of it."

I reckon he had, too, after slaving all those months for the State. I couldn't tell how Lily felt about sheep ranching. I couldn't even get her to look at me anymore.

She was glad to have him here, though. That much was clear enough. I came upon them one morning when they didn't know I was there. He was sitting on the porch rocker with her in his lap, saying nothing. Just the two of them sitting wrapped tight together, and him rocking her. It was chilly out, but they didn't either of them seem to notice it.

And from the sounds that came out of their room each night, he'd have her knocked up again before spring. Sometimes it kept me awake. Sometimes I had to go outside in the cold and walk around a while to cool off. Once I ran into Dane out there. He'd heard the racket, too, and had to get away.

"Disgusting," he muttered at me. "Purely disgusting, ain't it?" Compared to his feeling for Shot, Dane was plumb crazy about me.

I went on with what work I had planned. Dane was there sometimes to help me and sometimes not. He'd become pals with the Wilson boy and they went hunting a lot, after short varmints mostly, foxes and coons and ringtails. And God knows what all other mischief they got up to.

Shot pitched in with the work. We built a new corn-crib to make more room for next year, broke out the river pasture for rotating the cotton crop. I intended to let the old field lay out a season, and Shot urged me to sow it in sweet clover.

"Brings the minerals back up," he said. "And don't graze your animals on it till it sets bloom."

It was something he'd learned down south, though he never told me that for sure. He never talked about his prison time at all except to say that hell couldn't be any worse. But he was changed by it in small ways.

I caught him out in the barn one day, rooting around behind the grain bins. He acted bashful when he saw me, but said, "You don't got any liquor hid anyplace?"

"I don't keep it around."

"How come?" He laughed, like he thought that was hard to believe of me. To believe of any man.

I shrugged. "Don't wanna get like Pa."

He blew through his nose, and shifted. "You ain't nothing like Pa, Woody. Don't you worry over that. Pa wouldn't of never took such good care of my family like you done. I've been wanting to thank you for that."

It was me that laughed then, though there wasn't one thing funny in what he said. I heaved a chestful of air, and shook my head at him. "Hardest thing I ever did."

"I reckon it was." He grinned. "I'm gonna ride up to that store for a bottle of something. You wanna go with me?"

"I think I'll stay here and put away my tools."

"You've become a straight arrow, hadn't you? Lily said you even got religion."

"That was a passing fancy."

To prove to him I hadn't changed so much, I loaned him two dollars to buy his bottle. It was just the start of all the money I would come to loan him through the years.

After he'd left, Lily caught me coming in from the barn. "Where'd he go?" she said, and I answered, "He was thirsty."

I could tell she didn't like it, but she didn't complain, just kept trying to call him inside later that evening, when we were out on the gallery drinking the jug whiskey Riley had sold him.

"I'll be there in a minute, darling," he called to her just as sweet, but we stayed out on the front gallery till nearly midnight.

We smoked up my cigarette tobacco, and sipped his jug dry, and drunk as a spring bee on honey, I gave him Dash to pay him back for gambling Mollie away. While I was at it, I gave him the light wagon we'd come up here in and Sassy to pull it, since it was all bought with his money in the first place, or rather money he'd took as his in the first place. I thought he'd cry thanking me. And Dane, whose window it was we were sitting under, finally came outside to tell us to shut up and go to bed.

Shot had his birthday on the twenty-sixth day of February. On the twenty-seventh we packed up their wagon. It didn't take long with me and Dane helping. Em walked around in the wagonbed, throwing anything she could lift back out at us and laughing, till Lily spatted her hand. Em started crying then, and she could always get loud.

I lifted her out of the wagon and walked her, patting on her, saying goodbye. She was almost asleep when Lily took her from me.

"You'll write?" Lily smiled at me. A wisp of hair blew across her forehead. I resisted the urge to pull it back, to touch her cheek one last time. Shot was busy adjusting the mule's harness.

"Probably not," I said. "You know I ain't much with a pen."

She reached up to hug my neck, and I tried not to let it mean nothing. "I'll miss you," she said, and the smile still played at her cheek. "Me and Emmy'll both miss you."

It hadn't rained in so long the road had turned to dust. They raised a cloud of it leaving. I followed on foot until I couldn't take the choking. Dane stayed back near the house. Both of us waved them out of sight.

My feet seemed heavy to me as I walked back up the path. Dane had waited for me, sitting on the gallery steps. His knife and a fancy carved toothpick he was whittling on laid beside him. He had out his pouch of scratch tobacco and was stuffing his cheek full. He offered me some. I shook my head, blinked to get the sand out of my eyes. They were burning.

"You gonna stay here and work with me?" I said. "Or what?"

He shrugged, wallowed the wad around in his cheek. "Not for forty dollars, I ain't," he said. It was hard to understand him with his cheek packed so full.

I chuckled. "All right, then. What you think you're worth?"

He spit a big gloppy wad out onto the dirt, looked up at me, and grinned. It was the first time I believe I ever saw him smile. His teeth were brown with juice, but he had a dimple on his chin, in the exact same spot as his sister. "Half your profits," he said. I could tell he wasn't serious.

"The hell," I said, grinning too. "I'll ship you back to your pa."

"That bastard." He spit some more. "He don't want me."

I sat down on the step right above him. "You're turning into a real regular hellion, you know it?"

"You're one to talk."

I laughed again, and looked down the hill. "I reckon so. Do you cook?"

"For a snug price." He smiled his chocolate-toothed smile again. Two in one day.

I shook my head at him. "You're a hard man, DeLony. Too hard." My eyes shifted out to the dust still settling, down on the road.

The End

Author's Note

My first novel, *Lily*, dealt with events leading up to, and shortly after, the so-called McDade Christmas Lynchings of 1883. The lynchings and subsequent shoot-out were the culmination of an ongoing feud between a band of local outlaws and the townsfolk of McDade, Texas. The outlaws, mostly related one to the other, included the clannish Beatty brothers, two of whom were killed in the revenge shoot-out that took place the morning after the Christmas Eve lynchings. Two other brothers, Haywood and Marion Beatty, lived on.

In my research, I have been unable to learn much about Marion Beatty except that he was not present at the shoot-out that took his brothers' lives. In fear for his own life, he set out on the run. Three weeks later, he was found and arrested in Taylor, Williamson County, Texas. On June 3, 1884, he was given a two-year sentence for robbery. About Haywood Beatty, however, there is more.

In C. L. Sonnichson's excellent book on nineteenth-century feuds in Texas, *I'll Die Before I'll Run*, George Milton, one of the players on the other side in the McDade shoot-out, called Haywood the gamest man he had ever known. At the first sound of gunfire, the other members of the outlaw gang fled. But Haywood, standing alone and with the air around him thick with lead, returned the fire of his adversaries, even reloading his pistol at least once. Though shot in seventeen places, he walked away from the fight.

Haywood Beatty was arrested and held in connection with the murder of Willie Griffin, also killed in the street fight. But the jury hung and Beatty was acquitted. He moved north to Parker County. On June 1, 1941, after an unspecified illness lasting three years, he died at the home of a niece in Fort Worth.

The Parker County *Weekly Herald* called him "a pioneer of the county," and the Weatherford *Democrat* said in its obituary that he was "respected and esteemed by everyone with whom he came in contact." He never married and was survived only by nieces and nephews; however, his tombstone in the Cox Cemetery is one of the largest. Twenty paces away is another, less conspicuous grave marker. It bears the name of G. W. Dunkin, and its epitaph reads only, "FAREWELL."